MAKING A COWGIRL

CALLAHANS OF COPPER CREEK BOOK 1

NATALIE DEAN

Regular Print Paperback ISBN: 978-1-964875-64-4

Cover Design by Deborah Bradseth (who has been amazing to work with! Thank you Deborah!)

Photography by the fabulous Rebekkah Dubois

DEDICATION

I'd like to dedicate this book to YOU! All of my wonderful readers that have been following my stories over the years.

We're embarking on another new journey through Copper Creek. I hope you enjoy these stories as much as you've loved the Baker brothers!

Thank you to my biggest fans.... There's a lot of you! Jess, Bernie, Wren, Judy, Sherry, Vicci, Phyllis, Debbie, Indra, Jennifer, Carol, Jeanette, Margaret, Paul, and I know there's more I didn't list. But thank you all!

And I can't leave out my wonderful mother, son, sister, and Auntie. I love you all, and thank you for helping me make this happen.

Most of all, I thank God for blessing me on this endeavor.

AND... I've got a special team of advance readers who are always so helpful in pointing out any last minute corrections that need to be made. I'm so thankful to those of you who are so helpful!

EXCLUSIVE BOOKS BY NATALIE DEAN

GET TWO FREE BOOKS when you join Natalie Dean's Newsletter :)

Get Two Free Contemporary Western Romances:

1) The New Cowboy at Miller Ranch, Miller Brothers of Texas Prologue - He's a rich Texas rancher. She's just a tomboy ranch employee. Can she make him see life can still be happy without all that money?

2) Cowboys & Commitments, A Copper Creek Novella - She's a famous model. He's a small-town handyman. Can they find a way to be together and give love a chance?

Go to nataliedeanauthor.com and click on **FREE BOOKS** tab.

ALSO BY NATALIE DEAN

CONTEMPORARY ROMANCE

Copper Creek Romances

BAKER BROTHERS OF COPPER CREEK

Copper Creek Romances Series 1

Cowboys & Protective Ways

Cowboys & Crushes

Cowboys & Christmas Kisses

Cowboys & Broken Hearts

Cowboys & Second Chances

Cowboys & Wedding Woes

Cowboys' Mom Finds Love

CALLAHANS OF COPPER CREEK

Copper Creek Romances Series 2

Making a Cowgirl

Marrying a Cowgirl

Christmas with a Cowgirl

Trusting a Cowgirl

Dating a Cowgirl

Catching a Cowgirl

Loving a Cowgirl

Marrying a Cowboy

KEAGANS OF COPPER CREEK

Copper Creek Romances Series 3

Some Cowboys are Off-Limits

Some Cowgirls Love Single Dads

Some Cowboys are Infuriating

Some Cowboys Don't Like City Girls

Some Cowboys Heal Broken Hearts

Some Cowgirls are Worth Protecting

Some Cowboys are Just Friends

Some Cowboys Fall for Hidden Stars

Some Cowboys Come Home for Christmas

Some Cowboys Brave the Flames

Some Cowboys Fight for Love

PALMERS OF COPPER CREEK

Copper Creek Romances Series 4

Mateo & Nicole

Sophia & Cameron

Roman & Olivia

Miller Family Saga

BROTHERS OF MILLER RANCH

Miller Family Saga Series 1

Her Second Chance Cowboy

Saving Her Cowboy

Her Rival Cowboy

Her Fake-Fiance Cowboy Protector

Taming Her Cowboy Billionaire

BROTHERS OF MILLER RANCH SERIES BUNDLE

MILLER BROTHERS OF TEXAS

Miller Family Saga Series 2

The New Cowboy at Miller Ranch

Humbling Her Cowboy

In Debt to the Cowboy

The Cowboy Falls for the Veterinarian

Almost Fired by the Cowboy

Faking a Date with Her Cowboy Boss

MILLER BROTHERS OF TEXAS SERIES BUNDLE

BRIDES OF MILLER RANCH, N.M.

Miller Family Saga Series 3

Cowgirl Fallin' for the Single Dad

Cowgirl Fallin' for the Ranch Hand

Cowgirl Fallin' for the Neighbor

Cowgirl Fallin' for the Miller Brother

Cowgirl Fallin' for Her Best Friend's Brother

Cowboy Fallin' in Love Again

BRIDES OF MILLER RANCH, N.M. SERIES BUNDLE

Though I try to keep this list updated in each book, you may also visit my website nataliedeanbooks.com for the most up to date information on my book list.

CONTENTS

1

Sarah

ust swirled around Sarah's legs as she bolted into the stable. Her face burned with the heat of embarrassment she hadn't experienced since she was in middle school. The clamminess in her hands was just as irritating as the way her heart pounded in her chest.

What had she gotten herself into? She was trying to make up for what she'd done—and failing miserably at it.

Sarah strode about halfway down the aisle until she reached an empty stall. With both hands, she yanked the door open and shut it swiftly once she was inside. Her back dragged down the side of the stall as she lowered herself down and wrapped her arms around her legs. Unshed tears burned her eyes.

They were right. All of them.

Living here was harder than she'd expected. And doing it as penance for her wrongdoings seemed to only make it worse. She could feel it in the way Zeke, Adeline, and Brielle looked at her.

Yes, Brielle had been more welcoming toward her, but the others seemed to be judging her with every move she made.

She rubbed her nose on her knees, grateful she hadn't started crying. She was a lot of things, but she wasn't about to show any of them her weaknesses. Her saving grace was that she'd only have to be here for the summer. And the requirement to visit with the sheriff every week didn't *seem* so bad, but she couldn't be sure.

Sarah heaved a heavy sigh, closing her eyes. It was only a matter of time before someone came looking for her to see where she was. That was all they cared about, it seemed— making sure she was doing her job and pulling her weight. She was allowed to take a break. But up until now, they had been breaks dictated by the owner. She might get written up with this one.

One week. She'd only been at Slate Rock Ranch for *one week* and already it felt like months.

And why? Because some crazy rooster chased her out of the henhouse? The heat that had dissipated filled her face once more. The one cowboy who'd witnessed her frantic screaming as she ran from the murderous chicken probably saw her escape in here. And if he was the one who came to get her, things would only feel that much worse. He was handsome, strong, and emanated cowboy vibes with his worn jeans and cowboy hat and boots. How embarrassing that he saw her being so incompetent at something that should be easy.

"Hey."

A startled yelp tore from her throat and Sarah scrambled toward the far side of the stall. Her head whipped up to find *him*. Derek? Declan? His name started with a "D," right? There were too many people to keep track of here. On top of the seven girls who were raised by their single father, one of them was married, and then there was the staff. This place was so big that she wasn't sure she'd even met everyone who worked at the ranch.

She swallowed as she gazed up at the cowboy. His black hat made it hard for her to make out the color of his eyes. There was a dimple on his chin and his eyes danced. She glowered at him. "What do you want? To laugh at me?"

Her embarrassment often came out as anger, and here on the ranch she found it was no different. She was going to have to work on that if she expected to make it through the summer.

He arched a brow, then lifted and rested his arm on the top of the stall door. "Me? I don't want anything. But Chip here wants her room back." He nodded his head to the side where a large brown horse stood. The animal nickered and bobbed its head.

Her eyes widened and she immediately jumped up from her place in the straw and scrambled over to the door.

The cowboy moved out of the way, giving her a wide berth. His eyes watched her as she moved across the aisle and leaned against the stalls on the other side. His lips were quirked in that infuriating smile he'd worn when she'd met his gaze after the whole chicken fiasco. What she wouldn't give to wipe that smile off his face.

He turned his attention to the reins in his hands. The bridle was unbuckled and hung on a nearby hook. He kept making eye contact with her. Boy, he wasn't shy.

"Stop looking at me like that," she muttered.

A warm chuckle bubbled from his perfect, full lips. "Just how am I looking at you?"

"Like you think I don't belong here." It didn't matter if that was a true statement. She didn't like it when anyone laughed at her. She worked her jaw, clenching her teeth tight enough that it ached.

"I've not suggested any such thing." He continued working. "You're Sarah, right?"

"Yes," she ground out, then cleared her throat. "Why?"

He shrugged. "Just wondering what the sheriff's niece is doing *here* when she could be staying with him and his new family at Cedar Hollow."

She pressed her lips together. "People need to mind their own business."

Instead of the smirk she expected, a deep rumble and a frown came from the cowboy.

Sarah glanced down toward the entrance where she should probably be headed. But the thought of going back into that chicken pen filled her with more trepidation than she wanted to admit. Her eyes darted toward the cowboy again as he exited the stall and closed the door with a click.

He shoved his hands into his pockets and leaned against the door. Chip wandered up behind him and nudged his shoulder, pushing at him. He lifted a hand and rubbed her nose. "You've already had plenty of treats, Chip."

The horse must not have liked his answer because it shoved him harder, making him stumble toward her. He looked over his shoulder at the animal and scoffed. "You're not getting any treats tomorrow with that kind of attitude." He turned and gave Sarah another smile. "So why *are* you here?"

"I told you—"

"Right. Mind my own business." He sauntered closer to her. "The thing is, I don't do well with that. I like to know who I'm working with."

"Well, we don't always get what we want, do we?"

He shook his head. "I've been working here for going on eight years now. I would trust Zeke with my life. And you can bet that I would lay down mine for his. So, when I ask you what you're doing here, I'm not making a request."

She lifted her chin in defiance, although her trembling hands betrayed her. "Well, if you're so buddy-buddy with him, then why don't you go ask him?"

He reached out, and she gasped as she shrank back. His fingers touched her hair and tugged at something. Slowly, he lowered his hand to reveal the feather he'd plucked out of the mess that her hair had become. He stared at it, then lifted his gray eyes to meet hers.

"Zeke will tell me when he's ready. I just figured I'd save us some time and ask you myself."

Sarah scowled and folded her arms. This guy wasn't going to back down. He'd probably figure everything out anyway. But that didn't mean she had to make it easy on him. She stared at him, waiting for him to come to that same realization.

His gaze didn't leave hers, not even for a second. Her focus wavered, and she shifted beneath his stare until she couldn't handle it anymore. She threw her hands down at her sides and pushed past him. "I've got eggs to collect."

Sarah thought about her assignments as she left the barn. Once the eggs were collected, they wanted her to learn how to milk their dairy cow. She shuddered. Just the thought of having to do that sort of chore made her queasy. She wasn't a vegan, but maybe she should be.

Her steps slowed as she arrived at the chicken coop. The birds all *looked* somewhat tame. They clucked and bobbed their heads as they wandered through the fenced-in area. The miniature barn they laid their eggs in looked like a replica of the larger one she'd just left.

Fingers curling around the metal fencing, she searched with shrewd eyes. Where was the crazy chicken that had charged at her? She was the leader of the little pack of gremlins that paced within their cage. Sarah had been lucky to get out of there alive.

A flurry of feathers fluttered and cawed, bouncing against

the chain-link fence. Sarah's squawk mixed with the other sounds and she jumped backward, falling onto her backside. She muttered about the unfriendliness of chickens and clambered to her feet, not bothering to brush off the dirt that now covered her from head to toe.

"You okay, little lady?"

The voice came from behind her, causing her to jump once more. Sarah spun around and stared at the cowboy who'd been in the barn. "What do you want?"

He held a rope in his hands, coiling it slowly. His head was dipped so all she could see was the stubble of his strong jaw and his mouth set in a firm line. He tipped his head, giving her a quick view of his eyes before they were again hidden by his hat. "I don't think those hens like you much, little lady."

She bristled. "Don't call me that."

He wasn't fazed at all. Or maybe he didn't hear her. "I don't think I've ever seen those chickens take such a dislike to someone. What did you do to them?"

"What did I—" She huffed. "I didn't do anything. They hate me for no reason." She looked back into the coop. "There has to be an easier way. Whenever I go in there, they fly at me."

"They can sense your fear."

She stiffened. "I'm *not* afraid."

"Could have fooled me." He shook his head as one side of his mouth quirked up. "Eventually, you're going to have to figure out how to show them who's boss."

"Well, if it's so easy, why don't you go in there and get them?"

The cowboy's jaw twitched, though the humor in his eyes remained. "What are you gonna give me for doin' it?"

"Are you seriously bribing me?" She folded her arms tight across her chest. "Isn't that against your code?"

He arched a brow. "My *code*? I'm sorry, little lady. You're gonna to have to elaborate. What sort of code are you referring to?"

Ignoring the fact that he'd called her little lady again, she took a measured step toward him. "You know, like a code that all cowboys have. Like being honest and trustworthy. That sort of stuff."

The cowboy laughed. He actually laughed loud enough that the hens behind him fluttered and clucked with more urgency. He shook his head. "I'm no boy scout, little lady. I'm a cowboy."

"What's the difference?"

He cocked his head, his eyes drilling into her as if he could see into her soul.

She looked away and reached for the braid that had found its way onto her shoulder.

Taking a step toward her, he looped his rope onto his shoulder. "First of all, a cowboy is a man." His voice had lowered, holding a huskier quality. "Second, I'm not against doing something that has to be done even if in the process I find myself in a gray area."

A small chill raced down her spine. The way he'd said that sounded eerily familiar.

Just like the guys she'd hung out with when she'd been caught driving the people who were vandalizing the town. Her jaw tightened and she frowned at him. "I think most people would agree that they'd rather associate with boy scouts over a guy who doesn't mind playing in a gray area." What did Zeke see in this guy? There had to be something she was missing.

Yes, she'd been here for only a week. But while she had been staying under the Callahan's roof, she'd picked up on a few things. Zeke was strict. More so than anyone else she'd ever met. He didn't approve of his younger daughters dating before the older ones were spoken for. They had curfews, and according to him, they were perfect little angels.

Only, he wasn't quite as informed as he thought he was. There were a few of his precious offspring who liked to bend the rules.

Which begged the question, did he know? And did he look the other way when his employees did the same?

The cowboy, whose name she still couldn't place, scooped up a basket that she'd abandoned near the gate. He strode inside the chicken coop, leaving her gaping after him. Not one chicken charged at him. Not one feather was flung into the air as a show of aggression. He entered the coop and within minutes, he returned, his basket filled.

The gate swung open, then shut, and he shoved the basket at her. He turned his back and sauntered back toward the barn, whistling a little tune.

"I thought you wanted something," she called.

He didn't stop, though he twirled his wrist in the air and called back, "We can discuss that later."

"I'm not giving you anything," she threw back at him. "I mean it. I'm not."

She wasn't sure, but she thought she could hear his laughter again.

That was not how she expected a cowboy to act. Although, he had met her challenge and collected the eggs for her.

Sarah stared down at the basket in her hands. Not one egg broken. Not one feather. Maybe he'd had a point. Did the chickens sense her desperation? She sought out his familiar form, but he'd already disappeared.

Well, if he thought she was going to do him *any* favors, he was sorely mistaken. She already owed these people too much. She'd do her time and get out of there as soon as possible. Living under the same roof as her mother was starting to look like a much better arrangement than dealing with the hooligans covered in feathers.

2

———

Dax

Her dark brown eyes were the soulful sort of eyes that were only fit for an innocent creature. But Dax knew better. Sarah wasn't some harmless little doe who needed his protection. She was something else.

And he'd know.

He'd been to the darker side of things. There was nothing harder than returning and realizing just how good life was on this side of the fence. He couldn't put his finger on it, but there was something off about her. As much as he wanted to see it in her eyes, he couldn't.

Maybe that was why he needed to know more.

The problem was, either no one knew a single thing about her, or they knew but were remaining so tight-lipped that there wouldn't be any chance at getting the information from them. Not even Sean had seemed to know anything more about Sarah than what Dax had been told, and the man was *married* to a Callahan.

Oh well, it didn't matter. She'd slip up. They always did. And when that happened, she'd be booted from this ranch just like everyone else. Dax was the only one that Zeke tolerated on the premises despite his rough past. It probably had something to do with the fact that one of Zeke's sisters had practically raised Dax.

No, they weren't related. But Eve Callahan had a soft heart and no children of her own. She'd never married. And she'd never seemed like she missed out on any of that stuff. A twinge of pain sliced through his chest. The last time he'd seen her, he'd called her an awful name and ran away. When he finally returned like the prodigal son he was, the house she'd lived in was empty.

They said she'd had a heart attack.

He could read between the lines. That was code for she'd died from a broken heart. And he'd been the last one to leave. The pain that enveloped his heart grew stronger, and he had to focus even more not to let it overwhelm him. That was the trigger—the one thing that would put him on a spiral to a place he wasn't prepared to go.

Dax spun around and left the barn. He needed a meeting. Just over five years sober and he could still be hit over the head with the urge to find mind-numbing relief in the bottom of a bottle. He strode toward his truck, not making eye contact with anyone. A glance at his watch confirmed that he could still make the morning meeting that was held at the church in town.

He climbed into his truck. Zeke would understand. They had an agreement. Dax only ever left the ranch if it was important. He didn't hit any red lights, and by the time he pulled into the church parking lot, he was already feeling better. Dax yanked his keys from the ignition and strode inside. The meeting had already started. There were only half-a-dozen individuals in attendance—pretty normal for a Friday morning. Only there was one person who he didn't recognize.

His steps slowed as he moved toward the chair closest to the door. One of the usuals was sharing and all eyes were on him, giving Dax the opportunity to observe the newcomer. Her blonde hair was cut short, almost buzzed clean off. She had a tattoo of two interlocking hearts on the inside of her wrist that she seemed fixated on. Her thumb traced over the tattoo, back and forth as she listened to the man who was currently speaking. Her continued fidgeting was setting him on edge.

But then she stopped. Her whole body went still as if she'd been frozen by Medusa herself. Then she swung her eyes around to meet his. They were the color of the sky after a rainstorm— bright blue and so different from Sarah's dark brown ones. The woman's brows pulled together and she gave him a little wave.

Dax tore his gaze away from her and focused on the speaker. When he was done and had taken his seat, the woman stood. Her gaze locked on Dax, and she offered a small smile. "Hi. I'm Ann, and I'm an alcoholic."

The small chorus that welcomed her was drowned out by his own thoughts. She was tall and trim. Her clothing was more reminiscent of the sort of stuff a cowgirl might wear in Holly- wood. Her shorts were too short, and her boots looked like a fashion statement instead of being something that would actu- ally work on a ranch. If he had to guess, he would have said she came from the city.

By the time she sat down, he realized he hadn't learned anything about her. It was as if his brain had gone on autopilot and had decided to focus on other things. The room had gone quiet. This was usually when he'd stand and share his wisdom and experiences. But at the moment he didn't feel he could.

The organizer ended the meeting and reminded everyone to take a donut or maybe two before everyone left. Dax remained seated, ruminating on the feelings that continued to swirl without rhyme or reason within him.

The metal folding chair beside him screeched. He glanced over to find Ann holding a donut in one hand and a coffee in the other. "I was told you might be open to sponsoring me."

He stiffened. "What? No. I'm not ready for something like that just yet."

She shrugged, leaning back and resting her elbow on the back of her chair. "It was worth a shot." Her eyes lifted to his, then darted away. "You could probably tell, but I'm new."

"Yes, ma'am." He decided to keep things formal because he didn't want to give her the wrong idea.

A smile touched her lips. "Like I said, this was my first meeting, and I think I might need a friend."

He fought the surprise that threatened to paint his face. The last thing she needed was to feel judged by someone when she'd finally found the courage to come to the meeting in the first place. Dax leaned forward. "Well, realizing you need help is the first step in recovery."

She glanced at him, then away once more. "How long have you been in recovery?"

"I got my five-year chip a few weeks ago."

It was her turn to look surprised. She swung her attention toward him. "Congratulations."

"Thanks." He leaned forward, resting his forearms on his knees. "It's a lot of work, but it's worth it. I promise." As much as he wanted to ask her more about herself, he refrained. Getting too nosy wasn't good either.

The host for the meeting approached and pulled a chair to their little group. "Dax. Glad you're getting to know our newest resident. Ann Keagan just moved here. She and her brothers are taking over that ranch to the west of the Callahan's property."

Dax shot a curious look at her. "Really? Wasn't that place—"

"A hole? Yeah. It's going to take a ton of work to get up and running. I think my brother's going to be looking for some volunteers to do an official barn raising." She snickered. "That's still a thing, right?"

He nodded. "Sure. We've done a couple of them here. Let him know he should put up some flyers at the hardware store. Plenty of people should see it there."

She gave him a small smile. "I'll let him know. Thanks, Dax, was it?"

Dax nodded and held out his hand.

She accepted, giving it a firm shake. "Well, I should probably get back. If my brothers figure out I'm missing, they'll come looking for me. That's the last thing this town needs."

He frowned. "They don't know you're in the program?"

Ann got to her feet. "That's why it's called *anonymous*, right?"

He rose beside her. "But you ought to have a support system."

"I'll find a sponsor, and then I'll be set." She held up her coffee and nodded to Pastor Ben. "Thanks for the food."

Dax watched the woman walk away until she had disappeared out the door.

"I figured you'd be the best fit for her."

Startled, Dax glanced at the pastor. "You know I can't do that sort of thing."

"Actually, I don't. That's why I sent her your way. You've been at this a long time, Dax. You have a lot of wisdom to share."

Dax shook his head. "I'm too busy to have to worry about someone else on top of everything at the ranch. There's this new girl—"

"Sarah?"

He shot another look at Ben. "You've met her?"

Ben shook his head. "No, but I've spoken to the sheriff about her. She's his niece, right?"

Dax nodded even as his head hollered that was incorrect. There was no way she was the sheriff's niece.

Ben smiled. "How's she doing? I hear she's in need of some guidance too."

This was news to him. No one else had mentioned anything like that before. Why would Sarah need guidance? She was a grown woman. Dax lifted a shoulder. "She seems nice enough, if a little rough around the edges." His lips quirked up at the corners as that morning's memories flooded his subconscious. "The chickens sure don't like her... that's for sure."

Ben offered a smile in return. "Well, you be sure to keep an eye on her. I'm sure the sheriff had his reasons for asking Zeke to take her in." He gave Dax a pointed look. "And you know better than anyone how a second chance can mean the world to someone who needs it." He clapped Dax on the shoulder and wandered over to another small group.

Dang it. The pastor was right. Sarah might be a stranger. She might even be hiding something from the people at Slate Rock Ranch. But she was still trying. Sarah got up every morning and completed her tasks—even though she wasn't that good at it. He could cut her some slack. But that didn't mean he'd be doing her chores for her ever again. If she was going to succeed at life in the country, she needed to solve her problems on her own.

FROM THE SECOND Dax returned to the ranch, he was behind. He'd completely forgotten about the load of new horses, yearlings, that were being delivered to the ranch. That meant he had to oversee them getting situated and put on a schedule for training. But that wasn't all. There was a fence that had been broken out between the Callahan's property and the new owners to the west. He'd have to take a few men out there to get it sorted before they could move some cattle into the grazing pastures. All that along with several other chores were to be completed before the end of the week.

As much as he berated himself for attending that meeting, he knew he'd done the right thing. Skipping a meeting was the worst thing he could have done. Now he was in the right mindset to get his work done efficiently.

Dax sat in his saddle, overseeing the new yearlings that were being led toward the barn. They were a good group of horses—strong and spirited. It'd be some work to break them, but once they were trained, they'd make fine additions to the herd they had.

He touched the brim of his hat with his pointer finger, adjusting it on his head. Sarah darted from the barn just as a skittish yearling yanked and pulled away from the kid who was supposed to keep the animal restrained. She yelped and backed away from the horse as it charged forward.

She was going to be trampled. Sarah wasn't running nearly fast enough.

Dax wasted no time. He dug his heels into the sides of his horse and darted toward them. It didn't matter that the animal wasn't quite fully grown. There was still a lot of strength behind those legs. Not to mention, it had at least five hundred pounds of force behind it. There wasn't a doubt in his mind that she would get seriously hurt if he didn't intervene.

Sarah ran right to an area where the animal would corner her. It continued straight at her. Man, this woman had a knack for attracting the animals who wanted trouble. Dax charged forward, putting himself between the young horse and the fearful woman.

The yearling rose up on hind legs and retreated a few steps until the kid who'd let it get away finally caught up to them.

"Sorry," he mumbled, pulling on the lead rope.

Dax glowered at the kid. He should have known better. There was no excuse to let an untrained animal go like that. Someone could have been seriously hurt. Speaking of which, he turned and stared down at Sarah. Her wide eyes followed the yearling, and her chest rose and fell with such speed he was certain she would hyperventilate.

He let out a curse as he slipped from his saddle. "You need to slow your breathing. You're going to make yourself faint."

She stared at him with wide eyes and nodded, but her breathing only worsened.

Dax grasped her upper arms and peered into her face. "You need to slow your breathing. Hold your breath or make your lips small and blow out through that hole." The two of them were mere inches apart. "Can you do that? *Slow*. Fill your stomach, not your chest."

Something finally clicked and she got her breathing under control. Her skin was pale, and she reached out to grasp onto his forearms as she closed her eyes briefly.

"Are you okay?" he asked.

She nodded again but didn't say anything, nor did she open her eyes. Her knees buckled slightly, and her fingers dug into his skin.

"No, you're not." He scooped her up into his arms and headed for the house. His gaze searched for someone who could take his horse and tie her up. "Connie, put Chip away for me, will you?"

Constance Callahan had seemed to materialize out of nowhere. She must have been in the barn with Sarah. She hurried toward him. "Is she okay?"

"She'll be fine."

Sarah buried her face into his neck, but she still trembled. She must have been more terrified than he'd thought.

"She'll be fine," he repeated. "She just needs some shade and something to drink." He met Constance's worried gaze. "You can handle Chip?"

Constance nodded.

Dax offered her a reassuring smile and strode toward the main house. He'd have to have a serious talk with Zeke about training this girl. The sheriff wouldn't be thrilled about the lack of safety that had occurred today.

3

———

Sarah

*E*verything was foggy—like a gray cloud had descended around her—but one that smelled really good. There was something soft that rubbed against her cheek. She rubbed her face into it and a soft moan escaped her lips.

Something in the back of her mind seemed to be nagging at her. Fear. Terror. Her heart rate accelerated once more, and her breaths came out short and sharp. There was a horse. It was chasing after her.

Her eyes flew open and she attempted to scramble to her feet. Strong arms held her tight against that soft, good-smelling place. The fog lifted, and her head snapped up to find that cowboy holding her.

Sarah let out a squeak and bucked within his arms. "Let me down. Put me down."

"I can't do that," he grunted.

"Oh, yes, you can. Put me down, now!"

He sighed as if she were a child who didn't know that she had control over her own body. "Little lady, if I put you down, you're going to collapse."

"Don't call me that," she ground out. "And you don't know what you're talking about. I'm fine."

"You will be as soon as I get you out of the sun and get you something to drink."

She squirmed once more until he finally deposited her onto the porch swing. When she lifted her gaze to meet his, she found him shaking his head.

"What were you thinking?" he asked.

"Me?" she snapped. "I'm thinking I don't *know* you. I don't like that you think you can be so familiar with me. Who *are* you?"

"I seem to remember asking you that very question a few hours ago," he said.

She rubbed her arms with both of her hands. "Well, you got me here. Now you can go."

He still stared at her. His gray eyes doing that strange thing that she absolutely hated. It made her nerves light up with a tension that was almost painful. "If you're fine, then prove it. I'm not leaving you here until I know you won't do something stupid and end up flat on your face."

Her eyes narrowed. "What are you talking about?"

"Have you ever had a panic attack? How about carbon monoxide poisoning? Because I've witnessed it first-hand, and I can tell you it's no walk in the park."

She snorted.

"I mean it, Sarah. If you're okay, prove it. Stand up and walk over there." He pointed to the other side of the porch.

Sarah huffed. "Fine." She rose to her feet, and immediately stars filled her vision and her legs buckled. But before she could crumble to the floor, his strong arm slipped around her waist and pulled her back onto the porch swing.

She sucked in a sharp breath and stared at the legs that had betrayed her. It was like she'd been given some sort of paralyzing agent and the medication hadn't worn off quite yet. This was definitely something she had never experienced before. Her stomach knotted and she felt the blood slowly return to her head. Okay, so he was right. She wasn't ready to walk just yet. But now she knew. He didn't have to stick around.

Sara pressed her lips together. "Okay. I get it. I'll stay put for a little bit. You don't have to worry about me anymore. I'm not your ward or anything."

He folded his arms and shifted his weight so he stood more firmly in front of her. "I'm sorry. I can't do that. I'm going to stay here until Zeke comes out to discuss your training. We can't have you causing this kind of trouble at every turn. Someone is going to get hurt, and it might not always be you."

"What is *wrong* with you?" The question burst from her without provocation.

But to his credit, he didn't react.

"Seriously. Are you trying to mess with me? Do you get some sick pleasure from always hanging around me?"

This time his brows furrowed. "Is that how you treat the person who saved your life?"

A blush flashed across her whole body and she looked away. There was no telling what would have happened if he hadn't stepped between her and that charging horse. Today had to be the worst day of her life. Well, second to the day the sheriff had pulled her over. She took in a deep breath and let it out slowly. "Thank you." As much as she wanted to, she couldn't keep the begrudging tone out of her voice.

The front door opened. Then the storm door screeched as it swung open and banged closed, revealing Zeke. His hands were shoved in his pockets and his face looked lined and tired. He glanced from her to the cowboy. "What happened, Dax?"

Dax. That's right. That was his name.

Dax pulled off his hat and ran a hand through his dark hair before returning his hat. "One of the wranglers didn't have a good hold on his yearling, and it got loose. For some reason, it took a shine to Sarah here. It nearly trampled her."

"*Nearly?*"

"I got to her in time."

Zeke's gaze landed on Sarah again. "And you're okay?"

"That's what I've been saying," she said with exasperation. "I'm *fine.*"

"She's lying, sir. She nearly collapsed from a panic attack and I'm assuming a mild case of hyperventilating."

Zeke frowned. "Is this true, Miss Newton?"

Sarah broke eye contact to give Dax a dark look. "Yes, sir," she mumbled. "But I'm sure I'll be ready to head back out there after—"

"You're not going out there anymore today."

"But—"

Zeke held up his hand. "If Michael—your uncle heard about this, I'm sure he'd give me an earful if I let you get back to work. No. Don't the two of you have a lunch planned today?"

Her first meeting with the sheriff. She'd hoped they'd all forget so she could avoid it. But that wasn't going to happen. Not with so many people tasked to look out for her best interests. She sighed. "Yes, we do." She stared at the lines on her hands. Anything to keep her from looking into the dark eyes of the guy who both saved her and turned her in.

"Then when you're settled, Dax here can drive you to town."

Her head snapped up and she gaped at Zeke. "But—I'm more than capable of driving—" The look he gave her was enough to make a charging stampede reconsider their plans and turn in the other direction. Of course he wouldn't want her to borrow one of his vehicles. She *was* a criminal. But to have Dax take her?

Why did the universe hate her so much today? For heaven's sake, she wished she could just catch a break. Sarah gave him a sharp nod. "Okay."

"Sir?" Dax's hard voice drew her attention. His features gave away how much he didn't want to be her chaperone. Here it was. If he refused, then Zeke would have to find someone else to take her. That or let her finally borrow a truck. "We need to reevaluate what you're willing to let Sarah do at the ranch. She shouldn't be given tasks that she isn't equipped to handle."

Zeke glanced at her momentarily, and yet again, her flushed skin gave her away. "What are you suggesting?"

Dax didn't even bother looking in her direction. "She needs to be trained better. You can't just expect her to know how to do things with a quick overview of the task at hand. She needs to know what to do in an emergency. And she's far too scared to gather the eggs. Have Eloise keep doing that."

Zeke's lips twitched. "If you want Eloise to be the one gathering eggs, you're going to have to break the news yourself. I'm not doing it." He met Sarah's confused expression. "What do you think, Sarah. Do you agree with Mr. Heaton here?"

She blinked. "Agree with what? That I'm not a good rancher?"

Zeke chuckled. "No. Do you agree that you require better training? You're the only one who can decide that."

Oh, she wanted more than anything to tell the two of them that she could handle anything thrown her way. But there was no point in lying. They knew she wasn't ready to be a ranch hand. She'd grown up in a rich family with a housekeeper, tutors, and several other people who did things for her. The only thing she'd insisted they let her learn was driving. She refused to be the only person in her group of friends who didn't know how to drive.

The irony of this situation was not lost on her. She sat here, with two strangers making decisions about her life. How was that any different than the people at home doing the same thing? She'd gone to college to get away from that. She'd gotten into trouble with those guys she'd brought to Copper Creek because it had made her feel empowered and like she was in control of her own life.

Now she was right back where she'd started. She wasn't in control of her life. Not really. Sarah sighed. "I think some additional training would be nice." No, she wouldn't be getting paid for any of it. But maybe she could avoid the chickens and charging animals.

Zeke turned to Dax. "Well, I suppose you've got a new protégé, son."

Dax's eyes widened and he stiffened. "What? No, I don't have time for that. I'm already responsible—"

"I'm sure you can delegate some of that. Wasn't that why I gave you that promotion a few weeks back? Adeline hasn't been able to work as much, and we need more help. *She* knew how to delegate. Are you suggesting I made the wrong decision?"

Dax clamped his mouth shut.

Sarah couldn't deny the amount of pleasure she got from seeing him flustered. The best part was that he'd done this to himself. He was the only one responsible for the predicament he was in.

Her pleasure was short-lived. Dax taking her on meant she wasn't going to be able to rid herself of him. No matter where she went, there was little chance that she'd be alone. She bit back a groan. This was just great.

THE SCENERY FLEW by as they sat in Dax's truck in utter silence. The only sound she heard was the whirring of the engine. Dax had a decent vehicle. It was clear he took care of it. Despite being a work truck, it didn't have a scratch on it. How was that possible? She'd seen every car, truck, and ATV that had driven onto this property since she'd arrived and not one of them looked as nice as this one.

Sarah wouldn't be able to move even if she wanted to for fear that he would chastise her for doing something wrong in his precious truck. Without turning her head, she glanced at his hands, where they gripped the steering wheel. Tight enough to turn his knuckles white. His easygoing attitude from this morning had been completely wiped from his countenance. So, this was the tipping point. He only wanted to pester her if he wasn't being ordered to.

"Sorry," she muttered. Great. Now he had made her feel guilty over something she didn't have any control over. If she had told Zeke no, Dax would have most assuredly told Zeke she was a liar and that they needed to do something about her training anyway.

"Why are you apologizing?"

She lifted a shoulder.

"Well, don't."

"Okay."

He looked at her out of the corner of his eye. "I meant what I said to Zeke. I would still rather be stuck with you than see you get hurt."

Sarah huffed. "You have a strange way of showing it."

A strange kind of sound burst from his lips. It was like the combination of a laugh and a cough. She turned and stared at him but knew better than to ask him if he was okay. Instead, she turned her focus out the window. "How long did you say you've known Zeke?"

"I didn't."

She fought the instinct to look at him again. If he wanted to tell her, he would. She was slowly getting used to the way Dax communicated. He wouldn't use ten words when two would suffice.

"Tell you what, you give me something, and I'll give you something."

"I'm not interested in playing that game, Dax."

"Suit yourself. But the offer will remain open as long as you want it to."

"Like I said. Not interested."

At some point they'd arrived in town. Dax pulled up in front of the sheriff's station. "Enjoy your lunch with your *uncle*." He nodded toward the building. "I'll be back in an hour."

She pushed open the door and slammed it shut without saying a word. She didn't need a babysitter, and she was quickly getting the feeling that was exactly what Dax would become. Well, there was no turning back now.

4

———

Dax

Dax tapped his fingers on the steering wheel, then ducked his head and peered at the sheriff's station. Sarah was late. She was supposed to have come out about ten minutes ago. If the time on the dash got any later, he was going to head inside himself and remind both the sheriff and Sarah that the world didn't revolve around them.

Tap. Tap. Tap.

Where was she?

He let out a sigh and pushed open the door to climb out. Just as he put his feet on the sidewalk, Sarah and the sheriff emerged from the building but stayed on the top step. His eyes narrowed. Had she been crying? No. He was imagining things. Her eyes looked a little more pink than he'd remembered, but then again, he hadn't been paying much attention to her when he dropped her off.

The sheriff held out his hand and she shook it.

Weird.

He didn't know of any uncle who would shake the hand of their niece. Dax couldn't hear what they were saying, but it didn't matter anyway because one second later, the sheriff glanced in his direction. He smiled and gave Dax a short wave. "Mr. Heaton."

"Sheriff." Dax moved a little closer to them.

The sheriff turned back to Sarah. "I'll see you next week. Don't worry. He's not going to win this. You'll be fine."

She nodded. "Thank you, sheriff." Sarah hurried down the steps and brushed past Dax to get into the truck.

Dax locked eyes with the sheriff until the man returned to the building. Something was definitely going on. He shifted, but Sarah's hunched body in his front seat caught his eye. She wasn't looking out the window. Instead, she was focused on something in her lap. Her demeanor had completely changed from the time he'd dropped her off. He almost wanted to blame the sheriff for whatever it was. But based on the snippet of conversation he'd overheard, that didn't sound right.

He gave his head a sharp shake. None of this was his business. He should just accept that Zeke trusted this woman. It didn't matter that in his gut he knew something wasn't quite right. Whatever it was, no one would get hurt. Sarah deserved her privacy. Isn't that what he got with AA?

Dax climbed into the truck and started the engine. He glanced at Sarah out of the corner of his eye. "You okay?"

She nodded.

"Did you have a nice lunch?"

A sigh escaped her lips. "What do you want, Dax? I know you don't trust me. You probably even enjoy seeing me struggle. The happiest I saw you was this morning when those stupid chickens were chasing me. Honestly? I'm surprised by the way you reacted to that horse charging me. I don't need your help. I'm just going to keep my head down and do the chores no one else wants."

"No, you're not."

She groaned and her head whipped up so fast it had to have hurt.

He resisted the urge to laugh at her drama. He liked her spunk, even if it made her a handful—sort of like those new yearlings they needed to train. "I'm going to teach you every-thing I know about wrangling horses."

Shock filled her face, from the way her eyes rounded to her open mouth. "What?" she whispered. "I can't—"

"If you're going to be spending more time with your uncle here in the future, it's best for you to know how to handle horses."

"I can handle horses." She swallowed. "I've ridden them. I just..." A scarlet color filled her face and she let out a harsh breath. "I just fell off one once, and I never tried again."

Dax bit back the grin that rested just beneath the surface. "Well, you just broke the first rule of horse riding. Don't you know? When you fall out of the saddle, you're supposed to get right back on the horse."

"There's literally no reason I need to learn to ride. After this summer, I'm going back home, and I don't plan on coming back."

"But wouldn't you miss your *uncle*?"

A mixture of emotions crossed her face. First confusion, then understanding, then a flat expression that couldn't be read. "My uncle and I are not all that close. I mean, my mom sent me out here because..." She chewed on her lower lip.

This was probably the closest he'd get to finding out the truth as to why she was here. "Were you in trouble, Sarah?"

"Yeah. You could say that."

Dax pressed his lips together. "I get that."

Her eyes flew to meet his.

"I want to make something clear. I still think you're hiding something that you probably should just tell me, though I won't push you. But you *can* trust me when I tell you I will help you get back on that horse. By the end of the summer, you're going to be one of the best wranglers here."

She let out a laugh. It was the first one he'd ever heard from her, and it warmed him like the hot liquid of a fresh cup of coffee on a cold winter morning.

He gave her a crooked smile. "Okay, I can't exactly make that sort of promise. But I will help you be a better rider and a better ranch hand. You just have to listen to me—trust me. Do you think you can do that?"

"I don't see how I have any choice in the matter." Her tone didn't match the words that came from her lips. They were lighter somehow. He'd managed to cheer her up, even if it was only a little. Dax reached for the volume knob on the dash and turned on the radio.

A classic country song filled the cab and a tangible sense of peace settled on both of them.

Dax groaned. "No. Not like that. We've been through this, Sarah. You can't expect your horse to listen to you if you don't show her who's boss."

Sarah threw her arms up in the air in frustration. "I'm bossing her around as much as I can."

He shook his head, then dropped it. His forearms rested on the corral railing, dangling over the side. "I hate to break it to you, little lady. But the horse can tell your heart isn't in it. Even I can tell, and I'm all the way over here."

Her face turned that hilarious shade of red she was known

for whenever he used that term of endearment. Sarah's hands curled into fists at her sides. "This stupid horse won't do what I'm telling her to do because she likes you better than me, and she can tell you're watching."

He dropped his hands and slipped through the rails. "That may be. But you're the one in charge, and if she gets even a hint that you don't have any confidence in yourself, she's not going to do a dang thing that you tell her to. She's a yearling, Sarah. That means she's stubborn as all get-out. You have to actually work at this if you want to get anywhere."

"I don't understand why I can't just improve my riding skills. Why are you making me learn how to train these horses? It's not like I'm going to make this my career."

He took a deep breath to remain calm. "We've been through this. If you learn the basics of horse communication and how their minds operate, then you'll be able to ride anything. Now, run the drill again." Dax folded his arms tight across his chest, itching to step in each time he saw her misstep.

Zeke knew what he was doing when he'd saddled Dax with Sarah. He wanted someone to keep an eye on her. And he needed someone he trusted. Well, if that old man needed something out of this arrangement, then the least he could do was tell Dax what that was.

At this moment, a full week into their training, she wasn't making any improvements. She was still just as skittish as any of those yearlings they were working with. At this point in starting a colt, he would have been in the saddle. The trust would have been developed, and they would be making progress.

Instead, that yearling wasn't even willing to make the rounds in the corral, much less listen to her. Sarah's less-than-smooth movements were setting the animal on edge.

He strode toward them. "No, not like that." There was a bite to his voice he hadn't meant to let out, but it got her attention. He reached for the lead rope and placed his other hand on the horse's nose. Sarah stumbled back a few steps, putting distance between them. Dax ignored her frantic movements as he ran his hand down the yearling's head. "We're going nice and slow. No need to get restless. Nice and slow. I'm in charge." His murmured, low words had the exact effect they usually did.

The horse settled, only pawing at the dirt once more. Dax kept his hand firmly on the lead, close to the animal. They took a step forward, then another. Resistance seemed to seep from the horse into Dax's hold on her. The trust wasn't there. That much was clear. But he continued to murmur his soft, firm words and eventually they made it around the corral three times.

Dax released the lead rope and patted the horse on her neck. Almost immediately the spunky animal kicked up her hind legs and trotted to the other side of the corral. Dax turned to face Sarah. "That's how you do it."

Her glower was the only indication of her attitude. Sarah folded her arms and huffed, "Well, you've been doing this for a long time. You can't expect me to—"

"I can expect whatever I want. I'm training you, aren't I? You have the best teacher you could hope to have. So why aren't you doing what I tell you to?"

She opened her mouth and then snapped it shut. The combination of a groan and a growl left her lips and she charged toward the gate.

"I'm not done with you yet."

"Well, I'm done with you!" she hollered back.

He sighed. If Sarah wasn't willing to humble herself and accept that not everything was going to go the way she wanted it to, she wasn't going to get anywhere.

"You know, if you taught her the way you taught me, you might get somewhere."

Dax spun, finding Brielle perched on the corral. "You really shouldn't eavesdrop, Bri."

She shrugged, a smile on her lips. "I wasn't. Sarah saw me. Maybe you should be more aware of your surroundings."

He took off his hat, hitting it against his leg as he strode toward her.

Brielle nodded in the direction that Sarah had left. "I mean it. You need to go easier on her. She didn't grow up on a ranch. She's literally a fish out of water."

He peeked at her. "Not literally."

She rolled her eyes. "You know what I mean. And if you'd be a little nicer—"

"I *am* nice." A smile tugged at his lips. "You like me. The animals like me. Even your *dad* likes me."

"Okay, a little less condescending. You're not telling her what she's doing *right*. You realize she talks about how you're treating her, don't you?"

"And that should bother me?" He moved closer to her, keeping his chest a foot away from bumping up against her knees. They'd shared a few intimate moments over the years, but he'd long learned that Brielle was untouchable. She was damaged in her own right—a wild horse, never to be tamed. It was a good thing he'd figured it out before he'd fallen too hard for her.

Brielle adjusted her position on the corral and tilted her head. "Whatever it is you have against her, I suggest you get over it. She's a nice enough person, Dax. Trust me. She's trying."

He arched a brow. "Are you suggesting that you know more about her than you've let on?"

She shrugged. "All I'm saying is that you're better than this. If you could teach me how to handle an untrained horse, then Sarah is a walk in the park."

"That's an unfair assessment. You were never afraid of anything."

Her smile could light up a room. Maybe it was her green eyes that had the boys fighting over her. They could shine like emeralds or darken like a pine forest during a storm. She was the beauty of the Callahan sisters, and the one he would have done anything for.

But she knew all about the feelings he'd had for her, and she couldn't return them. Or she wouldn't.

Brielle gave him a pointed look that said he was going to follow her instructions to a T. "From what I understand, she doesn't have a strong family unit. She's always felt more on the outside than anything else. It can be hard finding a place where you belong. You know that better than anyone else."

Dang it.

Why did she have to play to his softer side? He stepped back and replaced his hat on his head. "I can't make any promises, Bri. You know that."

"*No*, what I know is that you're a whiz with this sort of stuff. Treat her like you treat me."

He snorted. "Okay, that's gonna be impossible." He gave her a meaningful look that made her look away. Guilt. He'd seen it in her eyes before she broke eye contact. "You are one of a kind."

"Everyone is one of a kind." She climbed down from her perch and put the rail between them. "I mean it, Dax. Patience and charity. You might be surprised at how that will change things." She took a step backward before turning and heading in the same direction that Sarah had taken.

What did she know that he didn't? Sarah was here because of some unfortunate living circumstances back home. She could be running away from something, or she had done something. Either way, this ranch was a chance to adjust her outlook.

And he knew more than anyone how much a person could use that when things got dark.

5

———

This place was supposed to be easier than dealing with her family. How was she ever going to learn all the ranching stuff they were trying to teach her? Failing miserably at everything she tried was turning out to be a good punishment for her criminal actions. She would have been better off just telling her family what had happened.

Sarah hurried into the house, hoping nobody saw her. There was a strong chance she'd get in trouble for not finishing her work with Dax today. She wasn't quite sure how everything was being calculated for her community service these days. It felt like she wasn't working nearly as much, but at the same time there was still a lot to do.

It probably had something to do with Dax and the way he made her stick with the drills over and over and over again.

She blew out a sharp breath. Well, Zeke was the one who signed off on those government documents. As long as all the numbers added up, she'd get out of here at the end of the summer and never have to see a horse or chicken again.

The original bedroom they'd put her in had been Adeline's old bedroom. But over the last two weeks, she'd opted to share with one of Zeke's daughters. Brielle was more than willing to bunk up. But Sarah had suspicions that it had more to do with the second eldest daughter's propensity for sneaking out at night.

To her knowledge, the girl wasn't doing anything against her father's strict rules besides breaking curfew. Technically, she could date whomever she wanted now that her older sister had gotten married.

Sarah settled onto the edge of her bed and glanced around the room. Her own strict upbringing didn't seem nearly as bad when she compared it to the way Zeke had raised his daughters. She *should* be grateful for that, right? Maybe the old saying was true. The grass wasn't greener on the other side, no matter how much it appeared to be.

The open door moved slightly, and Brielle ducked inside. She met Sarah's gaze and offered her a tight smile. "Hey."

"Hey." Sarah scooted back onto the bed and laid down, staring at the ceiling. "Is Dax always such a demanding boss? I can't seem to do anything right."

Brielle was quiet—so much so that it was clear Brielle didn't agree with Sarah's sentiment.

Sarah groaned. "So he only hates me."

"He doesn't *hate* you." Brielle moved over to her bed and stared down at her. "Scoot over."

Sarah obliged, and Brielle crawled onto the bed with her.

Brielle placed one hand behind her head and stared at the ceiling too. "He doesn't hate you," she repeated. "He just doesn't trust you."

A snort exploded from Sarah's chest. "Then he's a hypocrite."

"How do you figure?"

She twisted her head around to give Brielle a pointed look. "All he ever preaches is trust and making the animals trust me by having the right body language. But how can I do that? My body language is my body language. I can't exactly change it."

Brielle smiled. "Have you considered that he's like an animal himself? You aren't giving him much of an opportunity to trust you."

Sarah stilled. Brielle made a good point. She hadn't exactly been willing to give him any information about herself. Maybe she needed to tell him something that would make him trust her a little more. "He's not going to trust me if I tell him who I really am."

Brielle frowned. "Yeah, you're right about that."

"Then I'm stuck. He won't trust me, so he won't treat me better. And that means I'm never going to get to the point where I can excel here."

Her friend peeked at her. "Do you *want* to excel here?"

"I don't know. I mean, it would make this summer a lot easier if I did. If I could ride a horse better, maybe I could do other chores that I might actually enjoy. But he's not teaching me that. Why can't he just let me take a horse that is already trained?"

Brielle shrugged. "Sometimes Dax sees things we don't. He's good at that." Her voice was soft, almost in awe of the person she described. Did they have a thing going? Sarah hadn't seen any indication of it. Brielle didn't talk about Dax in a romantic way.

Then again, Brielle didn't talk about *anyone* in a romantic way. She only ever referred to men as a way to have fun.

Sarah glanced once more in Brielle's direction. "Do you like him?"

She stiffened. "What do you mean?"

"The way you're talking about him, it's like you have a thing for him." Sarah turned on her side and rested her head in her hand as she propped up on her elbow. "It's okay if you do. I won't judge you based on your poor preference of guys." Her lips lifted into a small smile. "You can tell me."

Brielle didn't move. Her eyes remained locked on the ceiling. There was no teasing in her voice when she finally spoke. "A couple years ago we got pretty close."

Sarah's eyes widened and she sat up. "Seriously?"

Brielle gave her a wan smile. "Yeah."

"What happened?"

Her friend sat up, folded her legs beneath her and met Sarah's gaze. "It was before Adeline got married. At the time, I thought I wanted a real relationship. And Dax was everything." Her sad smile tugged at Sarah's heart. Whatever had happened between the two of them must have been hard.

She waited, expecting to be told that Dax had broken her heart. He would. Dax with the smoldering eyes and the rumbling voice. "What did he do?"

Brielle straightened and let out a laugh. "Nothing."

"But... you seem so sad. I just thought..."

Brielle reached out and placed her hand on Sarah's knee. "It was me. Adeline's husband—Sean—"

Sarah gasped. "You didn't—"

Brielle laughed again. "Will you let me finish?" She shook her head. "Sean's dad was killed in an accident on the ranch."

Confusion swirled within Sarah. She hadn't been around long, but the other wranglers talked. From what she had gathered, the two families weren't the closest—even after they were joined by a marriage and a business contract. "Why would Sean's dad dying affect your relationship with Dax?"

Brielle withdrew her hand and clasped it with the other one in her lap. She stared at them, picking at her cuticles with her thumb. "It's hard to explain. We weren't close to them, but it hit me pretty hard. After I've reflected on it, I've come to the realization it has more to do with my mom." She lifted her gaze, her eyes shining with moisture. "My dad had to raise us without help. We were really little when my mom passed away. Adeline stepped up, but she was barely a teenager. I guess I got scared. I told Dax I wasn't ready for anything serious. We were sneaking around as it was, but I wasn't willing to step out into the light either. I cared about him—I still do. But no, I don't love him—not enough to put aside those feelings and get married." She lifted a shoulder and tilted her head as she peered at Sarah. "So for now, we're just friends."

There were no words that could make her friend feel better over this. Fears of losing a loved one were incredibly difficult to move past. If that was the root of Brielle's fear of commitment, it could take years for her to get over it.

Brielle brushed at her cheek with the back of her hand. "This conversation wasn't supposed to be about me. I came to talk to you about what happened out there."

Rolling her eyes, Sarah shook her head. "I'm a lost cause."

"No, you're not. You just need to adjust your outlook. You're gonna be here anyway, right? When is your community service done? The end of summer, right?"

Sarah nodded.

"And you have to meet with the sheriff again today?"

Another nod.

"What if I come with you and we come up with an additional plan? There has to be other things you can do to get your hours in."

"Dax wouldn't go for that. Apparently, he's my supervisor now and gets to decide what happens. I told the sheriff, and he doesn't have any problem with it as long as your dad had set it up. I feel like I don't have any say in this."

Brielle frowned. "That does sound like my dad." Her features brightened. "You know what? He doesn't have any say in what you do outside of your working schedule. I'm going to take you riding. I'm great at giving lessons."

Hesitation filled Sarah's entire being. She still hadn't gotten in a saddle since she was a kid. Dax was the only one who knew why she refused to do so now. As far as Brielle was concerned, Sarah had just never ridden.

Running the yearling in an exercise was a way for her to prolong the inevitable.

And yet as she watched the other ranch hands come and go from the trails, she couldn't help but wish she could go along. There was something about being around these beautiful creatures that filled her with longing and, at the same time, terrified her to her core.

Yep. She wasn't built to live or work on a ranch.

"Come on, Sarah. After you go to your meeting with the sheriff, let's go for a ride."

"But Dax—"

"Don't worry about him." Brielle's eyes sparkled. "And then tonight we should go out. There's an event at the country club. Karaoke, I think."

Sarah's brows furrowed. "But what about curfew?"

Brielle nudged her, then winked. "You'd be going with the best of the best. We won't get caught. I promise."

The ride to town was much like the one last week. While Dax had the radio going, he was as stiff as ever. He rarely spoke to her besides trying to get her to open up about her past. The only reason she was interested in going to her meeting with the sheriff was for an update.

She waited for the sheriff to shut the door behind her as she sat in the chair facing his desk. His feet clipped across the linoleum floor until he came to stand before her. He leaned against his large cedar desk and folded his arms. "How are things going this week?"

Sarah scowled. "It's like I said when Zeke—Mr. Callahan made me call you. They're switching up what they're having me do. I still have a set number of chores, but now half of my time is spent working with the new horses they got last week."

"And you're unhappy about it?"

She shrugged. "I'm not all that great at it, and I don't see how it's helping the community."

"Well, training horses is important around here. Are you aware that the owner of the country club is utilizing the property for equine therapy? They're due to open next spring with services geared toward special needs children and veterans suffering from PTSD."

"Okay?"

His eyes wrinkled as he smiled at her. "Those horses you are working with might end up at a place like that. Starting those colts is an important part of their training. If you can master that, you will set the foundation for working with any animal on these ranches."

She threw up her hands. "But I'm not going to work on a ranch. I'm here until the end of the summer. Then I'm gone." She blew out a frustrated breath. "Was there any update on Kenneth?"

The sheriff's hands dropped to his sides and he pushed away from the desk. He walked around it and pulled out his chair before taking a seat. "Unfortunately, they got him a deal similar to yours. He was given thirty days but got out early with a parole hearing. Now he's doing community service."

"But he *shot* you! And he threatened to come after me!"

"No one knows better than me that it's not a perfect system. We can be grateful that his community service will be served in Colorado Springs. He's not allowed to leave the city limits for the next six months. But after that…"

"It doesn't matter. If he wanted to come here, there's nothing stopping him. The drive isn't that far. What's to stop him from coming to find me? I hung him out to dry." The rate of her breathing increased and her heart thundered. That feeling of lightheadedness returned. Great. It was happening again.

Sarah leaned over and put her head between her knees. She'd never had panic attacks before, and now she'd had two in as many weeks. If she didn't get this figured out, she could end up in the hospital. When she sat up, the sheriff was holding out a bottled water toward her, concern etched in the lines of his face.

"I'll have my deputies keep an eye out for him. Perhaps it would be a good idea to let Dax—"

"Absolutely not. He already doesn't like me. I'm not about to give him another reason to hate me."

"Sarah," the sheriff spoke softly, "the people in this town have moved on. I don't see any of them doing or saying anything that would hurt you. They might be a town of gossips, but they aren't going to be nearly as dangerous as Kenneth might."

She shook her head fervently. "We agreed I could come and go under the radar. What is it they say? People need someone to blame—someone to hate? I refuse to be that person."

He studied her, his eyes piercing into her, but he didn't argue. That was one thing she appreciated about him. The sheriff didn't push her to do anything she wasn't comfortable with.

Sarah rose from her seat. "Are we done?"

The sheriff nodded. "I'll see you next week."

6

———

Dax

Dax nodded a hello to the Callahan's neighbors, Jess and Ruby, as they wandered down the street. His back was pressed against his truck as he waited once again for Sarah to be done with her meeting. She said she wouldn't be long today. Apparently, the sheriff was busy.

Sure enough, Sarah materialized and hurried down the steps. She looked just as upset as she had last week.

Dax looked up at the door, finding the sheriff watching him. Neither one of them appeared to be willing to break eye contact until Sarah came up short in front of him. She waved her hand in front of his face. "Hey. Earth to Dax. I'm all done."

His brows lowered and he stood aside to open the door for her. She climbed in, and he shut the door, then looked up at the sheriff again, only to find him gone.

When he settled into his seat, he held onto his keys, not putting it into the ignition. "Is everything okay?"

"Yeah. Everything is hunky-dory. Why?" Her tone was off and she was paler than usual.

He swallowed hard and glanced at her out of the corner of his eye. "I can't pretend to know what's going on—"

"Then don't worry about it. I'll be fine. I'm just frustrated at something the sheriff—I mean my uncle—told me."

Dax scowled. "I'm trying to help you, Sarah. Will you just give me the benefit of the doubt?"

She huffed. "I don't trust you. And you don't trust me. Let's not pretend anything has changed. Sure, we've had to spend more time together lately, but we can't even say we're friends." She gestured toward the keys in his hand. "Why don't you just get us home and then you can stop acting like you care about me."

"Will you just be quiet for a minute and let me talk?"

She jumped, turning wide eyes on him.

Dax grimaced and let out a sigh. "You're right. I've not been very welcoming toward you."

Sarah's jaw dropped open.

"But whether you like it or not, there are a few people who have been."

"So what are you saying? You get to treat me like I'm someone who can't be trusted because I won't tell you my life story? Well guess what? I've heard all of that before. I'm a grown woman who gets to make her own choices. I will graduate from college in a year. I'm just here for the summer—"

"Yes, you've mentioned that." He groaned and dragged his hand down his face. "But the fact is, you won't be leaving anytime soon. You might as well learn some new skills for if you ever decide to come back. And Bri seems to think that my idea to train you with horses is a good one. Don't you value her opinion?"

Sarah's shoulders slumped and she glanced at him out of the

corner of her eye. "Of course I value what she thinks. But it doesn't matter if you don't hold even a percentage of that opinion." Her eyes seemed to be pleading with him to care about her. To show her that she mattered to him. Not seeming to find what she was looking for, she turned away and looked down at her hands in her lap.

He faced her, waiting until she looked toward him. But that didn't seem like something she was willing to do so he began anyway. "I'm going to do better. It might seem like you're going to be here for a long time, but it goes by faster than you realize. And you know what else? I'll let you name that yearling."

Slowly, her gaze lifted to meet his. "Really?"

"Sure. You need to have some kind of connection with her."

For the first time that day, a ghost of a smile touched her face. "Okay."

"Okay." He gave her a short nod. "I'm not going to go any easier on you, though."

"No one asked you to."

That wasn't quite true. Brielle had basically done as much. She wanted him to teach Sarah like he'd taught her. Well, when he'd taught Brielle, he'd already developed feelings for her. It was easier to have patience and talk her through things. She wasn't nearly as combative as Sarah. Luckily, there was no way he would make that mistake twice.

He cleared his throat, still fingering the keys in his hand. "Can I ask you something?"

She visibly stiffened. "What?" Her voice was almost timid.

Dax nodded toward the sheriff's station. "Is the sheriff treating you with respect? He's not doing anything inappropriate, is he?"

Her eyes widened and her face turned scarlet. "Of course not! He's always been—he's my uncle, for heaven's sake." Her voice softened. "He's taking care of me."

"Then why are you always so upset when you come out after your meeting?"

She broke eye contact and shifted in her seat. "There's something else going on."

He waited for her to expound on her statement. Whatever it was, it had to be pretty bad to bring her to tears each time he'd picked her up. "Are you going to tell me?"

Sarah shook her head.

"Can I ask why?"

She scowled at her hands in her lap. "It's like I said, Dax. We're not friends. I don't need to tell you my life story. Just drop it, okay?"

His chest tightened and a weight settled on his shoulders that almost made it hard to breathe. Here he was trying to extend an olive branch, and she was pushing him back. At least he couldn't tell Brielle that he hadn't tried. She couldn't get mad at him anymore.

Dax put his keys into the ignition and shifted his truck into drive. Beside him, Sarah's stomach gurgled. She wrapped her arm around her middle and turned away from him. He let out a sigh. "Did you get anything to eat this morning?"

She didn't respond.

"Sarah."

"No."

"Why not?"

She shrugged. "I haven't been very hungry lately."

He shook his head. "Didn't they tell you that working on a ranch means you have to take care of yourself?" Dax made a sharp, sudden turn, causing her to let out a yelp and hold onto the armrest on the door.

"Dax! What on earth are you doing?"

"I'm getting you lunch."

She gaped at him. "I'm *not* hungry. You can save your money."

"It's not negotiable. Burger or chicken?"

"I'm not eating."

He shook his head. "I'm not against force-feeding you."

She gasped, and the corners of his mouth twitched as he turned his head toward her. Her body relaxed slightly, and she almost smiled back.

It wasn't going to be easy, but if Brielle wanted him to befriend Sarah, he'd try. It would just be so much easier if she'd let down the walls she insisted on building around her. Maybe he needed to reach her from a different angle.

They pulled into Sal's Diner and he climbed out. When Sarah had shut her door, he gestured toward the building. "They make the best pies here. I suggest the rhubarb, but Sean Baker's family is partial to the apple." He held out his arm. "After you."

She moved past him almost hesitantly. Once they were inside, she darted almost immediately for a booth on the wall with the large windows facing the parking lot. Dax removed his hat and gave a nod to the waitress before sitting across from Sarah.

He put his hat on the bench beside him and snatched a toothpick, placing it between his lips. Sarah glanced up at him. She must have felt his gaze on her. Instead of glowering at him like she was wont to do, she turned back to her menu. It rose up between them—yet another wall she had to put between herself and those around her. "Why are you looking at me like that?" Her voice was muffled behind the menu.

Dax placed his finger on the top of the menu and pulled it down so he could see her face. "It's been two weeks and I still know next to nothing about you."

She tugged the menu back in place. "You know as much as you need to."

He chuckled. "Why are you so scared to let anyone in?"

Her voice came from behind the menu, uncertain. "I'm not scared."

Dax tilted his head to the side. What, or who, was she hiding from? "That's what I said when I first came here." He'd caught her off guard with that one. Maybe Brielle had a point. He'd been more open with Brielle because he'd wanted her to see him. He couldn't say the same about Sarah.

Well, now was his chance to try a different approach.

He pulled the toothpick from his lips and twisted it between his finger and thumb. "Yeah. I was barely out of high school. My mom—if you want to call her that—she'd fostered me since I was ten. She never adopted me. Honestly, I don't think they would have let her. It was a headache to get approval to be a foster parent as a single woman anyway." He lifted his gaze, finding Sarah's big brown eyes peeking over the top of her menu and staring at him like he'd grown another head.

Dax chuckled and put the toothpick in the corner of his mouth. "Yep. When she passed away, her brother gave me a job." He left out all the nitty-gritty details of the darker moments of his life. She didn't need to know that he'd spent some time at juvie. Nor did she need to know that he was currently in AA. All she needed to know was that he could relate to her on some kind of level.

"Whatever it is you're trying to hide, you don't have to. I can assure you that the people here have seen it all. They're welcoming folks if you give them a chance. You're one of us, Sarah. You might not believe that yet, but you'll come around."

She stared at him long enough he thought that she might actually tell him something more. But all she did was lift the menu between them again.

So much for giving a little information and expecting to get something in return. This woman had to be the most stubborn person he'd ever encountered. He turned on the bench, resting his arm on the table and scanning the room.

"My mom had—*has* this plan for me."

His turned to look at her again, but the only view he had was the top of her head. She put the menu down, her face a strained mix of sadness and frustration.

"She's always wanted me to be perfect. I have to fit in this little box of hers. So, I moved out and went to a school halfway across the country."

"Where are you from?"

"Florida."

His brows lifted. "That *is* far. Did it help?"

She snorted. "What do you think?"

"I'm sure that was really hard. So what are your plans after this summer? Finish college and move home, right?"

Sarah nodded. "And I guess I'll be walking down the path my mother has paved for me."

His brows furrowed. "You know you don't have to—"

"Hello, honey." The waitress flashed Dax a smile and put the water on the table. "What can I get the two of you?"

Sarah glanced at Dax, then looked away. "I'm really not that hungry."

Dax looked up at the waitress, grabbing the menu from Sarah as he did. "We'll both have a burger and a chocolate shake."

The waitress nodded, retrieving the menus.

Sarah shot him a dirty look, and he laughed. "Humor me. Eat a couple bites. We aren't done with your training today."

"Actually, Brielle said that she'd like to go riding this afternoon. I was hoping that I could tag along."

He pressed his lips into a firm line. As much as that idea made him nervous, it was a way to get her more comfortable with horses without him breathing down her neck. "That sounds like a good idea. Mind if I come along?"

The way she squirmed in her seat and looked away made it clear she would rather he didn't.

"It's fine. I've got some other things I'll work on." He put his toothpick on the table and wrapped his fingers around the glass of water the waitress had brought. "So, your uncle. Is he helping you with this issue you have at home? Is that why he's the one your mom let you stay with?"

And just like that, the walls came right back up. Her eyes clouded over and she dropped her gaze. "I'd rather not talk about *why* I'm here."

Ugh. He'd pushed her too far. There would be no backtracking and getting her to open up about her family or her home.

They spent the rest of their meal in awkward silence while he tried to come up with another way to reach her. The only good thing that came from their lunch was making sure she got some food in her stomach. Apparently, she was hungrier than she'd thought. The woman could put away a burger, fries and a shake. On top of that, they each took a slice of pie to go.

Once they were in the truck and on the way home, Sarah finally spoke up again. "Thanks for lunch, Dax."

He offered her what he hoped was a supportive smile. "No problem."

7

———

"You're kidding. He took you to lunch?" Brielle laughed. "I never thought I'd see the day when Dax would take another girl on a date."

"It wasn't a date," Sarah said indignantly as she wobbled in her saddle. Her heart fluttered with unease. The horse's movements were far more uneven than she'd remembered. No wonder it was so easy to be thrown from the saddle. If this was how she felt when the horse was walking, then what was she going to do when the horse sped up?

Brielle turned in her saddle, looking over her shoulder at Sarah with a smirk on her face that rivaled all others. "Did he pay?"

"Well, yeah."

She laughed. "Think what you want, but Dax took you to lunch, ordered for you, and paid, it was a date."

Irritation simmered inside Sarah. "He took me to lunch

because I didn't eat breakfast and my stomach probably sounded like I hadn't eaten in days."

Brielle pulled on her reins and turned her horse so fast that Sarah's horse startled and stepped backward a few steps. "You *skipped* breakfast?"

Sarah's pounding heart refused to settle after she finally got the horse to stop its backward progress. Her hands gripped the reins so tight she was losing feeling in her fingers. She shot Brielle an irritated glare. How could Brielle not see that she was struggling? "Does it really matter? Like I told Dax. I wasn't hungry. You're not my mother. I can choose if I want to eat or not."

She shook her head. "It's summer and we do a lot of work—sunup to sundown. Be smart, Sarah. You wouldn't skip a meal if your job was a physical trainer."

"Stop with the judgment. I'm fine. He made me eat. Just drop it."

Brielle frowned. "Is something wrong? I mean, you're usually a little stand-offish, but lately you've been a little more angry than usual."

Sarah let out a sigh. "Sorry. I'm dealing with some stuff lately."

"Anything I can help you with?"

The horse beneath her shifted and Sarah sucked in sharply. "I just need to master something so I don't feel like such an idiot all the time. Everywhere I turn, I'm being told what to do and how to do it."

"To be fair, that's sorta what you signed up for. If you didn't want this, maybe you shouldn't have…"

Sarah froze. Her head snapped up and she stared at Brielle. Shock twisted her stomach in a way that caused additional pain. Even though Brielle knew about what she'd participated in, she had never pointed it out with such blatant disregard for Sarah's feelings.

Brielle's voice had trailed off and her eyes widened as if she realized what she'd just done. She shook her head. "I'm sorry, Sarah—"

"Just stop. You're right. I'm not like you. I made mistakes and as part of that, I get to be judged by people like you." She turned her reins and headed down the trail that they'd come.

"Sarah, wait. Where are you going?"

"I'm going back. I don't feel like going riding anymore."

"I'm sorry!" she called after her.

It wasn't even really Brielle's fault. Sarah had messed up big-time, all in an effort to prove that nobody could control her like her parents tried to. Who was she kidding, like her parents did. How embarrassing that she'd acted out so irrationally and gotten involved with the wrong people. This was why she refused to tell anyone about what she'd done. She'd made a mistake and now everyone would look down on her. And it could potentially irritate her parents if they found out. Would they disown her? Would it harm their business? She didn't know, and she didn't want to find out. For some reason, she was terrified of them learning about her mistakes.

She shut her eyes tight, and one tear slipped down her cheek. Thankfully the horse seemed to know where they were heading because the trail blurred in front of her. This was all her fault. She thought about how she'd acted since coming to Slate Rock Ranch. She hadn't exactly been trying to fit in here. She hadn't been kind to Dax, and she'd shut herself off from Brielle, too. The only thing that Brielle knew about her was the fact that she'd been part of the crew who had done damage here in town. Everyone else who had participated were faceless, nameless people.

If she wanted to make a change and try to fit in here for the remainder of the summer, she needed to make a better effort. That meant she'd have to open up a little more with Brielle. She'd like to have at least one person she could count on. With a renewed surge of energy, she brushed at her damp cheeks and straightened her back.

At some point she'd gotten more secure in the saddle. Her tears no longer threatened to escape, and the sun was sinking lower in the sky. Shouldn't she be getting closer to the ranch? There were still no buildings in sight.

That familiar feeling of anxiety flooded her chest. Weren't horses trained to return home? That was a thing, wasn't it? She turned in her seat, looking backward but didn't see any signs of the trail forking in any other direction. Nor did she see it in front of her.

She patted her jacket pockets for her phone, but they were empty. Where was it? She never left anywhere without it. If it fell out of her pocket at some point, how was she supposed to find it? Sarah pulled on the reins, stopping her horse.

Calm. She needed to remain calm. She could figure this out. At least she wasn't back home in the swamps where alligators could get her.

Somewhere far off the sound of a coyote howled.

Sarah jumped and a squeal escaped her throat. The horse shifted beneath her, growing restless. She moved forward a step, but Sarah pulled on the reins again. She should call for Brielle. Or anyone who might be close enough to hear.

She took in a deep breath and hollered, "Bri!"

Without warning, the horse lurched forward from beneath her. She lost her grip on the reins and slipped off the back of the saddle, landing on her back and hitting her head on the dusty trail with a whomp. Stars floated around her head and she couldn't breathe. Her lungs burned as she gasped for oxygen to fill them, but they wouldn't budge. Her fingers clawed into the dirt until she could roll onto her side. Finally, she was able to suck in a breath, but the dust filled her throat, causing her to cough uncontrollably.

When she was able to lift her head to search for her horse, she wasn't surprised to find that the animal had completely disappeared. Sarah could have cried if she hadn't expended those tears earlier. Why did everything seem to feel like it was only getting worse? Why was the universe working against her when she was trying to do the right thing?

Sarah collapsed onto her back, resting her hand on her stomach as she stared up at the sky. This had to be karma. Her mother had always told her if she didn't behave or if she treated her mother with disrespect, bad things would happen to her.

For once her mother might have been right.

There was no way she would be able to get to her feet and walk home right now. She needed a break first. Her lids were heavy, and the pounding in her head only made her feel sick to her stomach. She'd just close her eyes for a few minutes and then she'd figure out which direction to go.

8

———

Dax

Dax hung up the lead rope on a hook near the others, then pulled his leather gloves from his hands. The sound of horse hooves plodding on the ground drew his attention and he glanced over his shoulder.

Brielle wandered into the barn, leading her horse. He knew that grumpy expression. She didn't want anyone to speak to her. And if anyone did, they'd likely get their head bitten off. He faced her and headed in her direction.

His lips pulled into a smile. "Looks like you didn't enjoy your ride. I told you Sarah isn't as pleasant as you thought she was. Maybe she's better in small doses?"

"Just knock it off, Dax, will you? She's been through a lot."

"So you've said. Only you won't tell me any of the details."

Brielle shouldered past him. "She's got a right to her privacy just like you do. I don't ask where you disappear to whenever you go flying down that dirt road toward town." She led her horse into its stall and commenced unsaddling the animal and removing the reins.

Dax glanced toward the door, still not seeing Sarah. "Did she really get that far behind? I knew she wasn't ready for a long horse ride. She needs to build up more confidence."

Brielle stiffened visibly. She turned toward him, her face as white as a sheet. "Sarah isn't back yet?"

His brows furrowed. "No," he drawled. "She was supposed to be with you, remember?"

Her hands shook as she snatched the reins she'd deposited on the hook by the stall door. "Oh no. No, no, no. She was supposed to be back hours ago."

Dax's head swung back toward the barn door. Something wasn't right. His whole body felt tight, like he'd been restrained with little ability to move. He darted into the stall as Brielle fumbled with getting the saddle back on her horse. He grasped her upper arms. "What happened?"

"We got in a fight. She wanted to come home early. I thought she'd just follow the trail. Are you sure she hasn't come back yet?"

He groaned and shook his head. "Didn't I tell you that this was a bad idea? I knew I should have come with you. I just knew something like this would happen." He charged toward his horse's stall.

"What are you doing?" She stopped and came out into the aisle.

"I'm going after her!"

"But you don't know where to look."

"It's getting late. You know as well as I do that those woods just beyond the trails are *filled* with predators. Geez, Brielle, you should have known better than to let an untrained visitor wander the trails without supervision." He flung the saddle over his horse's back and cinched it tight.

Brielle's features faltered. Whatever had happened between her and Sarah was bad enough that Sarah hadn't wanted to come home. He shook his head. They'd have to work it out between themselves. For now, he had one purpose.

He needed to find Sarah and bring her back.

Brielle darted back into the stall. "Wait, I'm coming with you."

"No," he barked. He led his horse out of the stall and toward the door. "You stay here in case she comes back. If she does, you call me immediately."

He swung into the saddle and dug his heels into his horse's flanks. He was familiar enough with Brielle's favorite trails he had a good enough idea of where to start looking. The problem would be if it got too late, he wouldn't have enough daylight to find her, especially when it came to the trails that followed the perimeter of the woods.

Dax stood, hovering over the saddle. He leaned forward, letting his horse charge forward. They darted along the curved path and farther from the property. His sharp eyesight took in everything it possibly could. There was no sign of her anywhere. Overhead there were clouds moving in, making it feel later than it really was.

The horse she'd ridden knew how to get home, but it was also a horse that sometimes took people out hunting. There was a chance it might have gone in that direction, which meant there was a very real possibility that Sarah was wandering lost in the woods at this very moment.

He pushed harder, forcing his horse to run faster. The foliage on either side of him blurred into a deep green. "Sarah!" he bellowed. "Sarah, it's Dax! Can you hear me?"

The pounding of the hoofbeats probably drowned out his voice. He'd have to slow down, but he couldn't risk any lost time.

He closed his eyes briefly, praying for some kind of guidance on where to go. Deep inside, he knew something was wrong. He couldn't explain it, but instinctively he knew she needed his help. He didn't know what he would do if he came across her and she was seriously injured or worse.

His whole body was tense with worry. On top of not wanting her to be hurt while in his care, he knew without a doubt that Sheriff Donahue would have his hide if she returned to him next Friday with even one scratch on her.

"Sarah!" He pulled on the reins, causing his horse to rear onto her hind legs and whinny. "Sarah, so help me if you don't answer me—" What would he do? There was no threat that was likely worse than whatever position she was probably already in. He glanced at the sky as the clouds continued to gather and the temperature lowered.

His phone rang and he ripped it from his pocket. Brielle's picture filled his screen. He touched the answer icon and brought it to his ear. "Is she there?"

"No," Brielle's breathless voice sounded more scared than he felt, if that was even possible. "But her horse is back," she croaked. "Dax, the storm, what are we going to do if she—"

"I'll find her. If I don't call you back in the next twenty minutes, call the sheriff."

"But—"

"Just do it." He hung up and put his phone back in his pocket. "Sarah!"

It was quiet, and he wasn't sure if he'd imagined it, but a soft moan floated toward him. He spun his horse around, facing the direction that the sound had come. There were several other trails in that direction. He leaned forward, pushing his horse to jump over some shrubbery. "Sarah!" His voice was growing hoarse, and his throat was sore, but if he found her it would be worth it.

He arrived closer to the edge of the woods. That was when he saw a flash of color that didn't belong. He pressed onward, closer and closer, only slowing when he was within about ten feet.

Sarah's body was curled into the fetal position, unmoving. He all but leaped from his saddle, landing in a cloud of dust beside her. Thunder rolled somewhere in the distance but louder than he was comfortable with.

Dax dropped beside her, scooping her up so she sat upright. He patted her cheek. "Sarah. Hey, little lady, you need to wake up." He pressed two fingers to that tender spot on her neck, finding a strong pulse. That was a good sign. He patted her cheek again. "Sarah. I can't take you home if you're unconscious."

A breeze ruffled her hair and she shivered. Something splatted beside him. His gaze dipped to the small, dark spot in the dirt. Another thudded against the earth, followed by another and another. Rain. A large cold drop landed on his arm and then one hit Sarah's face, causing her to moan.

"Sarah," he muttered, "wake up." He moved to his knees and gave her a gentle shake. Her lashes fluttered open, and she stared at him in a daze. He sent a prayer of thanks heavenward.

"Dax?" she murmured. "Where's Bri?" Her eyes widened and she tore away from him, losing the contents of her stomach. She groaned, wincing as she pressed the heel of her hand to her temple. "My head."

He got to his feet. There was a good chance she had a concussion and needed to see a doctor. Dax pulled her to her feet, letting her lean into him as he pulled out his phone and sent a text to Brielle to call the doctor.

"Come on. We need to get you back before we get soaked by the storm."

"You came to find me," she said sleepily. "Does that mean we're friends, now?"

"Sure." He adjusted his grip on her. "I'm going to lift you into the saddle. You have to hold on while I get on."

"So sleepy," she yawned, then stumbled as he practically dragged her toward the horse.

"You can't fall asleep, Sarah. You probably have a concussion." By the time he got her in the saddle, the clouds were dropping fat drops of water. There was no way they wouldn't be drenched by the time they made it back to the ranch.

He didn't know how he managed to get her into the saddle without falling off. But the moment he got into the saddle behind her, he slipped one arm around her waist securely and turned the reins with the other. Sarah slumped against him, frailer than he'd remembered.

"Stay with me," he muttered.

9

____

old.

Ice cold.

Sarah moaned, shivering. She couldn't remember her head hurting more than it did in this moment. Each time she breathed, it was like hitting her head against a wall.

Every sound, big or small, added insult to injury. She winced and attempted to shrink away from the source of the sounds, but they surrounded her.

She whimpered, surrounded in darkness with voices floating around her.

"Don't we have to wake her up?"

"Where in the world is Dr. Henry?"

"He said he was on the way and it's probably okay to let her rest."

"I'm not going to risk her safety on a probably, Bri."

"She's shivering. Why won't she stop shivering? Do we need to put her in front of the fire?"

"Isn't body heat better for that?"

Sarah groaned again, the familiar voices dragging her from the dark recesses of her mind. "Don't talk so loud."

"Thank heavens. Sarah, can you open your eyes for me, please?"

Her lids still felt heavy, swollen almost, but she managed to get them to flutter open slightly. Light sliced through the slit in her eyes and she flinched. "Can someone turn off the light?" She didn't recognize her voice with how sore and coarse it sounded.

The lights in the room she was in dimmed, and she tried opening her eyes once more. The first face she found was Dax. His hair was wet, slick as if he'd just stepped out of the shower. His clothes were soaked too. His expression was dark, upset and exhausted.

"You look terrible." It was the only thing she could manage to say.

"Speak for yourself," he said, looking upset but she didn't know why.

She attempted to adjust her body, but found she was covered with several wool blankets and was propped up on the couch. A sea of faces surrounded Dax. Every one of the Callahan women and the one Baker. Beside her, Brielle seemed to hover as if she didn't know what to do with herself. Her face was puffy and red. She'd been crying.

Sarah's brows creased. "What's wrong?"

She flung her arms around Sarah. "I'm so sorry. I shouldn't have let you leave. It was my responsibility to get you back safely. I should have gone after you."

Sara didn't know what to say. She glanced at Dax, who sat in front of her on the edge of the coffee table. He didn't speak, and his expression didn't change.

In the corner of the room, Zeke hovered, his arms crossed. He didn't look all too pleased. The only person who was missing was—

"Sarah. Do you realize how worried we were?" Sheriff Donahue stepped into view.

"I guess the party's all here."

"This isn't a time for jokes, Sarah. You could have died out there. If Dax hadn't found you when he did, you most definitely would have caught hypothermia."

Someone knocked on the front door. Zeke left the room without a word. Why was it that when she'd nearly lost her life, they all managed to make her feel guilty about it? She wasn't the one who'd leaped from the saddle. The horse had taken off all on its own.

She frowned and looked away from everyone.

Adeline entered from the kitchen holding a steaming cup of something. She placed it next to Dax on the coffee table and then turned to the group. "Okay, everyone. Let's give Sarah some space. The doctor just got here. She doesn't need an audience."

Sarah gave her a look of relief as everyone in the room got to their feet and headed for the door. Everyone except Dax.

He remained perched on the coffee table. In fact, he'd shifted so he could rest his forearms on his knees.

"Aren't you going to get cleaned up?" Sarah's eyes darted to meet his, then away.

He shook his head slowly.

She tried not to get riled up. She really did. But it had been a terrible two weeks. No matter how much good she'd tried to do, there was always someone who told her she wasn't doing enough. Or they looked at her like she was some idiot.

Her heart rate accelerated. "If you're going to stay just so you can—"

"I'm staying because I want to hear for myself what happened."

Sarah scrunched her face. "Why do you care?"

"Does it matter? Can't I just be a good guy who doesn't want to see someone hurt?"

She closed her mouth. He made a good point. But it was hard to see that in the guy who only seemed to smile at her when he was laughing at her expense.

The closer she looked at him, the more she believed him. The worry was written in every line of his face. His cheek twitched as his eyes swept over her. He clenched and relaxed his hands before shaking them out and starting over. Dax was on edge, and he was filling the room with his own brand of tension.

Sarah tore her attention away from him just as the doctor arrived with Zeke and the sheriff on his heels. She attempted to toss the blanket aside, ready to escape from this room and the men who were controlling her life. "I'm fine. I'm feeling better, I promise." She rose to her feet, then wobbled and had to reach out to catch herself on the couch.

"Sit *down*, Sarah."

She had expected the sharp command to come from the sheriff or even Zeke, but it had come from the man in front of her. Slowly, she lowered herself onto the cushion and pulled the blanket over her once more.

The doctor came closer, and Dax moved from the coffee table to the seat beside her. Her heart fluttered as if responding to his closeness. But she'd been close to him before and hadn't reacted like *this*. She shivered and rubbed her arms up and down.

"Sarah, can you tell me what happened?" Dr. Henry was younger than she'd expected for a doctor. He couldn't be more than thirty. He smiled warmly at her as he lifted a flashlight and shined it into her eyes. Right, left, and right again. He frowned and made a soft sound that didn't seem very good.

Sarah glanced to Dax, who suddenly felt all too close. "I was riding out on the trails and my horse took off too fast. I lost my balance and fell. That's all."

Dr. Henry moved closer to her. "May I examine your head?"

She nodded slowly so the room wouldn't spin.

He moved his deft fingers around her head, lightly searching for something. She sucked in a sharp breath when he reached the back of her skull. He pulled his hand back and frowned. "It appears you're bleeding."

A gasp tore from her throat and her hand moved carefully to touch where she'd been injured. "Will I need stitches?"

The doctor had already moved around the back of the couch and was looking at the injury. "You're not bleeding a lot. We could probably get away with a little glue. You *do* have a mild concussion. Between the vomiting and your dilated eyes, I suggest you remain supervised so we can keep tabs on your symptoms overnight."

"Vomiting?" she asked. "No, I didn't throw up." She smacked her lips, tasting something a little rancid. Wait, had she thrown up? She couldn't recall.

The doctor glanced at Dax and back to her. "I believe Mr. Heaton witnessed at least one occurrence."

She swung her attention to her side, giving herself another wave of dizziness followed swiftly by nausea. Sarah covered her mouth and shut her eyes, willing the nausea to dissipate. When she opened her eyes, she wasn't surprised to find Dax still staring at her. She focused on taking deep breaths and finally found her voice. "You saw me throw up?"

His voice was soft, unexpected coming from his stone-like features. "When you sat up, you must have gotten dizzy. I don't think you were fully coherent. You slept for most of the ride back. Brielle had to help you get changed out of your wet clothes."

She looked down at her attire, finding herself in a nightgown that wasn't her own. A blush crept up her neck and she pulled the covers more tightly around herself. She turned to the doctor. "Okay. So I have to be babysat, but then I'm good? Anything else?"

The doctor tucked his little pen flashlight into his pocket and nodded. "Based on the fact that you can speak coherently and your abrasion isn't gushing, I'd say if you're feeling better tomorrow, then you're free to do what you want—within reason. You have to take it easy. Don't overdo it."

Sarah nodded. "Okay." She shot a look in the sheriff's direction. She didn't know how this would affect her community service hours. It would probably mean doing extra work on the weekends so she could still leave this forsaken place by the end of summer. She took in a deep breath and settled into the couch.

The doctor, sheriff, and Zeke moved out of the room, leaving her alone with Dax. He remained by her side, not saying a single word. The whole thing was very unnerving. She fingered the edge of the blanket, rubbing her thumb over the coarse fabric. "I guess I should thank you again for saving my life."

"You're welcome." His gruff voice was void of that softness from before. He'd returned back to that guy who didn't seem to think she could do anything right.

She let her eyes flutter closed, hoping he'd take the hint and leave. But when she peeked in his direction, she was dismayed to find him sitting there. "What do you want, Dax?"

"You really scared me today, Sarah."

She couldn't imagine why. They weren't close. He hadn't shown even a sliver of interest in her. She glanced at him with a fresh set of eyes. He was definitely attractive in that brooding, smoldering sort of way. His dark hair and dark eyes were something she was usually interested in. It was the playful smiles that threw her off. He could be laughing at her one second and berating her the next.

But there was more than just physical attraction. He'd risked his own health and life to save her. Twice. What kind of guy did that? Her heart leaped once more. She wasn't so naïve to think that he'd done any of that because he liked her. She'd seen the way he looked at Brielle. No one had ever looked at her like that.

No, Dax wasn't interested in her. He was probably just one of the last decent guys left in the world. That was far more likely than some kind of chemistry.

"Well, you don't have to be scared anymore. I'm home safe, and you can bet that I will *never* get on a horse again."

"Over my dead body, you won't."

Her eyes flew open, and she stiffened. "What? You're kidding."

He shook his head, rubbing his hands together in a slow, thoughtful way. "If I had been there, this wouldn't have happened."

She huffed. "Unless there's some magical power you possess that you're not telling me about, Dax, you can't control every animal on the premises. They're going to do what they're going to do."

"True, but I would have been there to help you right away. And if you think that never riding is going to solve this problem, you're mistaken."

This time she laughed, and goodness, did it hurt. "Of course it will solve my problems. If I don't get on another horse, then this won't ever happen again. I'll *literally* never fall from a horse if I don't ride another one."

He frowned. "And if I let you think that, then the next time something goes wrong, you'll just run from it like you're trying to do now."

"Why does it matter? You're looking at this so backward. You're not the boss of me."

He lifted his mouth into a half-smile. "Technically, I am. And if I say you need to be on a horse, you dang well better do it." He rose to his feet and stared down at her. There was something just beyond his eyes that she couldn't read. Whatever it was that he was trying to hide from her, it was working. There was no way she'd be able to break into his mind.

It didn't matter. Not really. It was probably something to do with how she was just a bad cowgirl. She wasn't meant to be here, and he was finally realizing it.

Only a matter of time. They all would figure it out eventually.

10

____

Dax

It took everything in Dax's power to walk out the door of the Callahan house and head toward the wrangler's cabin. And he couldn't figure out why.

Even the doctor had said she'd be okay. Brielle said she'd keep an eye on her tonight since they shared a room. He wasn't needed.

Was that why he didn't want to leave? He had invested so much into making sure she'd be okay that leaving felt like he was abandoning her?

He shook off the feeling.

This was Sarah. The infuriating, secretive woman who had a tendency to get under his skin when she wasn't in the throes of something hilarious.

Footsteps charged toward him from behind. Dax slowed and turned to find Brielle coming toward him. "What do—"

She flung her arms around his neck, colliding with him

much like she had a couple years ago when they'd been dating. He held out his hands, reminding himself that she'd made her decision. This hug wasn't a rekindling one.

No. The way she was trembling, this was a hug that was meant to comfort her. Slowly, he wrapped his arms around her, holding her close for only a moment before he stepped back. He had to be careful. It would be far too easy to easy for her to get the wrong idea.

He peered at her in the darkness. "What's the matter?"

Her voice hitched and she looked at the ground. "I upset her. I'm the reason she got hurt."

Dax shook his head, lifting her chin with his knuckle. "You grew up on this ranch. How many people get thrown from horses every single day?"

She hiccupped. "I let her go—she was inexperienced. You can't tell me that if I had stayed with her, this wouldn't have happened."

"No."

Her features faltered.

"But that doesn't mean you should beat yourself up over it. Sarah's a fighter. She's home safe, and she'll be fine. Don't worry about it." He nearly turned to head toward his cabin when something held him to his spot. "You can't leave her tonight, Bri."

Brielle's eyes widened. "I wasn't planning on it."

He tilted his head. "It's Friday. I know you, Bri. It's like you have this addiction to sneaking out."

She shook her head. "I wouldn't do that to her."

He took in a deep breath, staring at the house and then bringing his attention back to her. "I understand that need better than you might think. You like the escape, the rush. And after a day like today, I don't want you thinking it will be okay if you step out for even thirty minutes."

Her face flushed and she took an angry step back. "Who do

you think I am? Has it seriously been so long that you can't remember? If I said I'll watch her, I will." Her pained voice shot through him like a bolt of lightning. As much as he would have liked to take control and tell her to leave now if she planned on doing it at all, he refrained. It would have been easier to slip into Sarah's room and keep an eye on her in secret.

He took in a deep breath and let it out slowly. "This is your chance to make it up to her. Make sure she doesn't throw up in her sleep and that she doesn't get any of those symptoms the doctor mentioned. I'll swing by early in the morning and see how she's doing." He turned and took a few steps when her voice stopped him.

"Dax?"

Without turning to face her, he muttered, "What?"

"Do you—are you—never mind. Forget it."

When he turned to ask her what in the world was that about, he found that she was already halfway to the door. He watched her enter the house, shut the door, and turn off the porch lights. His gaze swept up to the window he knew belonged to Brielle. The soft yellow color of the light glowed behind a set of nearly sheer drapes.

Shadows passed in front of the window, but nothing he could make out. He shook his head and ran a hand through his still damp hair. His whole body was cold, and nothing would feel better than standing beneath a scalding shower to take the edge off.

He'd check back with Sarah in the morning. It was a good thing it was the weekend. Zeke would be crazy to expect her to do any work tomorrow, but just in case, he'd go collect the eggs in the morning before he headed for the house.

11

———

Sarah

Sarah could feel a difference in the air. The way people acted around her bordered on strange. As she sat at the kitchen table for breakfast, everyone acted like any sudden movement they made would cause her to shatter like a porcelain doll tumbling to the ground.

If this was the new normal, it was going to get old real quick. Brielle avoided meeting her gaze for more than a few moments at a time. It didn't matter how often she'd insisted she forgave Brielle; her friend wasn't accepting it.

The way they treated her was almost worse than it had been before. She'd rather be pulling her weight instead of being waited on. So the second they left her alone, she'd be heading out to the coop to get the eggs she was assigned to get daily.

Each and every Callahan sister sat at the table. Eating and speaking quietly. Maybe they thought too much noise would hurt her head. Or maybe she just made them incredibly uncomfortable. Either way, the silence was putting her even more on edge.

Someone knocked at the door and the youngest Callahan hopped up from the table. "I'll get it." Grace hurried from the room. She'd just graduated from high school a year early. She was sweet and soft-spoken. But that could change at the drop of a hat. Sarah found she longed for those days. From the moment she'd graduated from high school, things had gone downhill. Unfortunately, she didn't have anyone to blame but herself.

Sarah picked at her food. She wasn't all that hungry. In fact, the eggs on her plate seemed to make her nausea worse. It was either the color, the smell, or it could just be that she had collected it from beneath the underside of a angry hen a few days earlier.

She let out a sigh, putting down her fork and leaning back in her chair. All eyes at the table shifted toward the door. Brielle glanced at her, then once more toward the one area of the room Sarah couldn't see.

Turning around in her seat, Sarah locked eyes with Dax. Their last conversation had left a bad taste in her mouth. Why was it that every time she met someone, they wanted to wield power over her? She frowned and faced forward in her chair.

Great. If he was here that could only mean one thing. He was checking up on her. Boy, he must really want to know when she could get back to work.

"Mr. Heaton. To what do we owe the pleasure?" Zeke wiped at his mouth with a napkin and rose from the table. "Is there a problem on the ranch?"

"No, sir."

"Alright, son. What can I do for you?"

"I just came to check on Sarah."

She didn't think it was possible, but her whole body grew stiffer. Just as she'd expected, he was here to boss her around like he always did. He probably came to drag her off to the barn to put her on a horse like he'd talked about last night.

Sarah clenched her teeth, grinding them together, relishing in the pain the movement caused. It took away from the pain at the back of her head.

Zeke motioned toward the table. "Go ahead and take a seat. There's plenty to eat."

The chair beside her scraped against the tiled floor and Dax sat down. She didn't dare glance in his direction. It was absolutely ridiculous, and maybe she could blame her bump on her head, but some small part of her wondered if she stayed completely still, maybe he wouldn't see her.

"How are you feeling, Sarah?"

Well, it was worth a shot.

She focused on keeping her breathing regulated. There was no use getting worked up at the table. With her luck, she might end up passed out on the floor. She really should focus on keeping the pounding beats of her heart at a reasonable rate.

"Are you okay, Sarah?"

She jumped. "What?"

Dax touched her forearm and she startled. "I'm fine." Thankfully she'd been able to keep her tone light. "Just a little jumpy, that's all."

"Any dizziness? Nausea?"

Actually, she had experienced both when she'd walked down for breakfast. Her steps had been painfully slow, and when she moved even a smidge faster, the bright dancing stars behind her eyes made another appearance. The only way she seemed to be able to escape the symptoms had been to sit down.

But if she said *any* of that, Dax would likely berate her like he had last night. "Like I said. I'm fine."

The conversation at the table returned to a moderate hum as everyone who'd come down for breakfast dug into their food again. Dax shifted in his seat and leaned a little closer to her, causing her to experience what could only be described as some form of claustrophobia.

Her heart rate increased, her breathing grew shallower, and both of those responses made the stars return. Sarah closed her eyes and forced herself to take several deep breaths before she opened them again. When she did, she found Dax staring at her.

His brows were drawn together tight on his face. He frowned like he knew something she didn't and it concerned him greatly. Ha. He was probably worried he'd lost a worker ant. Well, the joke was on him because she couldn't afford to spend a single day extra on this ranch.

"Really, Dax," she muttered, "I'm fine."

"No, you're not."

His soft words were not what she expected. They weren't laced with judgment or disdain. She almost heard a note of genuine concern. But that couldn't be right. From the moment they'd met, he'd either been making fun of her or he'd been bossing her around.

"Did you get enough rest last night?"

"I think so."

"Are you drinking enough water?"

Her gaze darted around the room. "What's with the third degree? Don't you have somewhere else to be? I know I do." She pushed out from the table and stood up out of her seat. A blast of white blinded her and she sucked in a breath, her fingers tightening on the edge of the table. Sarah blinked, praying that everything would settle quicker this time.

Thankfully, her prayers were answered as the room came into focus once more. She reached for her dishes and carefully made her way across the room to the sink. The only problem was that Dax hovered at her elbow the whole time.

"Will you stop that," she said. "They're going to think I can't take care of myself."

"That's because you can't," he said, matching her tone. "I've seen this before, Sarah. I know what it looks like when a person tries to do too much so soon after having an accident like yours. And believe me when I tell you that if you do this today, you're going to end up hurting far more than you thought possible."

The conversation at the table hadn't been interrupted. Everyone still chatted about their weekend plans. She swung an irritated look toward him. "Well, what would you have me do? I'm here to work. I'm not going to bail on my responsibilities. If you don't like it, then I guess you're going to have to follow me around everywhere and make sure I don't drop dead."

She turned to face the sink and set to work washing her dishes. Dax must have taken her statement literally because he didn't move from her side. Sarah rolled her eyes, reaching for the hand towel to dry everything off. If there wasn't an audience readily available to witness her issues, she might have put him in his place and promptly gotten chastised for doing so.

With smooth, even movements, she headed for the back door. "If you'll excuse me, I'm going to gather the eggs this morning." Without waiting for a response, she exited out the door and into the cool morning air.

12

———

Dax

Dax barreled after Sarah, cursing his need to keep an eye on her. The woman was beyond annoying—if anything, she was infuriating to the highest degree. Couldn't she see what she was doing to herself? There was a reason doctors told their patients to take it easy.

He came up beside her. "You don't have to get the eggs."

"Yes, I do." Her breathing was heavier. It was clear that her injury had caused a great deal of strain on her body.

"I already did it for you."

She stopped so suddenly that he took a few more steps in front of her. "Why did you do that?"

"Why did I help you do your chore? Gee, I don't know, Sarah. Maybe it's because you went through a trauma yesterday and you're acting like an idiot by not staying in bed."

Sarah blinked.

Dax groaned and dragged his hand down his face. "Why

can't things ever just be easy?" When he met her gaze, she found the frustration from before, but along with it was that foreign substance she couldn't put her finger on. "You need to rest, Sarah. Did Zeke ask you to put in any work today?"

"No, but—"

He threw up his hands into the air. "Then what are you doing out of bed?"

She blinked again, clearly not grasping why this was such a big deal. "I have responsibilities, Dax. I thought out of everyone on this ranch, you would understand that."

"What are you *talking* about?"

Their voices continued to rise, and her face had now flushed to a worrisome shade of red.

Sarah glanced around, her focus sweeping over anyone who might be in the immediate vicinity. Was she worried he'd hurt her? The thought had his blood boiling. Then she took the few steps toward him and lowered her voice to almost a whisper. "I have to work a certain number of hours before I can go home."

To say he was bewildered was an understatement. None of what she was saying made sense. Why would the sheriff's niece have to work a certain amount before she got to head home?

She groaned. "It's no use. I can tell you're going to keep pestering and pestering me." The color in her face only deepened and nearly appeared purple. She grimaced and touched her head. "No one knows, and I don't want to tell a soul. Okay, that's not true. Zeke knows and so does Bri. But I guess letting... you... in on... the..."

He saw the color drain from her face only a moment before her legs crumpled and she collapsed into his arms.

Dax grunted as her entire weight sagged against him. This had been exactly what he'd been describing when he told her that she needed to rest. Why didn't people listen to him? His life would be so much easier if everyone would just trust what he had to say.

It took some finagling, but he managed to get Sarah in a position where he could scoop her soft body up against his chest and head back to the house. For the third time since this whole fiasco began, he was the one who had saved her. And for what?

The thought gave him pause.

Why was he so invested in helping her?

It took a great deal more effort to shove aside that question when all he wanted was to scrutinize it. Right now, he needed to get Sarah back to her room and force her to rest. He had some personal days saved up and something inside him innately knew if he didn't guard her room, she'd just end up outside passed out again.

Brielle was the one who opened the back door when he pounded on it with the toe of his boot. Her eyes grew wide and she gasped. "Is she okay? Should I call the doctor?"

"I think she'll be fine, but contact Dr. Henry just in case. She's probably just dehydrated and still trying to heal from her fall." Dax turned sideways to get past Brielle and head straight for the stairs. She followed, nipping at his heels. "Is there anything else I can do?"

"You can get her some water and maybe some aspirin. I bet you anything her head is pounding like she's been hit by a bus." The truth wasn't far off.

Brielle nodded and rushed away.

He was able to get her placed on her bed and covered with a light knit blanket fairly easily. Dax stared down at her with her long dark, wavy hair splayed on the pillow and her eyes closed. Her lashes brushed lightly against her still pale cheeks. Thankfully, her breathing had returned to a normal rate. A strand of her dark curly hair had managed to fall on her cheek.

With deft fingers, he grasped it between his finger and

thumb and moved it out of the way. Her features were relaxed into a peaceful expression, and it became almost difficult to tear his eyes away from her.

Everything she'd been spouting off just before she lost control stuck in his mind. Whatever it was had been bad enough that she'd been incredibly worked up over it. Who had Zeke hired? Better yet, why was the sheriff hiding it from the town?

Sarah's lashes fluttered and a soft moan escaped her lips. He took a step back. The last thing either of them needed was for her to get riled up again. Almost immediately, her gaze swung to meet his.

She started to sit up and he lunged forward, pressing on her shoulder to force her to lie down. "Like I was trying to tell you, you should be resting."

Sarah scowled, attempting to sit up again. "I fell off a *horse*, Dax. I'm not an invalid."

He gave her a dark look. "Do you know how many people die from that sort of thing?"

"Do *you*?" Her flippant remark escaped her lips with a sharp edge.

Dax lifted a brow and a smile stole across his face. There was her spunk and fire—the thing that had given him a mild amount of entertainment when she'd been chased by those chickens.

"What are you smiling at?" Sarah scooted back against the headboard and folded her arms. She eyed him with distrust. He could see so much of himself in those eyes. The suspicion, the inflexibility.

Dax moved a few steps back and sat on the edge of Brielle's bed. He rested his forearms on his knees and ducked his head, letting out a sigh. "When we were on our walk..." He peeked at her, noting the way she immediately stiffened. "You were about to tell me something."

Her brows pulled together and she shook her head. "I don't think so."

"If you don't want to tell me, that's fine. I get it." He lifted his face so their eyes could meet. For the first time she saw some semblance of vulnerability.

She glanced away and tucked that stubborn piece of hair behind her ear. "I don't."

Slowly, he shook his head.

The difference in her body language was like night and day. She took a deep breath and released it, then let her head rest against the headboard.

If he tried, he could probably piece together what she'd mentioned before she'd lost consciousness. She was here for a certain amount of time. She had to work a certain number of hours. That could mean anything from a probationary requirement to strict parents.

He straightened so suddenly that she stiffened, turning wide eyes on him.

"We haven't called your parents yet."

If he thought she was pale before, he was mistaken. The pallor of her skin worsened. "What?"

"Your parents. We need to notify them of your injury. Have you had a chance to call them yet?"

She was terrible at hiding the anxiety his words caused her. But she was even worse at lying. "Yes," she muttered. From the lack of color on her face to the way she clutched the covers beside her, there was no way she had contacted them.

His eyes narrowed. He took a step toward her with the intention of getting to the bottom of this whole thing when Brielle burst into the room with a glass of water and a bottle of aspirin.

"Sarah! You're awake!" Brielle hurried forward and pushed the items into Sarah's hands. "Are you feeling okay? I called Dr. Henry, but he won't be able to come by until later today."

Sarah glanced at Dax, then returned her focus to Brielle. "I feel fine. I think I just overdid it." She seemed to be avoiding his gaze as she murmured, "But maybe you could call my uncle?"

Brielle didn't respond right away. She shot a look over her shoulder toward Dax. "Your uncle... Oh, right. I'll go call the sheriff right away." She reached forward and squeezed Sarah's hand. "I'm so sorry... for everything."

Sarah nodded; the smile she offered Brielle didn't even come close to being genuine. "It's fine. I just need to talk to the sheriff."

Brielle hopped off the side of the bed, nodded to Dax, then headed from the room. Dax watched her go. Just as she disappeared from view, Sarah's words from earlier hit him across the head. Brielle knew something about Sarah—something the sheriff and Zeke knew as well—something Sarah didn't want anyone else to know.

As much as his curiosity burned within him, Dax had to push it aside. Sarah would tell him when she was ready. He turned back to face her, finding her gaze locked on him.

"Why are you helping me?" Her soft words took him by surprise.

"Why wouldn't I?"

Her hands moved to her lap and she twisted the hem of her shirt between her fingers. "It's obvious you don't like me very much." There was a sadness in the way she'd said it. And for some reason it made his stomach tighten.

"I don't *not* like you, Sarah."

She huffed, still not meeting his gaze. "You could have fooled me."

He moved to the edge of her bed—the place where Brielle had been sitting. "I don't trust you. There's a difference."

Sarah's eyes darted to meet his. "I guess that's fair."

One corner of his mouth lifted. "I think we got off on the wrong foot."

The scrunched-up expression on her face would have been comical if they weren't in the throes of a serious conversation.

Dax took in a deep breath and released it. "If you're going to be here for a while, we might as well change that. What do you say?"

She eyed him. "There are certain things I don't feel comfortable sharing—with *anyone*. I don't think you can accept that."

He blew out a breath through pursed lips. "How about we start with the easy stuff?"

A bark of laughter burst from her chest. "There is literally no such thing." She peeked at him. "Thank you."

"What for?"

She shrugged, then gestured toward the room. "You've saved me three times now and you didn't have to."

"I'm not a monster, Sarah."

A small smile touched her lips. Seeing her this way, free from the tension and the combative nature that seemed to be so natural to her, he couldn't deny how beautiful she really was. It was almost like some of her walls had to come down before he could truly see it—just like when she'd been asleep.

Dax looked away. He had no right thinking such thoughts. For all intents and purposes, Sarah was his subordinate. Not only that, but things could also get messy with her being so close to Brielle. It would be far better for him to keep his distance. Especially since she was set on being so private.

He'd have to fight the instinct to delve deeper into her past. It wasn't his business. Dax gave her a pointed look as he got to his feet. "I expect you to get some rest, and I don't want to see you out there working."

"But my hours."

"You have plenty of time to make them up."

She frowned. "I'm fully capable of gathering eggs in my condition."

He couldn't help it. Dax laughed. "With the way those mongrels chase you around the coop? I don't think so."

Sarah's face reddened, but she didn't argue.

"Besides, I gathered the eggs this morning. Just chill and hang out with Bri or something."

As if simply saying her name had the ability to summon her, Brielle floated into the room. "The sheriff said he could be here in the next few hours. He said if you needed him here sooner to let him know."

Both Brielle and Dax looked in Sarah's direction, expectantly.

"Whenever he gets here is fine."

Dax jerked his head toward the door. "Can I talk to you for a minute, Bri?"

She gave him a surprised look. "Sure."

He turned to Sarah. "I mean it. I'll not have you passing out on my watch again."

Sarah rolled her eyes, but the soft smile that hid just beneath the surface was enough to set off a warm sensation deep inside. There was something about being the source of that happiness that did something to him. He shook off the strange feeling and moved out into the hall with Brielle.

Dax pulled the door shut and lowered his voice so Sarah wouldn't be able to hear, then he faced Brielle. "Obviously, Sarah doesn't know what's good for her. She's more stubborn than that bull out in the pasture. I want you to make sure she doesn't do anything stupid."

Brielle's eyes narrowed and a smile played at her lips. "Oh. *I* get it now."

"You get what?"

"You like her."

His scoffed and shook his head. "What? No, I don't."

She lifted a shoulder. "Deny it all you want. But based on the way you were doting on her, I totally get it."

"Knock it off, Bri. I don't have feelings for her."

Brielle snickered. "I didn't say you had *feelings* for her. I said you *liked* her. But hey, maybe you *are* developing feelings for her." Her voice was teasing—the way she used to flirt with him when they'd been involved.

He took a step toward her, closing the distance between them. "I am her boss, and I'm responsible for her well-being. Your father entrusted me with her training and her safety, and I'm not about to drop the ball. That's it."

"Whatever, Dax. Don't forget that I *know* you. This is just the beginning. I don't know what it is about her that you like so much. But there's definitely something there. Just..." She glanced at the closed door. "Just be careful. There's stuff you don't know." It was like she'd caught herself from spilling a secret.

His cheek twitched just below his eye. He blamed this incessant need to learn more about Sarah on his own despicable past. Just like his other addictions, he'd have to quit this obsession regarding her past. Besides supervising Sarah's work on the ranch, he had several other responsibilities. "Just keep an eye on her until she's better. Then you can do whatever it is you do when you sneak out at night." He brushed past her, not letting her get in another word before he escaped down the hall toward the stairs.

He wasn't without his own secrets. Even Brielle didn't know *everything* about him, and they'd spent time growing up together. He'd chosen to keep his more sordid activities a secret. Dax rubbed a hand down his face as he exited the house and headed for the barn. Brielle was wrong. The way he felt toward Sarah, while improving, wasn't anywhere close to developing anything more than a professional relationship.

13

———

Sarah

The next few weeks were somewhat strained between Sarah and Dax. The way he'd treated her right after her fall had been strange, but at least she didn't feel like he was judging her at every turn.

Dax was the kind of boss who was strict but fair. He requested that she do her best work, pushing her to limits she never thought she could reach but at the same time supporting her. It was one of the many talents he seemed to possess.

Sarah headed toward the corral where he continued to train the yearlings. He'd sent her off to get a drink, something he was more insistent on since she'd gotten to the point where she could be on her feet without getting dizzy spells.

She stopped at the edge of the fence line and watched as Dax expertly maneuvered the animal into new positions or gaits with ease. The muscles on his arms rippled and the concentration of his brow was such that he looked like he was some form of divine being rather than a human being at all.

It wasn't any wonder that Brielle went on and on about him. As Sarah continued to watch him, it was like everything slowed down. Dax called out to the animal, clicking his tongue or whistling. The yearling galloped, tossing her head.

Dax was so different from all the guys she'd ever interacted with back home. The guys she knew usually fell on a spectrum from wanting something from her to dragging her into trouble. Those who knew about her family usually went for her money or recognition. It was the second most important reason she hadn't told Dax who she was. Money got people into trouble.

Here, no one recognized her. No one knew that she'd been involved in the criminal activity that had occurred a few months ago. Not even the Callahans knew about her family background. This was an opportunity to start over. It wasn't like her family had done much checking in on her. They probably thought she was still partying it up at college. The few times she'd called to check in, the conversations had been short.

Sarah climbed up onto the top rung of the corral, grasping it on either side of her with both hands. She dragged her attention back to the present, her eyes focusing on Dax. Her heart leaped into her throat when she realized he was watching her. She straightened, her hands tightening on the rail. How long had she been caught staring?

Dax patted the yearling's rump, releasing her from their exercise. He strode toward her, wrapping a rope around his arm. His languid movements had to be in her imagination. She most definitely wasn't developing a crush on this guy.

No, definitely not.

He flashed her a smile, and her stomach twisted. Okay, maybe she had a *little* crush. But that was normal according to all her psychology classes. When a guy did something nice for a girl, she couldn't help but find him more attractive.

"You okay?" Dax came to a stop and tilted his head as he peered up at her. He took off his hat and ran a hand through his hair, drawing her focus. He was only a few feet away and it wouldn't have taken much for her to reach out and brush a few of the longer strands from his forehead.

Wait a minute. Where had that thought come from? This was Dax she was speaking to. He was essentially her boss. He was the guy who had made fun of the way those blasted chickens continued to mess with her.

So why had her heart started to beat a little faster all of a sudden?

"Sarah?"

She jumped. "What?"

"You okay? You seem a little off today." His brows creased. "Do you need take off work early?"

Sarah shook her head vehemently. "I'm good. What else do you need me to do?"

Dax didn't look convinced. He took another step toward her as if he was going to reach out and touch her. She held her breath, but then he stepped back and she released the air in her lungs. Her body had gone rogue, and she wasn't about to let it take control.

Sarah jumped off the corral and held out her hands. "See? I'm fine. Didn't Sean say something to Adeline and Zeke this morning about needing to check on a few fields to make sure the fences are stable?"

"Yes, but I don't think you're—"

"I'm *fine.*" She moved past him, her arm brushing against his. Her breath hitched as the hairs on her arms lifted like some kind of electrical current had just jolted through her. She didn't turn around to see if he followed her. She knew he would as soon as he got ahold of the yearling's reins.

These reactions she felt were ridiculous.

More than ridiculous, she could blame it all on that one moment in her bedroom when he'd sat on the edge of her bed. Something about the words he'd said had gotten to her. And day by day, little by little, she was finding that he wasn't as bad as she thought he was.

Did that mean she wanted something stronger to develop between them?

Of course not. She was smarter than that.

Sarah glanced over her shoulder toward Dax, finding that her assumptions were correct. He followed the path she had taken toward the barn. They'd saddle their horses, and she'd get a chance to prove she wasn't as incompetent as he thought she was.

SARAH'S GAZE drilled into the saddle in front of her. Boy, was she *wrong*. She hadn't ridden since her fall, and now that she stood in front of the horse, preparing to mount, she wasn't so sure she was ready.

Her hands were slick and clammy. Her heart pounded fast, just not as fast as when she'd had a panic attack. She should be able to do this. She was an adult, for heaven's sake. *Stop being ridiculous and put your foot in the stirrup.*

"You don't have to go if you're not ready." Dax's soft voice sounded like it was mere inches from her ear.

Sara stilled, her hands clenched into fists at her sides. She squeezed her eyes shut, refusing to turn around. "I'm—"

Dax chuckled. "You're fine." His voice was still close—too close. "I get it. Getting back on the horse after an ordeal like yours isn't going to be easy, no matter how long you wait. Sometimes it's harder."

She spun around and immediately regretted it. Dax had been directly behind her and now he felt too close. Sarah took a step back, bumping into the horse behind her. She blinked a few times, trying to remember what she had intended to say. "You think I should go riding sooner than later."

He lifted a shoulder. "It doesn't matter what I think."

A lump formed in her throat and she swallowed hard. "It does, actually." At his amused expression, she elaborated. "You've been at this longer than me. I'd trust your judgment more than my own."

His smile warmed her, and she had to force herself to look away before her heart overreacted again.

"Glad we finally see eye-to-eye for once." He held out his hand, moving even closer to her.

She stared at his hand as if it were a rattler, ready to strike, then lifted her gaze to meet his. "What?"

He chuckled. Oh, how she wished he'd stop doing that. Every time she heard his laugh, it made her heart feel like it had up and morphed into a butterfly right there in her chest. "Let me help you up."

A refusal was on the tip of her tongue. She could do this herself. Only it might take a bit longer than if he was there. Sarah thrust aside the exhilarated voice in her head that seemed to insist he might actually like her. *Wrong.* He was just being nice. Sarah slipped her hand into his and lifted her left foot into the stirrup.

Dax's hand tightened around hers, steadying her. Strength and assurance emanated from his hold on her, and another thrill shot through her. Sarah yanked away her hand, furious for even thinking such things. Even if she wasn't going to leave in a few months. Even if he wasn't her boss. He had been involved with Brielle, and she clearly still had a thing for him.

Her eyes followed Dax as he swiftly settled into his saddle. He adjusted his hat on his head and then grinned at her. "We'll take it nice and easy. No running off."

She nodded. That was something she'd never attempt again. He led the way outside, and she followed. The horse she rode wasn't the same as the one that had bucked her last time, though she didn't know if that would have mattered. Being up this high was messing with her head again. Her pulse quickened and she held so tight to the reins that her hands turned white.

"You need to relax."

Sarah jumped, her eyes widening as her head swiveled around to where she'd last seen him ahead of her. How had he managed to get beside her?

Dax nodded to the reins. "The horse can sense everything you're feeling. And the way you have those reins so tight in your hands is going to put her on edge."

"Well, *I am* on edge."

"Remember when we discussed developing trust between you and your horse?" He motioned to the reins in his hands. "I have a firm hold, not too tight and not too loose. I want the horse to know I'm confident and in charge but that there's a mutual respect. I'm going to remain consistent in the way I'm carrying them. If I change too quickly, it can signal to the horse that they shouldn't trust me."

"First of all, I'm nowhere near being confident."

He directed his horse so that they rode closer together. "Just try to do what I'm doing. Release slightly, almost like you're pushing the reins forward."

She glanced down and made the adjustment, her whole body going stiff, preparing for something bad to happen. But nothing did. She eased her head up and grinned at him.

A smile stretched across his face. "Good. Now you need to relax your stance. Try not to be too stiff in the shoulders or in your legs."

That direction was easier said than done. She shook her head. "I can't do that. I'm going to fall."

"No, you're not." Dax's eyes met hers. "Lila is a good horse. She's the one we use when we're giving riding lessons. She's not going to just take off."

"Oh, so you gave me a training horse."

His crooked grin was almost enough to distract her from the realization that he was just as nervous about her getting back on the horse. "Let's start with your shoulders. Just release all the tension you're carrying there. In the unlikely event that you fall again, you don't want to be so tense. Try rolling your shoulders back."

She did as she was told, and surprisingly it helped. He didn't give her any more instruction as they rode, though he did stay close. She glanced in his direction more than once. And occasionally, she found him watching her.

It was hard to decipher if he was watching her because he was worried she'd end up having another accident or if he was proud of how she was doing. Each time, he gave her an encouraging smile.

They settled into an easy rhythm, and she lost track of the direction they'd come from with all the turns and forks they'd taken. Strangely, she was okay with it. Somehow, Dax being at her side gave her more confidence than she thought was possible.

14

———

Dax

"You're a very good teacher, you know that?"

Dax smiled, glancing toward Sarah. The compliment was a nice change of pace from where they had started. "Thanks."

She continued. "Have you ever considered doing it full-time? You know, teaching kids how to train and ride their own horses?"

One brow lifted. "I don't think their parents would be all that pleased to have me as their teacher." Not only did he have a colored background, but some of the people who saw him at AA probably wouldn't approve of him working with children.

She shot him a baffled look. "Why not?"

If there was one thing he knew, it was that people—more specifically women—were more judgmental when it came to that sort of stuff. How could he tell her without actually telling her?

The fact was, he couldn't. There was no way to keep all of his past hidden. Especially with the more one-on-one work they did with each other. Dax rubbed the back of his neck. He squinted as he peered at her, then toward the trail again.

"How much has Brielle told you about me?"

Her brows rose. "What does Bri have to do with you being a teacher?"

He laughed. "I'm just curious if she's given up any of my secrets."

"If your secrets include how good you are at your job or how much integrity you have or how hot—" She cut herself off and her face flushed. "It's not really a secret that the two of you are together."

"Were."

"What?"

His small smile didn't reach his eyes. "We were together. But that was a long time ago—like when she'd just graduated from high school."

Sarah's eyes widened. "Really? I would have thought it was more recent than that."

He shook his head. "Nope. But then Brielle never really gets over a guy because she never has really had a long-term relationship. Frankly, I don't think she wants one." And that was the biggest reason for their breakup. He'd needed to find someone who could be a better influence on him—especially after he'd started going to meetings.

Dax took in a deep breath, keeping his focus forward. "So she's not mentioned anything about my past?"

"Why would she?" She let out a nervous laugh. "What? Are you some kind of serial killer? Please tell me you're not a serial killer."

A laugh bubbled up from his chest. "You're funny when you wanna be."

She warmed with his compliment.

"But no, nothing like that. Remember when you mentioned that you were here because your mom sent you here for some kind of reform?" He didn't turn fully toward her, but he could see the blush on her face deepen. They were closing in on a topic that made her uncomfortable. It was ironic that he had similar experiences.

Sarah wasn't looking toward him anymore. And the way she sat in the saddle had once again grown stiff and unyielding.

He let out a sigh. "Don't worry. I'm not going to ask you about why you're here. I only brought this up because it will help demonstrate the answer to your question."

"Okay, so you have some kind of sordid past."

"Yes."

Her head snapped around to stare at him. "Really."

He gave her a crooked grin. "Let's just say that I have had my share of run-ins with the law."

"With the sheriff?"

"Actually, all my problems were in different states."

"States? Plural?"

He grimaced. "Yeah."

She blinked a few times as he gave her time to process this. He fully expected that she'd ask him for details. That's what every girl he'd dated seemed to want to know. Perhaps that was yet another reason why he'd been interested in her past. He didn't trust easily. And he'd been conditioned to need to know who or what he was dealing with.

Instead, Sarah just gave him a nod.

A nod. That was all.

She didn't push him. There was no judgment. Just an acceptance.

It was a strange experience, to say the least. He didn't have to put up any defenses and explain why he'd gone down that path or how he'd come back from it.

"You know? I think you might be right about some folks. But honestly? I think there would be a lot of parents who would be interested in your expertise. From what I can tell, your past hasn't followed you here. I haven't seen any evidence to say otherwise." Sarah gave him a timid smile. "Seems to me you were successful in getting a fresh start."

He nodded. "If it wasn't for Zeke, I never would have been offered that."

"I guess Zeke has a soft spot for troublemakers."

"Guess so."

They rode in silence once more. Sarah was different somehow. Yes, there were secrets she was keeping from him. And as much as he wanted to know every little detail, he was getting to a point where he was happy just to teach her and train her.

When she wasn't in a sour mood, she was just the kind of person he enjoyed working with. Sarah was bright—like more than a normal rancher or even college student. She must have had educated parents. She hadn't given up on doing any job that had been assigned to her. Once she'd gotten reasonably better from her accident, she was the first out to the barn and one of the last to head inside.

Hers was a work ethic some of his ranch hands could take notes from.

It was getting increasingly harder and harder not to notice every little thing that he discovered about her that made him want to get to know her even more. If their current situation was different, he could have seen himself asking her out on a date.

He let the silence continue to grow between them, almost itching to tell her more. She had a way of helping him feel validated that he hadn't experienced in years.

The landscape crawled alongside them the farther they went into Slate Rock Ranch property. Tall grasses filled empty areas, and wildflowers grew along the fence lines for the grazing fields they managed.

A breeze drifted around them, causing the hairs on the back of his neck to stand up and goosebumps to cover his arms. Sarah leaned her head back, letting the current of the air lift and tug at her hair. She seemed to fit in this world—the one filled with flowers and horses. It was strange to think she had another life separate from the one she led here.

"Tell me about your family." The request escaped his lips before he had a chance to consider what it might do to the easy way they were spending in each other's company.

Just like that, her body language changed. She gave him a suspicious look; everything from her boots up to her eyes were tighter than they had been at the beginning of their ride. "What do you want to know?"

He shrugged, hoping the gesture would be enough to convince her of his next statement. "Whatever you want to tell me. I figure you know my family."

Her brows furrowed and her eyes narrowed. "No, I don't."

"The Callahans are my family." He said it with a matter-of-fact tone. "I could have sworn I told you that Zeke's sister raised me. I spent some summers here, which is why Zeke hired me on when I was old enough."

"You might have," her voice was quiet, more contemplative than anything else. Then she took a deep breath and released it. "Well, I believe I told you about my mom—to a degree. She's always been a little more judgmental than anyone else. She always wanted me to play a role in the family that I wasn't ready for."

"I'm sorry."

"It's fine." She gave him a wry smile. "There's that word again."

He waited for her to go on. This was the most open she'd

been with him since arriving. He wasn't about to squander the opportunity he had to get to know her better.

"My dad was easier on me. But I guess that would be expected with me being his only daughter."

"Does that mean you have siblings?"

She gave him a strained smile. "I had a younger brother. But he died in a drunk driving accident. I barely remember him."

A twinge of discomfort sliced through his heart at her statement. Her story came dangerously close to an experience that used to keep him up at night. "I'm so sorry, Sarah."

"I guess the way they raised me would be the reason I am the way I am."

Dax reached out toward her, but immediately brought his hand back toward him. That gesture had been inappropriate, and he could only hope she hadn't noticed. "I guess I know who to thank then."

"What?"

"Your parents. If they are the ones responsible for how you turned out, then I suppose it's them I have to thank for raising such a strong person."

Sarah let out a soft laugh. "I'm really not all that great."

"Sure you are."

She shook her head. "You don't know what you're talking about."

He dug his heels into his horse, pushing her to leap forward and block Sarah from riding farther. She gasped, her hands tightening as he took over the trail before her. "I know exactly what I'm talking about. You are so much stronger than you give yourself credit for. Smarter, too."

Her gaze dipped to the ground. "Thanks," she murmured. "I appreciate that, even though you don't have to say it."

"No, I don't." He jerked his head toward another trail. "Let's pull off here and let the horses get a drink. There's a creek that runs through this side of the property." He turned his horse toward the trail, not checking to see if Sarah was close behind.

Since when had he become more generous with flattery? His jaw tightened. If he was getting soft, he'd have to reconsider how he led the ranch hands on a day-to-day basis.

When they reached the clearing, he hopped down from his horse immediately, then walked over to Sarah. He held up his hands, a gesture that made it clear he would help her down. She hesitated for a moment but gave in quicker than he'd expected. Her hands settled down on his shoulders and he lifted her from her saddle to deposit her in front of him.

His hands lingered on her waist as he gazed into her brown eyes. He could get lost in those eyes, *if* he was interested in her. *If* he was interested in a romantic relationship at all, it would be with someone who would be around for more than a few months.

As much as his head continued to spout out those thoughts, his heart disagreed.

The way his heart beat a little faster, the way his fingers twitched as they grazed her waist, the way his eyes dipped toward her mouth, his body was betraying him in ways he wasn't sure he disapproved of.

He jerked away from her. "See that your horse gets led over to the creek. We'll head back on the trail in a few minutes. The fields we're checking out aren't too far from here." Dax turned away from her.

Just because he could relate to her and had this undeniable attraction to her didn't mean a dang thing.

Brielle was wrong.

Dax strode toward his horse and grasped the reins in his hand, then led her to the water. His eyes met Sarah's, but neither of them smiled. The tension between them had returned with a vengeance, but this time, it was a little different. They weren't at each other's throats. It was more like they were two magnets that had been placed in a glass jar and now they danced around each other.

How had this happened? He searched his head for a moment in time when things had shifted, but he couldn't put a finger on it. The pounding in his chest grew more ragged. He hadn't wanted to be with a woman since... since he couldn't remember. And now, suddenly, he'd been blindsided by this girl.

Sure, if he really wanted to scrutinize what had happened, he might trace it back to when he'd seen her in the chicken coop for the first time.

Sarah was a spitfire. That was the thing that had drawn his attention to Brielle. She was a spitfire too, only in a different way. With Sarah, it was in the way she approached life, while Brielle had used her energies to attract the men she was interested in.

He ran his hand along his horse's neck and down her back as she dipped lower to take a drink. What if he allowed himself to open up more to Sarah? What would it hurt? He might just figure out that she wasn't his type after all. Then he could stop these traitorous thoughts from infiltrating his mind.

He'd been through this before. With Brielle, she'd overtaken every part of him until the point when they'd both had enough. That had to be the only solution.

Dax had to get her out of his system one way or another. Either he had to explore the possibility of something more, or he had to determine without a doubt that she wasn't meant for him.

But even as his gaze raked over her from this distance, he had a feeling the more likely of the two scenarios was the former.

There was only one problem. He couldn't fall for someone who refused to open up to him. Could Sarah find the courage to trust in him even a little bit?

He hated how much he hoped she would.

15

Sarah

Sarah loathed everything about the way she felt utterly caged in this moment—not by Dax, not by the Callahans, not even by the sheriff.

She had been cornered by her own stupid curiosity. This was downright ridiculous. She just needed to put some distance between them, that was all. Except how was she supposed to do that when her probation required her to be with him for most working hours?

Scowling at the water where she stood, Sarah tried to come up with as many excuses as possible to duck out early that day. It should be easy. She hadn't ever been the type of person who chased after a guy, and she still wasn't. As long as he didn't make any advances, she should be fine.

Sarah took a deep breath and released it. The relief that filled her took the edge off the worry. She'd overreacted. It was fine—this whole thing was fine.

Her horse wandered farther down the creek, leaving her alone to stare into the babbling water with unseeing eyes. There was a reason she was drawn to Dax. Even if he got on her nerves sometimes, he was a decent guy.

She rubbed her nose and attempted to glance over her shoulder with as much nonchalance as she could muster, only to find him missing. Her heart beat a little faster for reasons she wasn't certain of, and she spun around only to nearly bump into him.

Sarah let out a squeak and took a stumbled step backward. The heel of her boot slipped on a wet stone and her hands flew into the air, flailing. Eyes wide, she didn't have time to react before Dax's hand shot out and grasped her upper arm, yanking her back to safety. Heart pounding, she stared up at Dax as her breaths came out in short gasps. Immediately, she scowled at him and pulled away. "Why did you do that?"

"Why did I save your life? Again?" The corners of his mouth lifted into a grin.

"*No*. Why did you sneak up on me?"

He cocked his head slightly, amusement clear in his gaze. "I did no such thing."

"Yes, you *did*," she accused. "You were over there, and then suddenly you were behind me."

Dax turned his head to where she pointed. "I believe I was over there about seven minutes ago. And then I headed in this direction. May I point out that my boots crunched against the dirt and I snapped a few twigs on my way over here? If you didn't hear it, then maybe it's you who needs to reevaluate something."

Her eyes narrowed. There was no way he'd crossed the area like a normal human being and she hadn't heard him.

"I don't buy it." The beats of her heart still echoed wildly in her chest.

He didn't react to her words nor the bite in her tone like she had expected. The way he watched her was more unnerving than she wanted to admit.

Sarah moved to walk past him, but his hand shot out and grasped her arm. She stopped, looking down at where he held her as if she'd be able to see the electrical current that passed between them. When she lifted her eyes to meet his, the intensity she saw there was nothing like she'd ever experienced before. She could feel the warmth of her blush creeping up the back of her neck, and in order to prevent it from making an appearance, she tore her arm away from his. "Is there something you wanted?"

He opened his mouth, then shut it just as quickly. "No."

"Okay, then let's get going." She prayed he couldn't hear the tremor in her voice as she spoke. This was all in her head. There was no way he was experiencing the same thing she was.

It took her three tries to climb up in the saddle, but she managed to get up there without his help. The last thing she wanted was for him to touch her again and for her to find out there was, in fact, some kind of connection growing between them.

Would that be so bad?

The rogue part of her needed to stop questioning her common sense. Yes, it would be bad. It'd be really bad. What if he found out that she was some spoiled rich girl who fell in with the wrong crowd and wreaked havoc at his home? Based on the way he hadn't been willing to trust her when they first met, she didn't think that would go over very well. Sure, there were other issues that would be worse to confess, but this was more than maintaining an air of anonymity while at Slate Rock Ranch. This was about keeping her family name out of the limelight.

They started on the trail, but this time it had narrowed and Dax took the lead, allowing her thoughts to drift once more while she stared at the back of his head.

Dax didn't seem like the type to spill information about her family to others, but sometimes that sort of thing happened by accident. On top of that, money was a hot-button issue. She didn't know him well enough to gauge how he'd react to finding out she was an heiress to a fortune.

She'd managed to fall behind, though she didn't know how that was possible when her horse was the one to dictate how close they'd stay. Dax was probably five yards ahead, and when there was a slight curve in the trail, he disappeared for a few moments at a time. In those moments the anxiety from when she'd gotten lost returned.

Sarah urged her horse forward by putting pressure on the flanks of her horse. The distance between them shortened, easing the part of her that continued to relive her accident. The trail widened once more and she pushed forward until she was right beside him. "Tell me more about your childhood."

She wasn't sure, but she thought she saw his jaw tighten. He glanced at her out of the corner of his eye. "What do you want to know?"

"You said you were raised by Zeke's sister?"

He nodded.

"Tell me about her."

Almost immediately, his whole demeanor changed. He smiled as he swung his gaze back to the trail ahead of them. "Eve was amazing."

"Eve? You didn't call her mom?"

"Well, she never adopted me. She became my foster mom when I was about seven. She was always taking in kids that no one else wanted. And she'd let them stay as long as they needed to." Dax peeked at her again. "She was the kind of woman who only ever cared about other people even when she needed to worry about herself." The happiness in his eyes dimmed but only slightly. "She passed away just before I graduated high school."

Chills ran down Sarah's spine. "I'm so sorry."

He shook his head. "Don't be. She was always so vibrant and full of life. Sometimes I even wondered if she was *too* good to keep living here and God just came and took her home."

The chills changed into goosebumps and the hair on her arms lifted. Sarah shivered. "So I guess she's the one who helped you turn out to be the man you are today."

He lifted a shoulder. "I didn't turn out as well as she would have hoped."

Her face scrunched up with confusion. "How can you say that? I've only known you for a little over a month and even I can tell that you're one of the good ones."

Dax's eyes swung over to lock with hers. He worked his jaw back and forth, then returned his focus to the trail. "Sometimes people make mistakes and they have to live with them."

His words hit her harder than he probably meant for them to. As much as she knew in her heart that he was referring to himself, she couldn't help but relate to everything he'd just said.

If her mother could see her now, she wouldn't be pleased one bit. But then, her mother was always so much more judgmental than any mother ought to be. If she found out about this particular *mistake*, Sarah wouldn't put it past her to disown her own daughter. Sarah took a deep breath and shifted in her saddle, shoving down that thought before it could gain a life of its own and live side-by-side with the desire to get closer to Dax.

"Mothers are supposed to love you no matter what." She said the words softly, not expecting him to hear her, but she'd been wrong.

"She wasn't my mother, as much as I would have loved to be given the title of her son." His voice dripped with bitterness. "But yes, I believe you would be right. I think she would have forgiven me if she'd been given the chance. I was an orphan. She raised me to want more." He gave her a sad smile. "Everything I am wouldn't have been possible if she hadn't influenced my life."

The ache that sliced through her chest was only a drop in the bucket to the ache he must have felt after the only person who cared for him passed. If she could reach across to him and pull him into a hug, she would have.

Silence grew between them, cold, unsure, and palpable. There was nothing she could say to him. What could she offer? She had never lost someone that close to her. And her own mother didn't seem to share the same characteristics.

Her thoughts continued to spiral as she thought about what he must have struggled through. But they were shattered when he chuckled.

"Why do you look so sad?"

Sarah shot a look in his direction. Heat burst beneath her skin and she tore her gaze away from him. "I'm sorry."

"Whatever for?"

"For..." She shrugged. "I guess I'm sorry you had to go through that."

His grin went flat. Great. Had she just offended him? That hadn't been her intention.

"I'm sorry, I didn't mean to—"

"Don't apologize for being human, Sarah. It's nice to know there's a human behind the mask you wear."

She wanted to be insulted by his statement. But as much as the instinct to toss another snarky comment in his direction tempted her, she couldn't deny that he made a good point. She hadn't exactly been upfront with him about anything.

Sarah forced a laugh. "Yeah, well, what do you expect when you're raised different than everyone else?"

She felt his eyes on her, though she refused to meet his gaze. Swallowing hard at the lump in her throat, she fiddled with the reins in her hands and shifted in her seat. "I'm sure you've already made a fair number of assumptions about me." She grimaced and continued. "The reason I'm here is because I was sentenced to community service for some stuff I did a little while back."

This was it. The moment when he'd demand to know every detail and then judge her for it. That was the reason she'd avoided telling anyone. Because people were innately human and wanted to know the nitty-gritty of everything. When they drove by an accident, they slowed to watch. When flashing lights of cop cars were outside of a building, everyone waited by their windows to watch the officers retrieve the suspect.

She didn't blame him. But maybe it would finally do some good to get this secret off her chest.

Nothing.

Sarah forced herself to look toward him. "Aren't you going to say anything? Ask me what crime I committed to be sentenced to working on a ranch?"

He shrugged. "Can't be anything worse than I did when I was younger." He gestured toward the fence they came up to. "I'm going to open the gate and you head on in. We just need to inspect the fence perimeter and make sure there isn't anything that could harm the herd."

She gaped after him as he hopped from his saddle and pushed open the gate.

Had she seriously built up everything in her head and all for what?

Nothing.

No third degree. No demands. Just understanding.

Dang it.

Why did he have to keep surprising her?

16

———————

Dax

*P*rogress. That's all he could think about. Sarah had opened up to him about something small. Strangely enough, he didn't care *what* she'd done to get community service.

The only thing that rubbed him the wrong way was the fact that Zeke had kept this a secret from him. It might have been nice to know from the beginning about why she was at the ranch.

Then again, if he had been told, would he have developed an interest in her? Dax let his gaze linger on her, noting that she was far more relaxed than she had been at the beginning of their ride. He couldn't help but be impressed by her. But that was now. Deep down he knew he would have dismissed her if he'd found out she was a criminal.

An ache started in his chest and spread out. He had been in her shoes before, so judging her made him a hypocrite. Being around her made him want to be even better. He was a work in progress.

The whole ride back to the ranch, Dax studied her. Sarah didn't seem like the type to get into trouble. She'd hinted at problems with her family. Growing up, he had met a multitude of people who made poor decisions because the expectations at home had been too much to handle.

It wouldn't be a far stretch to imagine that Sarah had that kind of experience.

Sarah glanced at him and frowned. Dang it. She'd caught him staring. "What?"

He removed his hat and ran a hand through his hair, then shrugged. "Nothing."

"It's killing you, isn't it?"

"I don't know what you're talking about."

She heaved a sigh and shifted in the saddle, looking away. Her gaze remained on the trail in front of her, and she kept her spine stiff. "You want to know what I did. You want to know if I can be trusted."

Dax arched a brow. "Is that what you're worried about?"

Lifting a shoulder, she shot a quick look in his direction. Her hands fiddled with the rope in her hands as she twisted the cords around her fingers. The discomfort had returned and more than anything, he empathized.

"I want to make one thing perfectly clear." He waited for her to meet his gaze before he continued. "Like I said before, I did some pretty bad stuff, too."

She snorted. "I find that hard to believe."

"It's true. There was a time when I was in trouble with the law. I had a problem with alcohol and I got into some pretty bad drugs."

Her eyes widened, more shock than judgment.

"Yep." He sighed, dragging a hand down his face. "I had to

realize that I wanted to make a change. I needed to decide what was most important to me. Did I want to continue down the path I was taking, or did I want to be better?" Dax didn't know what had come over him. He shouldn't be telling her any of this. It wasn't something he even shared with Brielle.

Yes, Brielle knew some of it. She was aware that he'd fallen in with a bad crowd. But only because they'd practically been raised side by side. But did she know *everything*? No. Zeke had shielded them all from his bad influence.

Dax peeked at Sarah, her shocked expression like a slap in the face. He'd done so much to get away from that life—to forget it. But that's not what AA was supposed to teach him. He needed to remember each and every mistake he made so he didn't make them again.

Swallowing hard, Dax forced himself to continue. "As you might have guessed, I chose to walk away from that life and do what I could to make up for it. The road is not easy, but with family and friends to support you, it's possible."

Her features flattened. "You don't know my family."

"Right now, your family is at Slate Rock Ranch. *We* are your family. It might be hard to accept sometimes, but I would bet my favorite horse that those people care about you more than you realize. You just have to give them a chance."

If she needed any evidence, all she had to do was think back to her accident. He wasn't the only one who had been worried about her. He straightened in his saddle. "Maybe you just need to find a way to make that connection." He'd had to finally accept help and go to his first meeting. But that wasn't something he had to share. That's where he drew the line.

"You're a good egg, Sarah. Even I can see it."

"Thanks," she murmured.

The air had gone cold once more, and Dax found himself wanting to maintain that connection they'd managed to find earlier. He wasn't accustomed to feeling this way—not even when he'd been dating Brielle. But that didn't mean anything. He had just found a good connection with Sarah, that was all.

"What are your plans after you're done here?"

She didn't answer right away. It was as if she didn't trust why he might be asking this question. Dax nearly repeated the question, but she finally spoke up. "I used to think I wanted to go into finance. I took a lot of classes in college for that. But now I'm not so sure."

"What changed your mind?"

A ghost of a smile lit her face. "Honestly? I've sorta liked working here."

Surprise hit him over the head. "You're kidding."

"I know, right?" Sarah laughed. "You'd think with those crazy chickens and the whole being thrown from a horse thing that I would want to get out of here right away."

"You don't?"

She shrugged. "I mean, sure. I can't wait to be done. But I think part of me would miss this place." Her eyes landed on him, then darted away just as fast.

"What would your parents think? What about your uncle?"

The smile left her face again. Shoot. Why did he have to ask the wrong kinds of questions? He should have known better than to bring up her parents. Even the sheriff seemed to have a strained relationship with her.

"You don't have to answer that if you—"

"It's fine." She let her focus drift over the landscape as they lumbered along the trail. "I think my uncle wouldn't mind. Honestly, I think he loves it out here so much he would be impressed if I decided to make something of myself—you know, by doing honest work." She shook her head and shot him a wry smile. "But my parents? Oh, they'd be livid." She let out a sad sort of smile. The kind that sliced through his heart and tugged at his insides. "My parents would probably cut me off."

Sarah's hand clapped over her mouth and she glanced at him.

Her reaction was strange, to say the least. It was as if she'd said something that would give away too much information. And just like that his curiosity was piqued once more. If her criminal background wasn't what she was scared of revealing, then what was it about her family that she wanted to keep secret?

No. He wasn't going to go down that road again. They were just making headway and he wanted to get to know the real her.

But if you don't know what she's hiding, how can you really know the real her?

His subconscious made a good point.

Nope. Nope. Nope.

If he wanted to know more about Sarah, she'd have to tell him on her terms. "You don't have to tell me anything you don't feel comfortable saying."

"Why are you being so nice to me?"

Hadn't she asked him that question before? He couldn't remember. It didn't really matter. The answer would have been the same regardless. "Because everyone deserves a chance to prove themselves. And I like you."

The words slipped from his lips before he could contain them. He didn't mean he liked her in a *romantic* sort of way.

Did he?

Brielle would have told him he was in complete denial.

And lately the evidence seemed to agree with her. He couldn't bring himself to meet Sarah's gaze. Doing so would be a disaster. If she had a smug look on her face—if she was making fun of him, that would be a hit to his ego.

But what if she was considering what he'd said, contemplating whether he was worth the risk?

Well, he wouldn't risk it. Not yet. Not until he figured out what it was that she meant to him.

It was all his fault, really. The entire ride back to the barn, the silence continued to grow between them. Even the birds seemed to hold their breaths to see what big mistake he'd make next. But with each passing step, the feeling that he was doing something wrong persisted. He needed to take action if he thought there was a possibility of something more.

The concept was laughable until it wasn't. He'd spent the better part of six weeks with this woman, and while their relationship had been strained in the beginning, they'd found a good place to settle.

So why was he so keen on messing it up? She'd be leaving in a few months. Starting anything would most definitely end in disaster.

Dax climbed down from his position until his boots hit the ground, displacing dirt and dust. He led his horse toward the stable, his thoughts battling in a cacophony of wills. Sarah continued riding until they made it to the stalls where they'd brush down their horses.

Out of habit, Dax moved to her side and reached for her. It was something he'd done for Brielle and several of the Callahan women over the years when he was charged with the brush down after a ride. Sarah stared at him like he'd grown antlers.

"What?"

"I'll help you down."

She shooed him off. "I can do it myself, thank you." Sarah rose up and moved to take her right foot from the stirrup, but something caught. The momentum put her off balance and she teetered, a small sound of surprise escaping her lips. Dax's arms shot out and wrapped around her waist before she had a chance to tumble from the saddle.

Still, Sarah fell against him, their bodies colliding until he could put her securely on her feet. Her hands remained on his shoulders and she stared at him with wide, nervous eyes. It wouldn't have been a fall that caused another concussion, but he could understand why she might be a little shaken.

Where his hands held her at her waist, a spark ignited. The energy flowed from her body into his. Time slowed as he gazed at her, waiting for her to react to him even a little. Her big, brown eyes looked just like a doe in the woods and she remained frozen. Was she experiencing what he was in this moment?

His focus lowered to her mouth as she brought in her lower lip between her teeth. The quiet intimacy that clung around them seemed to nudge him into a completely new train of thought. He could steal a kiss, bridge the gap where he lacked *really* knowing her.

Dax dipped his head, lowering slowly, getting closer and closer to her as his fingers dug into her soft waistline. Sarah blinked rapidly and she swallowed but didn't pull away from him. Was this it then? Was he really doing what Brielle had accused him of? Could the walls be crumbling right before his eyes?

She lifted on her toes and exhaled through parted lips. Two more inches and their lips would graze against each other. His pulse roared through his body. There was nothing wrong with developing a relationship with this woman. There was nothing to hold him back, not really.

A stall door about fifteen feet away from them burst open and a cowboy backed out, leading a horse, saddled and ready to go.

Sarah tore out of his grasp, her face flushed and her eyes darting to the ground.

Sean glanced from Dax to Sarah and back. His eyes narrowed and he adjusted his hat. Clearing his throat, he nodded to them. "Dax. Sarah."

Dax swallowed at the lump in his throat. "Sean. I thought you were out at the country club today. Aren't you training a fresh set of horses?" He could see it in the way Sean hesitated. He probably thought something shady was going on between himself and Sarah. Well, nothing was and based on the way Sarah continued to edge away from him, nothing would.

Sean gave Dax a short nod. "I was. But Adeline mentioned that a few pastures needed to be checked, and I finished early so I thought—"

"We already checked on them." Dax moved swiftly past Sarah, a scowl on his face. He retrieved the reins of each horse they'd ridden and gave Sean a pointed look. "While we appreciate you helping out here and there, the Callahan ranch is in good hands, I assure you."

"I never said it wasn't." His mouth twitched, spreading into a small smile. Sean's brows remained pinched. "May I suggest going on a date outside of working hours? Then you might not be interrupted in such an awkward manner."

Sarah's blush darkened and her eyes flew open as she shook her head. "I—we—we're not—"

Sean held up a hand. "There aren't any rules prohibiting you two from dating. I merely make the suggestion because you're going to find it hard to get some privacy in here." He flashed Dax a smile and led the horse toward the door.

Dax bristled. "Like I said, the pastures checked out. You don't have to—"

He waved toward Dax with a dismissive hand. "I'm here. She's saddled. I'm sure we can find something to do." He disappeared out into the sunlight, the clopping sound of his horse's hooves dissipating.

Dax watched him until Sean could no longer be seen, the reins still in his hands. When he turned to face Sarah, she leaned against the stall door a few feet away. One foot was propped up against the frame behind her and she had her arms folded. She avoided his gaze, but he didn't expect anything else.

He led the first horse into a stall, turning her around and then shutting the door. When he got the other horse into her stall, he reached for the belt beneath the saddle, letting himself go on autopilot.

They'd nearly kissed. His body still hummed with nervous energy. It probably shouldn't have gotten that close. Thankfully, Sean had interrupted them when he had. Dax was Sarah's supervisor. That was enough to make their relationship a bad idea, right?

Right.

He grabbed the brush, praying that Sarah would leave and go find something else to do. With the way he was feeling, he wasn't sure how he'd react to her if she stayed. He needed to clear his head.

"Dax?"

Dang it.

17

____

Sarah

I almost kissed him! Oh my goodness, I almost kissed Dax Heaton. What am I doing?

Dangerous thoughts swirled around and around in Sarah's head. She should take off—run from the stable and go find Brielle.

No, that would be very bad. She didn't know how Brielle would react to this information. What if she got upset about it? Well, then she would talk some sense into Sarah. It wasn't too late. She hadn't kissed him.

Not yet.

They could be adults about this, and she could tell him she hadn't meant to—to what? To lean into him and show him that she was interested.

She cleared her throat, peering over the side of the stall door as he brushed the horse with agitated movements. The horse sidestepped and bobbed her head. She was probably more nervous with the pace at which he was brushing her, not due to any discomfort.

"Dax?" she repeated.

He grunted.

"Can we talk?"

Dax's eyes lifted to her, guarded. She couldn't tell if he was upset because they'd been interrupted or if he was upset because of the line they'd nearly crossed. Her heart leaped into her chest.

He'd told her he *liked* her. The way he'd grown quiet after that confession had made her consider that he might be interested in something more. But there was still a part of her that was content to stay in denial.

Until he nearly kissed her.

She could still feel the weight of his hands on her waist, feel the warmth of his body against hers, and a thrill shot through her. She could do so much worse than Dax—like Kenneth. Once, she'd thought she liked *him*. He still hadn't made any attempt to contact her, and her anxiety about seeing him had settled into something more like a quiet unease.

Sarah shook her head to clear it. Dax's steady gaze remained locked on her, and she squirmed beneath it. How was she supposed to bring any of this up and not sound like some dumb, lovesick teenager? Being near him made her feel so small and insignificant already.

"Well?" he demanded.

She jumped.

Dax let out a sigh. "What do you want to talk about?"

Sarah swallowed hard. It was obvious, wasn't it? "We almost —" Her voice died in her throat when he tossed the brush to the side and strode toward her.

"What do you want me to say?" His voice lowered to something huskier and goosebumps prickled on her arms and legs.

She took a quick step back, even though the stall door remained between them. "I just—I guess I want to know why."

"Why what?" Dax tilted his head. "Why we almost kissed?"

She nodded. Finally, someone was able to voice what her tongue was unwilling to.

He let out a frustrated sigh. "I don't know."

"You don't—" Her brows knit together. "You don't know."

"Look, I'm not interested in a relationship. At least I wasn't until..." He frowned and his jaw tightened, the muscles in his neck twitching. "No. I still don't. I'm too busy. You're not..."

Her stomach plummeted and she looked away. "I'm not what you're looking for—because of my *history*." She knew she should have kept that part of her life private. Dax hadn't needed to know that about her. What made this whole thing worse was how disappointed she felt over his confession. He had seemed so understanding about it.

"What? No. That's not what I was going to say." Dax darted out of the stall, causing her to stumble back a few more steps. He closed the distance between them, standing close enough that it wouldn't take much to pick up where they'd left off. His eyes searched hers. "If anything, knowing about your history is something that helped me relate to you." He snatched his hat from his head and raked a hand through his damp hair. "I was going to say that you're not going to be here that long. You'll be leaving at the end of the summer. The last thing I want is for either one of us to get hurt."

That actually made sense. There was so much she had to consider if she were to allow herself to fall for him. Like what she'd done to deserve community service, her wealth, and whether or not she wanted to stay here. She took in a shuddering breath. She pressed her lips together, gnawing on them between her teeth. "Oh."

"Yeah," he muttered. "But honestly, if you did decide to stay, there could be other problems."

Confusion mingled with the disappointment.

"I'm technically your boss, Sarah. I don't like the idea of mixing business with pleasure."

Her eyes dropped to his mouth as his lips formed that last word. The desire from before hit her with a vengeance. She had to be honest with herself. She had *wanted* him to kiss her—more than she wanted to leave this place. More than she had wanted anything.

Sarah squeezed her eyes shut and nodded. Backing up a few more steps, she pressed up against the cool wood of the stalls behind her. "You're right," she rasped. "Of course you're right." Her eyes remained shut, but she couldn't seem to get her mouth to obey the same rules. "I shouldn't be thinking about what it might be like for you to pull me into your arms." Never had she been so brash with her words, but they kept coming. "I shouldn't even entertain the idea of being with a guy like you. But I do." She opened her eyes to find his face inches from hers.

Dax's hand rested over her shoulder against a wooden pole. She hadn't heard his steps as he maintained the same distance while she spoke. Her heart fluttered angrily in her chest, demanding to be satiated.

He expelled a long slow breath. "Why did you have to do that?"

She blinked and whispered, "Do what?"

"Make things so complicated." He shook his head, then let it hang as he continued. "I can't explain it to you other than to say that I had no intention of developing an interest in you. When you got here, you were supposed to keep your distance. I figured that you'd keep your head down and do your work and I wouldn't have to get to know you."

Her stomach knotted. They'd been thrown together as if

against their wills. She had been content to do exactly what he'd described. But then the incident with the runaway horse had happened, and that set off a domino effect of what had resulted in the last few weeks. As much as she tried to keep her attention on her chores, she had entertained an alternate reality where Dax was someone who would sweep her off her feet.

Dax lifted his head, his gaze more serious than she expected. "It's not a good idea, Sarah."

She swallowed at the stubborn lump in her throat, but it wouldn't go anywhere. "Don't you think I know that?" She bit down on her lower lip. "But I don't care anymore."

He gave her a sideways look with a boyish grin on his face. "Why do you have to be so deliciously stubborn one second and infuriatingly desirable the next?"

Her breath hitched. No one had ever said that sort of thing to her before. Her pulse roared in her ears like an angry river racing down the side of a mountain in the spring.

This was crazy. They both knew it. But one kiss didn't a relationship make. It wasn't like he was proposing to her. They could find out that their chemistry was imagined. There wasn't any real harm in one kiss, was there?

Dax let out a chuckle, sending a fresh wave of chills rocketing through her. "I can't make you any promises."

"Same."

His smile widened and he chuckled again. His warm breath fanned against her face, and he reached out to grasp her chin with his thumb and finger. "You don't know how much I want to kiss you right now."

"I think I can guess," the words escaped her lips breathily. Her legs trembled and she itched to grab his face with both hands to just get the kiss done and over with. It would be so simple, so easy. What was he waiting for?

"But I can't." He pulled back, his hands dropping to his sides.

It was as if he'd punched her in the gut. The air whooshed out of her chest, leaving her lightheaded and dazed. "What?"

"I'm not going to kiss you."

"Why?"

"Because you deserve better than a stolen kiss in the Callahan's stable."

"I do?" She took a step toward him, confused and hating how hurt she was beginning to feel.

Dax nodded. "I'll kiss you, Sarah. Make no mistake. But I'll do it right."

"But—"

"Go on a date with me." His mischievous grin was something she was very familiar with. It was the same kind of smile he gave her the first time she was attacked by the stupid chickens. It was the same one he gave her when he teased her. She'd grown to hate that smile.

Until now.

Now, that crooked grin made her stomach loop around as if competing for a world championship in gymnastics.

"You want to take me on a *date*?"

He folded his arms. "Is that a yes?"

"Are you—do you know how crazy you sound right now?"

Dax shrugged. "You're avoiding my question."

"Fine."

"Okay." He turned on his heel and headed back toward the horse he had been tending to. "I'm going to get back to work. You're welcome to run your yearling through some exercises, then call it a day."

She bit back an argument that sat on the tip of her tongue. He'd flipped this whole conversation around, surprising her, keeping her on her toes. She couldn't deny how exhilarating it had all been, and she found herself looking forward to whatever he had in mind for their date.

S ARAH SAT on the edge of her bed. Today had been taxing but fulfilling all the same. From the emotional rollercoaster to the energy-zapping labor she had to complete, she wouldn't be surprised if she fell asleep the moment her head hit the pillow.

Her feet bounced against the wooden floorboards as she waited for Brielle. Her roommate hadn't come to get ready for bed yet, and she didn't know how she was going to broach the subject of an official date with Dax.

The way those two acted around one another—man, she should have discussed that with Dax before. She'd been so thrown that she hadn't even thought about it. Obviously, Dax wasn't concerned or he would have brought it up. Even still, Sarah knew she had to discuss it before the actual date.

She wrung her hands together. Guilt had started to grow like a wildfire, spreading to the most vulnerable parts of her. If Brielle wasn't pleased, Sarah had no intention of backing out. She wanted to go on a date with Dax. Even she wasn't so blind to see that he was good for her. He'd pushed her to do things she wouldn't have otherwise attempted. He made her feel better about her situation, almost like he'd helped her give herself permission for forgiveness.

Dax made her happy.

The bedroom door opened and Sarah's head snapped up. Brielle smiled at her and tossed her hat on the dresser near the door. "Hey. How was your day?"

Sarah pulled up her legs beneath her, folding them and turning to face Brielle's bed. "It was good." The last word hung in the air, noticeably different than the rest of the sentence. Sarah grimaced. Why was it so much harder to brush off what made her nervous around Brielle?

Brielle paused what she was doing and glanced over her shoulder. "What's going on?"

"Nothing."

Brielle snorted, pulling out her pajamas from her drawer. "Something is definitely up. What happened today?" She moved to her bed and sat on the edge. "I know you might not realize it, but you can tell me anything. I promise. I'm here for you."

Her words were likely due to the guilt she still harbored over the argument they'd had right before her accident. It didn't matter that Sarah had told her all was forgiven. Brielle still seemed to step lightly around the subject, never directly discussing it.

Sarah pursed her lips together and pulled them to the side. "Can I ask you something?"

"Of course."

"You and Dax…"

Brielle tilted her head to the side, "What about me and Dax?" She didn't appear to be apprehensive at all. It was almost like her small smile was one that said she already had a feeling about where this conversation was going.

"You two were involved."

"Yes."

"Do you still have feelings for him?"

Time dragged on as Brielle considered her. The longer she waited before she answered, the more anxious Sarah became. "Sure."

Sarah's heart stuttered, tripping over itself. "You do?"

"Yeah, but not in the way you're probably thinking."

Brows furrowing, Sarah moved closer to the edge, letting her legs dangle over the side. "There aren't many ways I can take that statement."

Brielle's smile stretched over her whole face. "I care about Dax like anyone would care about their ex when things ended on good terms. If he wanted to get back together and have some fun, would I be up for it? Absolutely. Do I want something serious right now? Nope. Why? Did he say something?"

She frowned. "You could say that."

"Something *bad*?"

"Not exactly." Sarah sighed, dragging a hand down her face. "We almost kissed."

One of Brielle's brows lifted. "*Almost*." She let out a soft chuckle. "Man, he's changed."

"He has?"

Brielle tossed her clothes onto her bed and moved over to sit beside Sarah. "Okay, maybe *changed* is the wrong word. You have to understand the two of us know each other *really* well. I probably know him better than anyone he's dated. He has always been more comfortable around me. If he's taking it slow with you, that is probably a good thing."

"Wait, you're not mad?"

She tossed her head back and laughed. "Of course not. Dax and I aren't together. He doesn't owe me anything. If he wants to date you, I'm not going to stand in his way. That man deserves every bit of happiness he can get."

The way Brielle said that, it sounded like she thought Sarah made Dax happy. A warm sensation replaced the trepidation she felt inside. Maybe all her worry was for nothing. She offered a shy smile at Brielle. "Do you really think I make him happy?"

She shrugged, then got to her feet. "All I know is that he hasn't dated anyone seriously since we had our fling. He tends to keep to himself—likes his privacy. So if he's willing to open his heart to you, don't take it for granted.

18

———

Dax

Dax stood and walked to the front of the room. Only half-a-dozen people showed up to this meeting. It wasn't the usual one he attended, but he had needed it. He shouldn't even be nervous, but he was. His date with Sarah meant far more to him than he'd let himself believe.

There was something intangible that made him realize just how much he wanted this to work out. Yes, she was pretty. But it was more than just her looks. It was everything she offered—the complete package.

He cleared his throat. "I'm Dax, and I'm an alcoholic."

"Hi, Dax," the chorus of voices welcomed back.

Dax rubbed the back of his neck. "It's been five years since my last drink, and I find myself wanting just a sip to take the edge off." He continued explaining how Sarah made him feel. Each time he met the expectant gazes of those in the group, he grew a little calmer. "I don't want to mess this up. For the first time in my life, I know what I want, and I'm terrified that I'll sabotage it. But I know if I take that one drink, I will head down a road I don't want." He forced a smile. "I'm keeping a lot about myself from her, and that might be making matters worse. I'm worried that if she sees this side of me, it will scare her off."

All of his worries tumbled from his lips, worries that he couldn't tell her or Brielle or anyone really. But just getting them off his chest made things a little easier to bear.

Dax took a deep breath and let it out through pursed lips. His smile morphed into one that was more genuine. "I'm taking her out on a date tonight. If everything goes well, I'll be able to take more steps to share this part of my life with her." He ended his turn and returned to his chair.

The pastor patted him on the shoulder and gave him an encouraging smile. Dax nodded to him and turned his focus on the next speaker. He could do this. He was a different man than he'd been when he was younger. And he'd continue to be that guy—the one who deserved to have someone like Sarah.

Silence.

Awkward, nerve-wracking, and irritating silence filled the truck. He could taste it, breathe it in and all he wanted to do was get some fresh air.

Up until Dax asked Sarah out, their interactions had been more carefree. Sure, there were moments when he'd have to teach her something new and she grew frustrated. But once the lesson was over or she'd grasped the concept, everything settled.

But now, in his truck as they headed toward the country club, he was second-guessing everything. The only way he could describe it was that there was this pressure to be something—do something that would guarantee he wouldn't mess anything up.

He knew better. Nothing was ever perfect. So why couldn't he shake that feeling?

Dax glanced at her for what seemed like the hundredth time, and his eyes met hers.

She let out a soft laugh. "So why is this country club so special? Is it like the nightclubs in Colorado Springs?"

He shook his head. "There's dancing and food, but it's not seedy like the places you might have seen in the city. The guy who owns it is a pretty good guy."

"Do you know him?"

Again, Dax shook his head. "Shane has some local fame. We all thought when he opened this place, he'd turn it into some hoity-toity golf club for the elite. But it turns out he has different plans."

"Oh?"

"Sean got hired to help train a bunch of horses for therapeutic services there."

Her features scrunched up, and she shifted in her seat so she faced him a little better. "How do horses and therapeutic services go together?"

"You know how people might have service dogs?"

She nodded.

"It's kinda like that. Turns out horses can be therapeutic. He wants to help people with learning disabilities or military vets with PTSD. I'm sure he'll provide other services, but from what Brielle has mentioned, those are the top of his list."

"Brielle, huh?" Her voice grew more distant and she looked away, lost in thought.

"What?" he chuckled.

Her eyes shot to his and her face flushed pink. "Well, you two were involved. Was she involved with him too?"

He stiffened. Why was Sarah bringing up his old relationships? Had Brielle said something to her? Obviously, she had.

Otherwise, Sarah wouldn't have said anything. "I don't think so. I believe she only met him once."

"Oh?"

"Yeah. I think Adeline introduced them, thinking they might hit it off." He chuckled. "Boy, she was wrong on that front. I don't even think they clicked on a friendly level. But I could be remembering wrong." He gave her a sideways glance. "Does it bother you that she and I dated a while back?"

The way her blush spread across her face was a clear indication it had been on her mind.

"Don't even worry about it. She and I never really clicked that way. We were too close as friends to ever make a relationship work. Besides, she doesn't want to settle down any time soon. I believe her exact words were that she'd rather have fun. But that's going to create a lot of problems moving forward."

Confusion filled her countenance. "What kind of problems?"

"I'm sure you've heard of Zeke's rule when it comes to his daughters getting married?"

Her face remained a blank mask.

"Oh, I would have thought Brielle would have mentioned it." He rubbed his jaw, turning his focus to the road as they came up to the turnoff. If Brielle hadn't talked to Sarah about the rules her father had for her, he wasn't so sure he should be the one to tell her. Then again, it wasn't like the whole ranch didn't know. Probably the whole town was aware.

Dax peeked at Sarah out of the corner of his eye. "Zeke's wife passed away when Adeline was a teenager. He had to raise all the girls on his own, so it's understandable that he got a little... strict."

"I suppose."

"Well, he won't let his younger daughters get married or even date until the older ones are taken care of. Adeline was the oldest, and she married Sean. Brielle is next."

Sarah snorted.

A smile tugged at his lips. "So you see the dilemma here. Brielle doesn't want to get married, but if she doesn't settle down, her younger sisters might end up old maids."

Sarah's grin fell. "Zeke can't possibly hold them to that, could he?"

Dax shrugged. "I've seen him be more stubborn on issues that matter far less. That man is ten times more stubborn than any of his daughters. I wouldn't bet against him at all."

She settled back in her seat and let out a low whistle. "Wow."

"Yep. I think it's his way of compartmentalizing everything and keeping them safe. If he only has to watch out for one daughter in the dating pool, then he can rest assured the others aren't going to be taken advantage of."

"And I thought my parents were tough. But to be fair, they were probably trying to control their legacy. All of their rules had less to do with keeping me safe and more to do with their own selfish desires."

Her words didn't make a lick of sense. "What kind of legacy are you talking about?"

Sarah's eyes widened and she stiffened, her face looking visibly paler as if she were sick to her stomach. "Would it be okay if we didn't talk about my family tonight?"

His brows creased and his cheek twitched. There it was again, the feeling that she was holding back on more than what she ought to—especially seeing as they were on a date. Dax bit down on his cheek hard, wincing as a sharp pain ran through it. He wasn't going to mess this up because he had mild paranoia. Sarah had proven that she could be trusted in other ways. She deserved her privacy.

Dax nodded and turned the steering wheel to pull into a parking space in front of the country club. It was dusk and people were coming and going, chatting happily with one another.

If tonight was to be a success, he had to settle a few things—get some things off his chest. He pulled the key from the ignition and faced her. "I want to make something perfectly clear."

"Okay?"

He chuckled at her hesitancy. "It's nothing bad. I just wanted to say that while we're out tonight, I don't want you to view me as your superior. I want this to be fun. Let go. Be yourself. I want to get to know the real Sarah."

She stilled, every part of her once again stiff. Then again, maybe he imagined it. While she didn't appear to be at ease, that could be due to any number of reasons. Once again he admonished himself. Sarah needed space and a reason to trust him. She needed to know that he wasn't going to push her to do or say anything she wasn't comfortable with.

He offered her a reassuring smile. "Does that sound good?"

"Sure," she hedged. "But there are still parts of my life I'm not ready to discuss." Her eyes darted away from him and she let out a shaky breath. "I don't want that to upset you."

Dax didn't know why, but he reached for her hand. He laced his fingers between hers, igniting several sensations at once, causing him to stare where they were connected instead of continuing with his train of thought. It felt like it took almost a full minute before his head was clear enough that he remembered where he was going with this conversation.

He squeezed her hand. "This is a first date. I don't have any expectations."

Well, that was a lie, but she didn't have to know that. He fully expected to find out by the end of the night whether she was someone he wanted to share more of his life with. It seemed strange, and a little rushed, but that's how he'd always been. He was pretty good at figuring that sort of thing out from the beginning. And based on what he knew about her so far, all he had to learn was whether or not they were compatible.

Dax was relieved to find her smiling at him and not pulling away. His heart beat just a little faster, then returned to its normal pace. "Okay. Let's get going." He climbed out of the truck, letting the cool evening air bathe his face and calm his heart.

He opened her door and held out his hand, pleased and excited when she accepted and again didn't pull away from him. It appeared that Sarah was just as invested in tonight going well as he was.

They headed toward the front entrance and up the stairs. Sarah stuck close to his side, and he tightened his hand on hers. Whatever she was nervous about, he would be there to shield her from it. Already he had this connection with her when it came to her safety and wanting to be the person that took care of her.

It wasn't too far of a stretch to believe that after tonight, things would be very, very different. The country club was far more congested with people than he thought it would be. A lot of the people on the dance floor weren't local. He could pick out anyone in a crowd if he'd seen them around town, and at least sixty percent of the people they passed were new faces. Was Copper Creek really growing that much? Or had the city kids found out about this place and come to make it their own?

Dax frowned at that thought. He'd come out to Copper Creek to get away from the drama that was the city. There were too many people who were bad influences on others. Out here, people were generally good, kindhearted, and hardworking folk.

"Dax?"

He jumped and stared down at Sarah.

"You're holding my hand a little too tight."

Shoot. He released her hand and muttered an apology.

Right away, Sarah reached for his hand again. "You don't have to be sorry. I just wanted to make sure you were all right."

Her kind words were one more reason he knew that she was worth the effort. The Sarah before him was someone who deserved a second chance to show the world that her mistakes were simply that. Mistakes.

He brought her hand up to his lips and brushed a light kiss across her knuckles, relishing in the way she sucked in a soft, sharp breath. Her eyes and her complexion brightened along with her smile. "What was that for?"

Dax lifted a shoulder. "I'm just impressed by you."

Sarah glanced away. "You don't have to say stuff like that."

"I know."

That prompted another smile to cross her face.

He jerked his head toward the dance floor. "Do you want to dance with me?"

"I'd love to."

19

———

Sarah

This whole experience tonight was surreal. It couldn't be happening. She wasn't supposed to serve her sentence here in some tiny town and end up finding a guy. Something was off. She'd get comfortable, and then the rug would get ripped out from under her.

But the logical part of her brain that knew all of that to be the truth was being overruled by her heart. She wanted to believe that maybe karma had decided she'd had enough. She'd slung horse manure, worked until her palms were blistered and cracked, and those dang chickens.

Yes, those murderous chickens who seemed to hate only her should have made it possible to shorten her community service alone.

As much as she had wanted to leave this place and go back home to start fresh, lately she found she wanted to stay more than she wanted to go. Copper Creek and the cowboys at Slate

Rock Ranch had shown her that there was more beyond college parties and fitting in with a popular crowd.

She'd learned to work hard, befriend people who were more down-to-earth, and all because she'd made mistakes first.

It didn't seem fair that she was finally settling in after all the trouble she'd caused.

Her thoughts shifted to Kenneth and a chill crawled up her spine. No, everything hadn't been wrapped up in a pretty little bow. He was still out there somewhere, and there was a very real possibility that he could come looking for her. He'd served at least a few months in jail, and he was bound to be upset with her for outing him.

She forced her breathing to remain steady. Dax would be able to sense her discomfort if she wasn't careful. Besides, Kenneth had no reason to come looking for her *here*. The country club would be the last place she would think to look if she was searching for someone who had gotten in trouble with the law.

Sarah shook off the strange feeling that she shouldn't let her guard down. She shouldn't let these thoughts ruin her night with Dax, but she most certainly should remain alert.

Finding Dax's gaze on her, she basked in the way he could set her insides aflame with just one look. His hand was around her waist, holding her near. His other hand held hers as they danced like he was about to sweep her across the floor. He may not be a prince and she wasn't a princess, but tonight she might indulge just a little and pretend.

"I'm surprised you wanted to take me out." It was the first sentence that had popped into her head, and she immediately regretted it. She sounded like an utter fool.

He chuckled. "Well, maybe I'm surprised you accepted."

"Why?"

Dax spun her around and put her into a dip, leaning over her with a boyish grin. "Because we got off to quite a rocky start."

She bit back the impulse to giggle. "I suppose you're right."

"I'm glad things changed."

"Me too." She let him continue leading her through some basic dance steps, nothing like the two-step sway that most people did when they slow danced at weddings or concerts. "Who knew a cowboy could dance so well?"

His beaming smile turned everything inside out. "There's a lot about me that you don't know." The moment those words left his mouth, his smile faltered. "I guess there's a lot about you that I don't know as well."

Guilt.

Hot and uncomfortable roiled within, dousing the happy, giddy flame that had once danced in its place. "Yeah, I suppose so."

"Do you think we'll get to a point where that's something we don't mind sharing?"

"I hope so." But probably not. She cringed to think of what Dax might do when he found out just what she was involved in. She also had no idea what he might do if he realized who her family was. It was best to keep that sort of thing private. Yes, she felt there were parts of his life that he purposefully hid from her, but she wasn't in any place to even ask about them.

"Okay, tell me more about you—things like your interests and hobbies. Friends or siblings."

"I can do that." Sarah tilted her head and grinned at him. "Even though I never wanted for anything, my favorite food is something that my family can't stand."

"What is that?"

She made a face. "I love Spam. And it isn't even a little bit. In college, I would buy and eat it at least once a day. My specialty is Spam tacos."

This time he grimaced. "Okay, I can get Spam with potatoes. But *tacos*?" He chuckled. "That was definitely an unexpected confession."

Sarah laughed. "Don't knock it 'til you try it." She let her thoughts wander some more. "I told you I took a lot of finance classes in college."

"Right, and you don't know if you want to go into that."

"Correct. I think I've figured out what I would do if I didn't go back to that."

He gazed at her expectantly.

"I think I'd try doing what you do. Training yearlings."

Dax's feet slowed, though the music continued to play. "Really?"

She nodded, but then her gaze swept around them. "I think we should keep dancing though."

He jumped. "Right." Once they'd found their rhythm again, he studied her. "Why would you want to train horses?"

"Well, it's a little bit of two things, really. I want to train yearlings, but I'd also want to volunteer at a place like that therapy thing you were talking about. Remember when I told you about the time I fell from that horse? Well, I would want to help kids gain their confidence with horses, too."

"Training yearlings is a little different than training the horses to work with people. We set up the foundation—"

"I know. We train the horses to listen to their future trainers. But I think working with both the yearlings and then with the people who need help would give me a more rounded experience, don't you?"

"I guess so."

She beamed at him. "I never thought I'd even enjoy being here, but I'm beginning to forget what it was like back home. I feel like if I left, a piece of me would stay behind."

"I can understand that," he said quietly. "This place seems to have figured out how to crawl into your heart and make you realize you can't live without it."

"Yeah. And I can respect that." The music stopped and a song with a faster beat started up. The bass grew louder, making it more difficult for her to hear his response.

Dax nodded his head toward the back doors. "Do you want to get some fresh air?" He didn't exactly wait for a response. Instead, he grasped onto her hand and tugged her off the dance floor.

They found themselves outside on a wrap-around style porch that oversaw the biggest property she could imagine. Slate Rock Ranch was large, but a lot of it was contained in the woods where they couldn't develop it. The scene before her reminded her of the scene in that animated movie where the lions discussed their kingdom.

The sun had already set, but the sky still reflected enough sunlight to show just how far Shane's property extended. There were several barns already constructed along with pastures that were fenced in.

Sarah's eyes narrowed, squinting as she made out the trails that snaked through and around different grassy areas. It wasn't completely developed, but she could tell that Shane had a vision for this place. It was more than impressive; it was extraordinary.

She let out a sigh. "Wow."

Dax huffed, turning and leaning against the rail. "It's not all that great. Don't get me wrong, the guy is practically a saint for wanting to create this place for those who need it. But he's not doing the hard work."

Sarah snorted. "Do I hear a hint of jealousy?"

He shook his head. "Hardly. That guy has money. That's all. He brought his money here, made the place his own and he's making a difference, but do you think he ever had it rough?"

And just like that, Sarah knew she'd made the right decision.

Dax had a prejudice against Shane solely because he had money. If he didn't like the guy when the guy was a "saint," what would he think of *her*? Especially when he found out that not only did she have money, but she was also a miscreant who harmed others with no sense of consequences.

All these thoughts churned in her mind. Her family's money had never done anyone any good. They'd kept it for themselves and their own selfish reasons.

She swallowed thickly and stared out at the property even as it got so dark that she couldn't see it. "What would you do if you had money?"

He let out a bark of laughter. "What?"

Her tone was serious, drawing his focus even more. "If you were in Shane's position and you had money. What would you do with it?"

His brows pulled together, low over his eyes. "No one has ever asked me that before."

"Well, I'm asking you now. What would you do with, say, a million bucks?"

This time his laugh was more sarcastic. "What kind of question is that? I would never see that kind of money in my entire life."

"It's just a getting to know you question."

"Okay, I'll play." Dax turned around, resting his elbows on the railing and staring out at the black fields in front of them. "If I had a million dollars, I'd buy a ranch."

"You'd buy a ranch."

"Yeah. But you know what I'd do with it? Instead of making it a dude ranch, I'd turn it into a halfway house for juveniles."

Her head whipped around, and she stared at him.

"I would teach kids real life skills and the value of working hard, just like Eve did for me." His face contorted into a grimace. "Kids who need a second chance at life and who might end up on the wrong side of the tracks because the system failed them. Those kinds of kids."

"Dax?" she whispered, reaching to cover his forearm with her hand. "Were you one of those kids?"

He stared down at where she touched him but didn't pull away. "Yeah," he croaked. "I was a kid who got into trouble despite all the love and support that Eve gave me. I made every mistake in the book. I hurt people, I stole, I got high. I was a regular drain on society."

"What changed?"

Dax shifted his focus once more to the field. His jaw was hard and his cheek twitched every few seconds. "Eve got sick. After everything she did for everyone else, she didn't even get to live a full life." His voice broke and he swung his attention back to Sarah. "Now, do you think that guy in there had to experience anything like that even once in his life?"

Slowly, she shook her head though she had absolutely no clue. Granted, people with money usually had a different set of problems, but they were less likely to turn out like she had.

"Exactly. If Shane wants to be philanthropic with his money and help the public, he can do so. But having money and using it in the right way is not nearly as hard as experiencing something like what I went through as a kid. I *know* what it's like to be on the outside looking in. And I bet you anything I could do more with a million dollars than that guy ever could."

Sarah reached for his hand. "I'm sure you could."

He let out a dry chuckle. "You know what I kept telling myself the whole time on the ride over here?"

She remained quiet.

"I told myself not to mess this up. We needed to have some fun so we could loosen up around each other. And now I'm standing here telling you how I'm better than Shane Owens. I don't really paint myself in a very good light, do I?"

Sarah traced her finger over the back of his hand. How could she express to him that she related to what he'd said more than he could imagine? What would he say if he knew she actually agreed with his opinion on how having money doesn't make a person genuinely good? Sometimes people have to walk through the fire to overcome their weaknesses on the other side.

But admitting any of that was dangerous for several reasons.

Instead, she offered him a smile. "I think you are a man who has the biggest heart out of everyone I've ever met. The fact that you had to go through such hardships only made you stronger. And I know that if you were to get that money, you'd succeed."

Dax faced her and placed his hand against her cheek. "How did you get to be so amazing?"

She dipped her head, avoiding his searching gaze. He hooked his finger under her chin and lifted it, forcing her to meet his eyes. As much as he appeared to be enthralled with her, she was ten times that with him. Dax had proven himself a force to be reckoned with. He had a heart of pure gold and he hadn't let the world crush him. She could only hope to end up as sweet as he was.

Dax studied her, the silence between them growing with each passing second. Even the cicadas that were native to the area seemed to stop their chirping. The earth grew still as Dax moved closer toward her, his focus dipping to her mouth only once.

This was it. The kiss she'd wanted him to steal a few days earlier.

Her heart leaped into her throat, racing, soaring, ready to finally experience what it was like to be held by this amazing man. Sarah's legs trembled, losing the will to keep her upright. If it weren't for her grasp on the rail at her side, she might have sagged to the floor.

"Sarah," he murmured, "I want to kiss you."

"Okay," she whispered, and her heart sang along with that one uttered word. Motion out of the corner of her eye caught her attention, and for a split second, she glanced in that direction. Someone stood in the shadows at the far end of the porch. Someone whose form she recognized.

The hairs on the back of her neck stuck straight up and she gasped, stumbling back a few paces on wobbly legs.

Confusion filled Dax's eyes and he took one step toward her.

Sarah gripped the rail even tighter and peered once more in the direction where she could have sworn they were being watched by someone. Her heart hammered but for a completely different reason than the near kiss she'd almost been given.

It couldn't be.

Not now.

Not *Kenneth*.

"What is it?" Alarm laced Dax's words and he glanced over his shoulder in the direction she focused on.

There was nothing there. A figment of her imagination, maybe? Someone peeping on what was supposed to be their first kiss? Either way, the shadows were empty now. She met Dax's worried stare. "It's nothing, really. Can we please go back inside?"

He nodded, though he didn't look at all convinced. She forced a smile, jittery and on edge. Disappointment was a present emotion as well. Another potential romantic moment had slipped away.

20

___

Dax

It didn't matter what Sarah said; Dax knew deep in his gut that something was off. There had been terror in her gaze he'd never seen before—not even when she'd nearly been trampled. Sarah was scared, but of what he had no idea.

The only way to find out would be to get her to say it, but how was he supposed to convince her to talk when she clearly wanted nothing more but to forget what she'd seen.

Dax glanced back toward the shadows. Five steps away. He could cross that distance in fewer strides. Had she seen someone there? He should just drop it, but there was this feeling he couldn't shake. He needed to know.

Sarah strode through the doors to the dance floor, and his steps slowed. One more glance in her direction and he shot toward the corner of the building.

At the far side of the wrap-around porch, someone darted around the other corner. The figure was tall and slim, but that was all Dax could make out. Male or female, he wouldn't be able to pick them out in a lineup.

A tightness constricted his chest. He could cross that distance in a matter of seconds even with the peeping Tom's head start. Whoever it was had startled Sarah, and she deserved an apology. He moved forward, but Sarah's voice stopped him.

"Dax? What are you doing?" Timid and unsure, Sarah hovered in the doorway.

He glanced once more where the figure had disappeared. He wasn't here to chase down miscreants. He was here to be with Sarah, and their romantic moment had already been lost. He took in a steadying breath, willing his heart rate to settle. The blood pulsing through his veins had been prepared, his fight or flight response triggered.

Sarah's nervous gaze grounded him, and he flashed her a smile. "Would you like to dance again?"

She shook her head. "Actually, can we go home?"

Dax reached for her hand and brought it to his lips. "Whatever you want."

Just like the previous times when she'd been in trouble, he knew he needed to be there for her now. He wanted to wrap her up in his arms and shield her from whatever it was that made her hands shake and her jaw tremble.

An upbeat country song played inside, and all the dancers were moving with more energy. Sarah pressed up against him, clinging to him as if her life depended on it. She was definitely not fine.

By the time they made it into the parking lot, his hand ached from her holding it so tight. Her eyes darted back and forth, shifting with each sound they heard. He picked up his pace and walked her straight to his truck to get settled, then he got in behind the wheel.

Dax faced her, waiting for her to focus on him. She stared straight ahead, her whole body tense. "Sarah."

She jumped. "What?"

"You're not fine."

"I don't see why that would matter to you."

Her words struck him harder than he'd expected. A backhanded retort was on the tip of his tongue, but he knew that wouldn't do him any good. Instead, he took another deep breath. "What did you see back there?"

"It doesn't matter."

"Clearly, it does."

She blew out a frustrated breath. "I'm seeing things. That's all."

Except she wasn't. He'd seen the figure escaping plain as day. Whatever reason she had for lying to him wouldn't do her any good. "I can help."

Sarah shook her head. "No, you can't. This is my problem, and I'm going to deal with it the way I feel is best."

His jaw clenched. Why did she have to be so dang stubborn? Hadn't he proven that he could be there for her when she needed him to? Why was she holding back?

Hypocrite.

He was holding back, too. Why hadn't he told her about his issues with alcohol, drugs, and his criminal past? He'd merely hinted at the topic. Because he thought it would make him a lesser man, that's why. A girl like Sarah deserved better. It didn't matter that she had her own mistakes to work through; they probably weren't as bad as the havoc he'd wreaked in his younger years.

Dax faced forward, placing his hands on the steering wheel. As much as he wanted to get it all out in the open, he wasn't ready. And if he couldn't bring himself to show her his skeletons, then he couldn't demand she show him hers.

He forced his key into the ignition and started the engine. The oxygen had been sucked right out of the cab and his mood had been completely altered. Who was he kidding? He wasn't strong enough to date a girl like her, and she wouldn't want anything to do with him. He'd always be the guy that girls were embarrassed about or ashamed to bring home.

They drove all the way back in utter silence; neither one of them had bothered to turn on a radio station. He scowled at the road, hating himself for his cowardice. The truck pulled up to the main house and Sarah launched from the truck before he had a chance to open the door for her. He climbed out and slowly walked around the front of his vehicle, then leaned against the headlight, his arms folded.

Her steps slowed as she made it to the porch and up two steps. Sarah was bathed in the golden glow of his truck's lights. He could see just how broken she had become since they'd nearly kissed, and his heart ached from being locked up. As much as he wanted to march over to her and pull her into his arms, he couldn't. That's not what she needed, and it was probably the furthest thing from her mind.

Sarah's fingers tapped on the wooden railing, and she turned around to face him. "Dax?"

He straightened. "Yeah?"

"Thank you."

"For what?"

She didn't meet his gaze, didn't move from her spot. "For being there—for me." Her voice could barely be heard over the engine from behind him. "I'm having a hard time sharing a lot about myself. But I want you to know something." Her eyes lifted, and he pushed away from the truck to move closer to her, making it easier for her to find his gaze. "I wanted you to know that I really like you."

The tightness in his chest moved through his whole body, from the way his toes curled to his throat closing up.

Sarah blushed. "Out of everyone I know, you are the one I feel closest to."

He took a few more steps toward her. "You know you can tell me anything, right?"

She offered him a small smile. "We say stuff like that, but we don't mean it. This is the real world, Dax. Sometimes there are things about us that we have to keep to ourselves for whatever reason. I don't ever want you to stop looking at me the way you did tonight."

Her words reflected his concerns almost perfectly and hearing them come from her lips made the ache in his heart even worse. He swallowed the lump in his throat. It burned, begging for some alcoholic elixir that would ease the sharp jagged reality they found themselves in. "Maybe one day that could change."

"I hope so," she breathed. "Do you think you could look past those secrets I want to keep hidden and still want to see where things might go between us?" Her voice hitched and a tear slipped down her cheek.

He closed the distance between them and took her hand in his. "Of course I do." He reached up and brushed the tear on her cheek. "You might be surprised how much I can relate to what you're going through. Our past may be something that molds us, but those experiences are just that. You are not your mistakes." The irony of how hard it was to listen to his own advice was not lost on him.

Dax climbed up one stair so that their gazes were level. She was hurting and wouldn't let him in. He'd have to accept that she wanted to handle this on her own because he had no right to demand that she change when he wouldn't do so.

He placed his hand gently on her cheek. "As far as I'm

concerned, today can be day one." It would be difficult to rein in his curiosity, but if it meant being with Sarah, he could do it. He had to. "I've said it before, and I'll say it again. You don't have to tell me anything if it makes you uncomfortable. Let's just make it easy."

Sarah's soft smile crashed into him, washing away the tension and the worries that had so easily suffocated him moments ago. "I like easy." She glanced over her shoulder toward the house. "I'm not really tired. Would you like to go for a walk or something?"

"That sounds pretty good right about now." Dax tugged her from the steps, toward him. They wandered along some of the paths closest to the house rather than following the trails they used when riding.

Sarah seemed to grow more comfortable as she leaned into him. "Where did you learn to dance?"

A slow smile spread across his face. "I figured you'd ask me something like that." He peeked down at her. "Eve was really a hopeless romantic at heart. She taught all of the kids who came through her care how to dance and treat each other when we were out on dates. They were her own little etiquette courses."

"Tell me more about her."

That was an easy topic. Eve was the closest thing he'd had to a mother. She was the most important person in his life growing up, and every choice he made, he did so with her in mind. Dax found himself relaying stories of his childhood more readily than he'd expected. By the time they'd completed their rounds and had returned to the house, he'd probably given her enough stories that she knew more about Eve than she did Zeke.

"The best part about Eve was how she knew exactly what we needed even when we didn't realize it ourselves." Dax led Sarah to the porch swing, letting her settle on it while he leaned against a column on the porch. He rested his shoulder against the pole. "Remember when I said I wasn't an easy kid? Well, she was literally an angel."

Sarah gave him an empathetic smile. "You must really miss her."

"I really do. I wish I would have come home sooner. Or realized she was struggling and had been there to help."

Sarah swung back and forth, her toes grazing the wood porch. "What do you mean?"

"She worked too hard caring for others, and no one was there caring for her." He still blamed himself for not being able to prevent what happened, but he wasn't about to get into that.

"If it was a heart attack, then there was nothing you would have been able to do."

"There are always signs." He shook his head. "It doesn't matter. I can't change it now. All I can do is live like she would want me to."

Sarah stopped her swinging. "I don't think there's any way that she wouldn't be proud of the man you've become."

His smile was wistful at best. "Thanks."

She rose from her seat and closed the distance between them. "I mean it, Dax. I'm not just being nice. You've made a name for yourself here. Zeke trusts you with so much. And look at how good you are with the horses. If Eve were here, she would most certainly be proud of the man you have become." Sarah poked him in the chest right over his heart. "What matters now is that you forgive yourself and accept that you've changed."

Dax's hand wrapped around her finger, holding it steady.

She stilled and looked up at him, lifting her chin to meet his steady gaze. Her warm brown eyes were like two pools of hazelnut he wanted to dive into. They were the kind of eyes he wanted to tell everything to. And one day he might.

At some point his body had decided it had waited enough. Dax's breathing grew sharp and uneven. His heart beat at an irregular pace as he dipped his focus to her lips. Those luscious, pink lips were just begging for him to taste them.

Dax tugged on her finger, pulling her a step closer to him. "I don't know if you feel what I'm feeling," he rasped, "but I need you to know that I can't get you out of my head, and I don't want to." He gave her a wry chuckle. "You are adoringly stubborn and exasperatingly exactly what I want in my life."

She snickered. "And you have a way with words. Do I have Eve to thank for that as well?"

"Probably."

Her lashes fluttered and her focus darted to the ground. "And if she knew that I had found someone who makes me feel this way, she wouldn't want me to squander the opportunity."

She looked up to meet his gaze. "The opportunity for what?" she whispered.

"For this."

Dax lowered his face, his eyes closing as he lightly brushed his lips against Sarah's. They tasted faintly of strawberry, and they were as warm as freshly baked bread. He released her finger and moved his hand to her waist, pulling her in for an embrace that sent fireworks rocketing through his entire being.

Each second that ticked by was another moment he locked away in his mind. Sarah was warm, inviting, and everything he could ever want. What had taken him so long to finally let down his walls?

Oh yeah.

All of those secrets.

21

———

Sarah

Stars and glitter exploded behind Sarah's eyes.

I mean, of course she'd been kissed before. Her first kiss was when she was ten and little Michael from school had insisted they needed to at least try what all the big kids liked so much.

At the time, she'd absolutely hated it. Michael tasted like peanut butter sandwiches. She hated peanut butter.

But even after that failed attempt at testing the waters, Sarah had let several other boys kiss her throughout high school and even college. Kenneth was one of them.

She shut out that memory the second it appeared. Kenneth was in the rear view. Right now, she was with Dax. All she wanted to think about was the way it felt to have his strong arms around her, the way her stomach did a complete gymnastics routine as they deepened their kiss, and her reasons for not wanting this moment to ever end.

Dax broke off their kiss first. She let out a soft moan, her eyes not willing to admit that their little slice of heaven had ended.

He was an excellent kisser, but then that opinion could be due to her developing feelings for him. Sarah's eyes fluttered open and locked on his bright blue ones. Another loopty-loop took place where her stomach had been.

Sarah took a deep, shivery breath, and an embarrassed smile touched her lips. She tucked a strand of hair behind her ear and looked away. Funny how even after they'd shared such an intimate moment, she found it hard to meet his gaze.

Did this mean he wanted an exclusive relationship?

Great. One kiss and immediately she was thinking about the future. Wasn't that one of the reasons she'd gotten in trouble with Kenneth in the first place? She'd wanted to impress him, and one thing led to another.

Once again, she berated herself. She needed to stop dwelling on the past. Dax might just be someone who could be part of her future—if only she could get past her insecurities.

Sarah worried her lower lip, allowing Dax to take both of her hands within his own. "I hate to be the person who brings this up—but where do we go from here? I'm going to be leaving in—"

He shook his head, successfully cutting her off. "Let's approach that when the time comes. Maybe you decide that you want to stay when all is said and done."

Right now, that idea made her heart soar. But wishful thinking didn't make something possible. She couldn't stay here past summertime or her parents would have a cow. Their plans for her future didn't give her the opportunity to turn into some cowgirl—or date a cowboy for that matter.

This was not the time to bring that up. In fact, there might never be a good time for that sort of conversation. How would Dax react when he found out she was just some spoiled rich girl?

He had morals.

He'd grown up with barely anything to his name.

They couldn't be more different if they had been born on opposite sides of the world. They literally were raised on opposite sides of the track—a regular Romeo and Juliet. The only difference was that they didn't currently have their families fighting to keep them apart.

She *should* be grateful. But as she gazed into his eyes, all she wanted was for the slate of her past to be wiped clean. Dax hadn't specified any of the things he'd done criminally. In her eyes he'd been through a lot. He was an orphan and in the system.

What excuse did she have?

Nothing.

"Hey," Dax's soft voice stopped her from spiraling further.

She jumped and met his eyes once more.

"What do you want this to be?"

Sarah let out a strangled laugh. "You can't ask me that."

"Why not?" The corners of his mouth lifted into a grin that had her heart racing once more. "Whatever this is or will be has to be a partnership."

If she wasn't already warm and fuzzy, his words only added to what she currently experienced. "I want..." She took a deep breath and let it out. "I think I do want to stay."

"So stay."

She shook her head. "It isn't that easy. I can't just leave my family and—"

"The family that doesn't treat you with respect? The family you have yet to tell me more about? It doesn't seem like you want to be with your family at all."

With each sentence he spoke, she continued to feel more and more backed into a corner. She couldn't exactly tell him now, after being with him for a month and a half, that she came from money—especially now that she knew the extent of his upbringing. Not to mention his strong feelings on the matter.

But the more she squirmed under his scrutiny, she knew that this wasn't something she could keep hidden. Eventually, she'd have to decide to stay or go back home.

Sarah swallowed hard, but the lump in her throat remained stubbornly lodged right where it was. She guessed it was now or never. "I have to go home because of *who* my family is, not how they treat me."

"You're not making any sense."

"My parents own one of the biggest finance firms in the state. They are probably the most wealthy power couple within a hundred-mile radius."

"Okay, I'm still not following." Dax shook his head. "So your family is rich. Were you worried that your family's wealth would bother me?"

"A little," she admitted. "Okay, a lot. But it's more than that." Like the fact that her parents were unaware of the reasons she was at the ranch or that they didn't even know she'd gone to the ranch in the first place. As far as they were concerned, she was still on campus. If they found out about her indiscretions, they'd take away what freedom they'd given her. "My parents have certain—expectations. I'm supposed to follow in their footsteps. After my brother died, I think it triggered something in them. They expect me to be... I don't know... just like *them*. If I told my folks that I wanted to stay here and train horses, they'd disown me."

There, she'd said it out loud, making it even more real. That was the biggest problem with keeping this whole thing a secret. Yes, she didn't want the town—or Dax—to know that she was the reason for the sheriff getting shot. But she also couldn't risk her parents finding out what she'd been up to.

If they cut her off, she wouldn't know what to do with herself.

She had never worried about money or where her next meal would come from. She'd been pampered; she could admit it.

Maybe it was working here alongside Dax that had helped her realize that she might be able to do more with her life than be a little puppet. But right now, even that concept seemed unattainable.

"You don't really think they'd do that, do you?" Dax's soft voice ripped her from her thoughts.

"What?"

"Your parents. You don't honestly believe that they'd cut you off from them. They're your only family. You're their only daughter."

She lifted a shoulder. "I've seen them do a lot of things I didn't think they'd be capable of. But I'd like to think I know my parents a little better than the average person. Not to mention, my lawyer was able to hide this whole thing from them from the beginning. What do you think? Would a guy do that if he didn't think there was at least some risk involved?"

Dax's mouth dropped open. She could see it in his face. He was finally starting to realize that her family wasn't the norm. The realization was written all over his face. If she'd been raised by such people, then what prevented her from being just like them as she got older?

His hands still held hers, but the air had suddenly grown a little colder than she expected. She pulled her hands out of his and rubbed her arms up and down. "There, you wanted to know more about me, and I told you. My parents are crazy. I'm selfish. And even if I wanted to stay, I can't." Sarah turned and continued walking. She fought back the emotions that threatened to erupt.

She had come to several realizations today. She wanted to stay—to be with Dax and see if they might be able to work it out. But doing so risked her inheritance, her reputation, the reputation of her family, and even the relationship she had with her parents, however strained.

Dax jogged after her, his heavy hand landing on her shoulder, forcing her to stop and face him. "Why are you walking away?"

"Because I can *see* it, Dax. There's just too much baggage to make a relationship with me work. If we decided to stick it out this summer, what then? Would you move to the city to be with me?"

His brows pinched and he didn't say a thing.

She let out a sharp laugh. "*Exactly.* You couldn't move to the city any more than I could convince my parents that I should stay here. There is no life for me here. And I'm not interested in doing anything halfway. I don't want to open my heart to you only for things to end abruptly when I leave."

"Why not?"

Sarah blinked. "Did you just ask me that?"

Dax shrugged. "We don't know what the future holds. Summer ends in a few months, and then we can figure things out. The city isn't that far away. Maybe your parents wouldn't be upset with you relocating out here. We *don't* know."

She couldn't tell if it was awe or shock, but one of those two sensations had made her completely freeze up. Dax stood before her, the words coming from his mouth more logical than anything she'd ever considered. Somehow, she'd managed to make this huge deal out of what could possibly be nothing. Dax didn't care about how she was raised or that she had money. At least that's what he was saying. He wasn't buying into any absolutes either. She found herself drawn to his clear-headed thinking and a weight was lifted from her shoulders. Not even Brielle or Zeke knew about her parentage. The only one privy to that information had been the sheriff.

And now Dax.

He reached for her hands and held them firmly within his own. "Besides, what if the end of the summer arrives and you decide you can't stand to be with me anymore?" Dax chuckled, then lifted his thumb to trace the length of her jawline. His touch left a wake of tingles just beneath the surface of her skin. "I'm not saying that we'll end up together, and I'm not saying we'll break up. All I'm suggesting is that we give whatever this is a decent chance."

Her throat closed up, not allowing any words to tumble from her lips. Sarah nodded and threw her arms around his neck. No one, not her parents, not her past relationships, had ever been this supportive. Perhaps that was the main reason for her anxiety with oversharing. She'd held her cards so close to her chest for so long that when she finally found someone who was willing to accept her for who she was, she didn't know what to do with herself.

Dax's arms wrapped around her, pulling her close. He cupped the back of her head as she buried her face in his chest. Dax smelled like soap and mint with a hint of leather and dust. The more time she spent with him, the more secure she felt.

He'd been there for her multiple times, always showing how much he cared about her. She'd stupidly let her worries get in the way of something good. While she still couldn't fathom confessing to the mistakes of her past, she felt confident in moving forward with him. There was nothing she needed to learn about him that she wasn't willing to overlook.

She pulled away from him and they headed back to the house, each quietly locked within their own thoughts. Rather than the tension that had filled the air between them, there was an almost sense of peace. She felt lighter, happier.

Dax squeezed her hand as they arrived once more at the porch. He tugged on her until she stumbled against his chest.

Their eyes locked and her lungs refused to operate. Dax tucked a stray hair behind her ear, his fingers tracing along her jawline.

Heat tickled deep in her stomach, lighting along each of her nerves. Dax dipped closer to her, grazing her lips with his. The kiss was an echo of the one they'd just shared. Soft, sweet, and almost hesitant.

Sarah wrapped her arms around his neck and leaned into their kiss, letting it deepen with her desire. The heat that had started as a trickle burst into a flame that consumed her. Everything fell away, all the worries, all the anxiety, all of the unknowns—leaving behind just Dax. He wrapped her up securely in his arms, and with each kiss he bestowed on her, it was as if he was making another promise.

This was not a typical infatuation.

This was something better.

This... was worth the risk.

22

———

Dax

Dax couldn't remember a time in his life when he was happier. His whole life seemed to be leading up to finding someone like Sarah. She was everything he wanted in his future. It wasn't just the connection he felt either. It was the way she'd managed to impress him from the first moment he'd watched her in that chicken coop.

Sarah was the kind of woman who continued to strive to reach a greater potential. He stood outside the corral, watching her work with the yearling he'd assigned to her, and he couldn't deny the pride that continued to fill every free part of him.

Her brows were creased in the most adorable show of focus as she moved that stubborn horse into the steps that were required to earn the trust and respect between both parties.

Someone moved in beside him, leaning against the corral fence.

Brielle.

Dax's eyes cut to her for a moment before returning to Sarah. "She's actually pretty good at it, isn't she?"

He nodded.

"Wow." They stood there, and Sarah glanced at them for a moment before she continued working. Brielle turned, leaning her shoulder into the metal bars and smiling at him. She tilted her head in that teasing way she used to. "So... you two seem to be hitting it off really well."

Dax didn't bother meeting her gaze. "Yup."

"What are you going to do when she has to leave in a few weeks?"

His jaw hardened. He'd done so well up until now not thinking about the one thing that could hurt their relationship. Sarah still planned on leaving. And he had no intention of moving just yet. A small part of him secretly hoped he still had enough time to convince her to stay here. There had to be a reasonable compromise she could make with her parents.

But even if she couldn't, he would like to think that their relationship was more important than the money they'd cut her off from. It wasn't an easy life, but money wasn't everything. The thought that she might return home just for her inheritance made his stomach churn.

"Oh." Brielle's soft voice made it clear that she understood the fact that he didn't have any answers for her. "It'll work out. Things like this always do."

"Not always," he grumbled. Dax worked his jaw. "There's a lot going on with her family that might prevent things from going the way I'd like them to."

Even though he wasn't looking directly at her, he could tell she was surprised. Her body stiffened and she grew suspiciously quiet.

Dax heaved a sigh and faced her. "What?"

"She's talking about her family?"

He lifted a shoulder. "So?"

"I just thought it was odd. She hasn't told me anything about her family. Just why she's—" She shook her head. "Sarah must trust you a lot if she's sharing more with you." Brielle nibbled on her lower lip and glanced away, brushing some hair from her face. "What are you doing with the horses after you get them trained?"

It was odd the way she changed the subject so quickly, almost like she knew something that Dax wasn't privy to. He almost asked her to expound on what she had almost said, but he shook off the urge.

"Shane Owens, the guy who owns the country club—"

"I've heard of him."

"Right. Well, his equine therapy program is due to start here soon, and the horses that Sean is working with won't need as much training. I'm preparing a few more to start their program."

A soft smile touched Brielle's lips. "You've always been pretty good with that sort of thing. I have to admit the way you are with horses is one of the reasons I was drawn to you." She reached out and pushed his upper arm with her fingers. "It's too bad you're taken now."

He chuckled. "You have no interest in settling down."

"True. But you've been one of those constants in my life that I think I'll have a hard time letting go of." She pressed her lips together into a thin line and her eyes grew serious. "Do you think if I had been ready to settle down like Adeline, that we could—"

Dax held up a hand and shook his head. "Don't go there, Bri. You know as well as I do that going down the path of 'what if' will only get one or both of us hurt." There was a time when he'd thought about proposing just because they'd always been so close as friends before they'd experimented with their romantic feelings.

Those feelings were gone now, and he had no desire to dredge them up again.

"You're probably right." She heaved a sigh. "What am I going to do, Dax? Adeline is married and now it's my turn, and I'm…" Brielle shook her head and then rubbed her nose.

"You're not ready."

"No. I'm not. I have zero interest in the white picket fence and a house filled with little kids." She made a face.

"You don't have to get married. Just because you're second in line doesn't mean it's up to you to say 'I do.'"

Brielle rolled her eyes. "You know my dad better than most. What do *you* think would happen if, say, Constance decides she wants to get married? My dad is stuck in the stone age. There's no way he would let Constance go out and start dating someone when he only wants one of us out in the dating scene at a time."

"That didn't stop *you*. I seem to recall that you dated plenty of people under your father's nose, myself included, before Adeline got married to Sean."

She rolled her eyes. "What do *you* think? Is Connie the type to go against Dad's wishes?" Brielle made a good point. Constance was probably the most well-behaved of the lot. She wouldn't go and get into a mess like falling in love with a guy before it was her turn.

"What if you got married just to—"

"*What?*"

"Hear me out. Like a marriage for—"

"If you say convenience, I'll slap you right here and now." She gave him a pointed look. "I may not be ready to get married, but I won't do it just so my sisters can have their turn. When I marry, it will be because I love the guy more than I'm terrified of everything else. It will be because he will look at me like I'm the only thing worth caring about in the world. And it will be because I want to be with him forever."

He offered her a wry smile. "Who knew you were such a *romantic*?"

Brielle slugged him in the shoulder. "Don't you start." She turned, her focus on Sarah again. "I want what you guys seem to have found."

A pleasant warmth coursed through his body, and he turned his attention toward Sarah. It was funny that Brielle had noticed whatever it was he had found with Sarah, though he didn't know if he was strong enough to label it with that formidable "L" word.

His heart leaped into his throat. Was that what this was? He wanted to be with her for the long haul. He was willing to share things about his life with her that he kept private from others. And he knew if it came down to it, he'd risk his own life for hers.

Was that love?

His throat closed up as his eyes continued to follow Sarah. She moved closer to the horse, speaking softly to the animal. She rubbed the horse's nose and then patted her neck, giving the animal a preliminary rubdown. Sarah was so completely in her element with this yearling, he knew if she stayed, he'd have to figure out a way for her to get a horse of her own.

"I *knew* it."

Dax shot a look in Brielle's direction, surprised to find her staring at him with the smuggest expression he'd ever seen. "What?"

"You're in love."

He swung his focus toward Sarah. "Maybe I am."

"No *maybes*, buddy. You're in *love*." She let out a laugh. "You're in trouble, too, 'cuz if she moves—" Her features sobered. "Sorry. Do you think you would move with her?"

Dax shrugged. "I don't know. I guess we have to see if it comes to that." He ducked down and stepped through the corral fencing.

Brielle's hand shot out and touched him. "Dax?"

"Yeah."

"Word of advice? Make sure you tell her. Don't wait. The sooner she knows, the better. That way she can make plans too. There's nothing worse than being blindsided with information like that."

"We haven't been dating that long. I'm not going to give her an ultimatum. *That* would be a bad idea."

"No one said you had to give her an ultimatum. You just need to be very clear about what you want and how you feel. Don't hold anything back. That sort of thing can hurt you more than you realize."

"Thanks for the advice," he muttered.

"I mean it, Dax. No secrets."

Her final words gave him pause and he shot a surprised look in her direction. Did she know about his AA meetings and why he went? Did she know that he'd nearly killed someone with his stupid mistakes? He nodded, feeling a little sick to his stomach. If she knew, would she admit to it? Or even worse, would she tell Sarah?

Based on Sarah's past experience with losing someone in an accident where a drunk driver was at fault, he wasn't so sure he could tell her that part of his life.

Dax swallowed hard and headed toward Sarah, his hands deep in his pockets and tightly clenched. He'd already resigned himself not to tell her about the accident. Sure, one day he'd tell her about the meetings, but that would be the extent of his confessions.

Sarah grinned at him as he neared. "Did you see that? She's getting so *good*."

He patted the horse down her back, letting his hand trail along the animal's spine. "She has a good trainer."

She beamed, her cheeks filling with color at his compliment. "You're just saying that because you like me."

Dax folded his arms and rested them on the horse's back. He grinned at her, still fighting off the thoughts that swirled in his head over those secrets he'd kept from her so far. "Maybe it's more than that."

Her head popped up and she gazed at him with uncertainty.

Lowering his voice, Dax forced his focus on her to remain consistent. He didn't want her to have any doubt in her mind about how he felt. "Maybe it's love."

A lot of things could have happened in that moment. She could have said she loved him back. Or she might have told him that she appreciated the sentiment, but she wasn't ready to say it back. Instead, she laughed.

Sarah actually laughed at him. Her head tossed back, and she let out a sweet but heart-wrenching sound that brought him back to the days when he was a bumbling middle school kid with his first crush.

But then her eyes found his and turned solemn. "Oh, you're serious."

Dax wandered around the animal, closing the distance between himself and Sarah. "Of course I'm serious. Why wouldn't I be?"

She glanced away. He should probably be grateful that she didn't step back from him and turn to run for the hills.

Reaching for her hands, he held them tightly in his own. "I've been trying to come up with a way to explain how I feel about you. The only thing I've been able to come up with is that... I might be in love." She absolutely looked like one of those woodland creatures in the middle of the road on a cold night about to be hit by a moving truck.

An ache shot through him, starting in his gut and ricocheting through his body until it nestled into his heart. She didn't feel the same. At least not yet. At this point he wasn't about to draw attention to his realization. She might need time to process this.

So instead of making her respond, he released her hands and pulled her close for a hug. Dax rested his chin on her head and fought all the feelings of inadequacy and the returning trauma from when he'd had strong feelings for Brielle and the way that had turned out. Sarah wasn't Bri. She was her own unique person, and when she figured out what she wanted, she'd tell him. He just had to have faith.

He'd done what Brielle had recommended. He'd told Sarah how he felt about her, and that was what mattered. After a brief hug, Dax released Sarah and reached for the yearling's reins. "The day is about over. I'll finish up with this one. You can take the rest of the evening off."

Dax guided the horse toward the gate, not looking back.

And that had to have been the hardest thing he'd done to date. He'd jumped the gun and told her before he'd given it much thought himself.

No, he wasn't wrong. He knew he loved her. He was absolutely in love with Sarah Newton, and he didn't have any regret over telling her.

Okay, maybe he had a *little* regret. But not enough to wish he could turn back the clock. She needed to know, and he was glad she did.

23

———————

Sarah

Sarah blinked, watching with her mouth hanging open as Dax wandered toward the barn. To say she was stunned was an understatement. Neither one of them had bothered to label their feelings for the other.

What had happened to doing things the easy way?

Dax couldn't just drop a bomb like that and walk away.

And yet that was exactly what he'd done.

Her head was still reeling, and she didn't know what she should do. She could chase after him and make him admit he was teasing her. Because that's what this felt like. He was making fun of her for some reason only he knew.

Unless he wasn't.

Her stomach knotted in an almost pleasant way. She hadn't even thought about what it might mean to be loved by a guy like Dax. A future with him had been the furthest thing on her mind.

But the more she lingered on his words, the more she grew to like them.

Then all at once the blood drained from her body. He'd said he loved her and like a stupid person, she'd laughed.

And what did he do? He hugged her, kissed her head, and gave her the rest of the afternoon off. That didn't sound like Dax at all.

Sarah scrambled through the dusty corral toward the fencing that was closest to the barn. She launched between the bars and continued running even though she nearly tripped over her own feet on at least two occasions.

By the time she'd caught up to him, he was already getting ready to brush the yearling down. The muscles in his shoulders rippled, showing off his strength and many hours of labor he'd put in on the ranch.

"Dax."

His head turned and he glanced at her in such a nonchalant way that she almost got distracted. But not quite. He had some explaining to do.

Sarah placed her hands on her hips and scowled at him. "What do you think you're doing?"

Dax had the audacity to look confused. He lifted his brush as if it were obvious.

"I didn't mean that, and you know it."

His brow arched and one side of his mouth quirked into a smile. "I'm afraid you're going to have to elaborate."

She moved closer to him, stepping into the stall with both him and the horse. The enclosure felt even smaller the closer she got to him. "How can you admit something like that to me and then just walk away. It isn't fair."

"I feel like we've had this conversation before. Life isn't fair."

A groan left her lips in a huff. "Will you knock it off? I'm trying to have a conversation with you?"

"Really? Because it sure seems from your tone that you'd rather get mad at me for something that I have yet to figure out."

His teasing smile both made her heart leap into her throat and beat faster than was recommended by any decent cardiologist. "You can't tell me you love me—"

"Oh, that." His grin widened and he turned back to the horse. "If it's the truth, I don't see why I can't."

Okay, this conversation was getting out of hand. She closed the distance between them and grasped the brush right out of his hand. Her fingers grazed his, setting off the electrical current she'd grown to love and hate at the same time. Her eyes drilled into his. "You can't tell me you love me and expect me to just let you walk away. We should probably discuss it."

"With all due respect, you didn't seem all that keen on a discussion."

Her face flushed. "You caught me off guard. What did you *expect* me to say?"

Dax grasped her chin with his finger and thumb in that gentle way he did when he wanted her to focus on what he was about to say. "I didn't *expect* you to say anything. Would I have *liked* it if you told me you felt the same? You bet that pretty mouth I would. Did I understand if you weren't ready to say it back? Without a single doubt in my mind. But I'm certainly not going to wait around for you to figure out how you feel before I admit my feelings. I'm also not in the business of forcing how I feel on anyone who isn't experiencing the same."

His words brought Brielle to Sarah's mind. Those two had a history, and even seeing them having a quiet conversation earlier had triggered some insecurities she'd rather not deal with at the moment.

"You really don't care if I say it back?"

"Of course I care. I care very much. I also *love* you, Sarah. I'm willing to wait for you to come to your own conclusions no matter how hard it is."

"Why are you so good to me?" She hadn't meant to whisper that question out loud. They'd just seemed to appear. And even before he spoke his answer, she had predicted it.

"Because I love you." He said it with such a matter-of-fact tone that she had no choice but to believe him.

The words were there, hiding just beneath the surface. She wanted to admit to him that she loved him. But for some reason they wouldn't come. They got caught in the back of her throat and refused to budge.

"Well, I'll say it when I'm good and ready."

Dax's lips twitched. "I wouldn't expect anything less."

"Fine." She spun on her heel, listening to his chuckle as she strode down the aisle between the rows of stalls. The horses seemed to be laughing with him, nickering and tossing their heads. What was it with the animals on this ranch? First the chickens, and now the horses.

Was she so emotionally damaged that she couldn't bring herself to tell the one guy she could actually see a future with that she loved him?

No. That wasn't it. She couldn't remember a time when she'd told any guy that she loved them.

Sarah charged from the barn, but instead of turning toward the house to clean up for dinner, she went in the opposite direction, opting for a walk to clear her head instead. She'd grown more familiar with the trails around the property, loving the peace they seemed to offer. They were one thing that she knew she'd miss when she ended up leaving.

Unless she didn't.

That wasn't going to happen, and she knew it. Deep down, she knew she'd been raised to do right by her family. She'd leave Slate Rock Ranch and Copper Creek behind. Along with the landscape, animals, and overall beauty of the countryside, she'd be leaving the people she'd grown to care for.

A sharp twinge rocked through her. She couldn't imagine what life would be like without the surrogate family she'd found while living here. Not only would she leave Dax, but she'd leave Brielle, her sisters, Zeke, and the sheriff, all of whom felt more like family than the people who raised her.

Maybe she could convince her parents that there was a future for her out here. Would that be so bad? It wasn't just the money she'd be losing. While she had felt judged and put down by her parents all these years, she still loved them and knew they loved her in their own ways. She couldn't bear the thought of losing everything that she'd come from.

Sarah charged down a trail that took her toward a grove of trees. The smell of pine and lavender was stronger over here, and it was more soothing than the smell of the barn. With each step she took, she grew more agitated.

Why did Dax have to go and make everything so much more real?

She slowed her steps, realization hitting her like a slap to the face. She was agitated because she already knew the decision she'd be making. Deep down, there wasn't another option. Not a logical one, anyway. She knew from the moment she'd kissed him.

Sarah wasn't a quitter. She'd speak to her parents and hope that they understood where she was coming from. She'd lose all her inheritance, but maybe they'd still support her. Then she could find happiness with the people of Copper Creek. It would be the perfect fresh start.

The more she thought about it, the better she felt. The old Sarah might have just returned home for the easy life that had been carefully planned and curated for her. But not anymore. She had grown, and she knew what she wanted.

Someone stepped out of the tree line when she made another turn along the trail.

Sarah clapped her hand over her mouth, stifling a scream that would surely draw attention from those at the ranch—something that could ruin everything she had created while living here.

Kenneth stood before her, a smug, sinister smile on his face. His gaze swept over her as if he were seeing her for the first time, but she knew better. He *had* been at the country club that night. She should have known better than to think it wasn't him. More than that, she should have told the sheriff immediately.

Sarah swallowed at the lump that had formed in her throat. He'd convinced her to be the getaway driver for what had been their final night as a Bonnie and Clyde duo. Only it wasn't just the two of them. He'd brought along a friend who had a gun, and they had wanted to do more than just graffiti, flatten tires, or tip over some cows.

She couldn't prove it because she hadn't been there, but she suspected the dead cattle that had been reported was their doing as well. Her stomach seemed to twist in inhuman ways at the thought of those poor creatures. Up until she'd worked on the ranch, she hadn't cared much about what happened to a herd, but now it was different.

Her head swiveled around, almost expecting another person to pop out of the bushes with him. Kenneth never did things without backup.

Her eyes narrowed and she folded her arms as she edged backward. "What are you doing here, Kenneth?"

He took a step toward her. "Now, is that any way to treat your boyfriend?"

"You stopped being my boyfriend the moment you threatened me with that gun."

Kenneth rolled his eyes. "Come on, Sarah. It was a joke."

"Sure didn't seem like a joke." She hated the way her voice trembled as the memories of that night came flooding back with a vengeance. "Didn't seem like a joke to that sheriff you shot."

"He didn't die, though, did he?" Kenneth sneered. "Seems like you have gotten pretty cozy with folks around here, haven't you?"

"What do you want?" she ground out through gritted teeth. Kenneth *probably* didn't have a weapon, but that didn't mean she would hand over the trust he'd stolen from her before. No one knew they'd been dating, not even the sheriff. It was one more secret she had told her lawyer not to divulge. And since neither one of them went to trial, it was never brought up.

He stepped forward again, like a predator cornering his prey. "You ruined everything, Sarah. We could have kept this whole thing going if you hadn't swerved into the other lane right in front of that cop."

She shook her head. "I wanted out, and you know it. I swerved because you were swinging that gun around like it was a toy."

Kenneth sighed. "Get over it already. You didn't even have to serve time."

"Because I didn't assault a police officer!"

His demeanor shifted and he glowered at her, causing her heart to stutter. She clamped her mouth shut. There was no telling what he was willing to do to her at this point. She'd basically handed him over to the authorities on a silver platter.

Kenneth's voice lowered, resembling a growl. "Money."

"*What?*"

"Don't play dumb. I know you're loaded. I know your parents are practically billionaires. I finally put it all together. Your nice car, your nice clothes—and your name. There's no way you're not related to them. I want you to give me half a million dollars."

She scowled at him. "You're a bigger idiot than I gave you credit for if you think I'm going to give you *anything*."

His eyes sparked with a fury she hadn't seen before and he launched toward her, grabbing her wrist. She sucked in sharply, attempting but failing at pulling away from him. His words were laced with venom as his hot breath fanned her face. "You will give me every penny I'm asking for. Otherwise, I go to the press."

Her brows creased, confusion consuming the fear.

"I reached out to your parents yesterday." His grip on her tightened. "Imagine my surprise when they said they'd never heard of me. Not only that, but they let me know I was invited for your next family dinner." He clicked his tongue. "Now why would the only daughter of a well-known wealthy family keep secrets like this?"

Sarah's jaw locked tight. She wasn't going to give him any satisfaction over the answers he sought.

"You want to know what I think? I think it's because they have this beautiful little story of their perfect little girl being the best student and an upright citizen. Finding out that she was involved with a criminal like me, or worse—that she had instigated the whole string of crimes a few months ago—now that might ruin their family's reputation."

He'd hit the nail on the head. He knew right where to strike her and strike hard. This was yet another reason why she'd made a deal rather than go through the courts. If her name was in the papers, it wouldn't take much for people to connect the dots.

She'd been a fool to believe that Kenneth wouldn't come looking for her and figure out about her family. She could kick herself for not being more careful about her identity.

Lifting her chin, she spewed the only words that came to her mind. "I have an army of lawyers. I can make one call right now and get them on this."

"But you won't. Because you'll lose *so* much more." He leaned in so close she almost thought he was going to kiss her. But instead, he whispered. "If you tell your parents, you lose their respect. They lose the reputation they've built on strong family values. That would lead to articles in the paper—everyone loves a good local scandal. How hard do you think it would be to get that information over to the local news in Copper Creek? How do you think people will treat you when they realize what an awful person you really are? What would Dax think?"

Her blood ran cold as ice. His words had made it perfectly clear that he'd been watching her for weeks, not days. Sarah might have changed a lot since arriving here and starting her community service. But that wouldn't do her any good when the truth came out. Some of the townspeople might shrug off that sort of thing, but not all of them. There was a great deal of gossipy and judgmental members in this community.

And what about Dax? How would he react to knowing all of this? He might have alluded to having a colorful background as well, but it couldn't be as bad as being the one person to target a whole town of hard-working people. These were his friends and family.

Her stomach roiled. She didn't have the money to pay Kenneth. That money would only be made available after she accepted a job at her parent's firm.

Sarah yanked her hand out of his grasp. "Unfortunately, I won't be able to get you any money. I don't have it."

Kenneth's eyes narrowed. "You'll figure out a way, or I'll tell everyone your secrets."

"I'm telling you the truth. I don't get a cent of that money until I start officially working for my parents."

"Didn't you say you only had one or two more classes to take? You're smart. You can figure out a way to make this happen."

He took a step away from her, his features now smooth as if

he hadn't just blackmailed her, holding everything that was important to her over her head. "I want it deposited into an offshore account by the end of the summer." He winked at her. "Or everything that you love will be ripped from your grasp." He whistled, wandering down the path in the opposite direction from which she came.

Her heart pounded angrily, and her hands shook. She'd seen all the movies. If she gave in and paid a ransom, he'd just come back for more. The only way to stop him was to take away his power.

And that meant doing the one thing she had fought so hard not to.

She'd have to tell her parents everything. She'd have to confess to Dax. And she'd have to get out ahead of the tabloids and press.

Sarah's shoulders slumped, a tear finally escaping from behind her eyes. Deep down, she knew she wouldn't be able to do any of that. When the time came to be done with her community service, she'd be going home and taking a job from her parents at the firm. She'd leave behind everything she'd grown to love about this place and return to the life she now realized was an empty shell of what she really wanted.

24

———

Dax

Dax hung the rope he had coiled on a nail near the barn entrance and leaned his forearm against the entrance as he stared out at the ranch surroundings. This view really was a little slice of paradise.

One day he could see a life with Sarah by his side as they ran a ranch together. Granted, they would have to start out small, but that wouldn't matter as long as they were together. Sarah had a knack for training. Maybe they could start a little business together.

He smiled. He had his work cut out for himself with a girl like Sarah. But he'd known that from the first moment he'd met her. She was exactly the kind of fire he wanted in his life.

There was only one problem with the way he felt about her.

His past.

At some point he'd have to tell her about his past. If it ever came out from someone else, he didn't know if she'd forgive him.

Really, he wasn't so sure she would be willing to look past it now. Which was why he hadn't been able to bring himself to tell her earlier.

The folks at AA would probably tell him he was making a mistake in waiting. But they didn't know Sarah. He'd weighed the risks, and he knew deep down that he was making the right decision. It wasn't like he *wouldn't* tell her. He would. It just had to be the right time.

A familiar figure charged across the property in the distance. Sarah moved like she was running from something but didn't want anyone to know. His arm dropped and he took a step toward her, but she moved too fast. By the time he would have gotten to her, she would have already been in the house.

A chill ran down his spine and he glanced in the direction from which she came. There wasn't anything there. Of course he wouldn't see anything. What did she have to run from? His eyes followed her as she stormed up the steps and hurried inside.

He could call her and ask her if everything was okay. But chances were she wouldn't want to talk about it. Sarah was the kind of girl who only talked about something if she wanted to.

Dax let out a sigh and shoved his hands in his pockets. He'd have to get used to this kind of worry if he wanted to be with her. Sarah was far too independent for him to become her knight in shining armor. The only way he could help her was when she was utterly incapacitated.

He could call Brielle and ask her to keep an eye on Sarah, but something told him he'd already maxed out his favors with her. Besides, he had no idea if Brielle was out on one of her dates. Tonight he would just have to shove down the anxious energy that swirled within him.

Already he could tell that these feelings wouldn't just go away. They were the beginning stages of losing his cool and wanting to go raid the fridge where all the wranglers kept their after-work beers.

As if his tongue had heard his thoughts, it became dry, tasting sour. He shook off the temptation. He hadn't felt this triggered in a long time. Everything had been going so well. There was just something about seeing Sarah so riled up after their conversation that put him on edge.

His stomach lurched, echoing the unraveling thoughts in his mind.

It was silly, this feeling of foreboding that had suddenly settled over him. He needed a meeting before he did something that he'd regret. Dax glanced at his watch. There was a meeting in town in about thirty minutes. If he finished up his work, he could slip over there and recharge. He shot one more look over at the house, itching to knock on the door and demand to see Sarah, if only to give her a hug and remind her that he was here for her.

But he'd leave her be. He knew better than anyone how important it was to collect one's thoughts before discussing them with someone.

Dax's gaze swept over their small AA group until it landed on a guy that looked vaguely familiar. He couldn't place the young man, but that didn't matter. The kid could be just like Sarah—working in Copper Creek for the summer. He was probably just here temporarily.

The stranger's eyes found his and Dax offered a welcoming smile. The kid didn't return it. He shifted in his seat and returned his focus to the person who was currently talking at the front of the room.

That was fine. Newcomers typically didn't like talking on the first day. They were still under the impression that attending these kinds of meetings somehow made them bad people. He'd come around. They always did.

He'd have to approach him and introduce himself after the meeting.

Dax got to his feet the second the current speaker finished. He smiled widely and stared at all the friends he'd made over the last few years. This support system was like a second family to him, and he would love for all of them to meet Sarah in person. But then that would defeat the purpose of this being anonymous.

"I'm Dax, and I'm an alcoholic."

The group murmured their hellos.

"Life is good. But it wasn't always that way." He glanced at the stranger. But the kid wasn't meeting his gaze. Instead, he got to his feet and headed for the doors.

Dax frowned, losing track of his train of thought. He scrambled for the right words to say next, attempting to remember why he'd needed to come for a meeting in the first place, but his thoughts were elsewhere. When he finally got his bearings, he finished up his little speech quickly, then hurried across the gym floor toward the door. He poked his head outside, swiveling so he could look both ways. The kid had disappeared.

Strange.

Dax returned to the meeting and took a seat, but his focus had once again left him. He couldn't pinpoint why seeing the kid had pulled his focus. He felt like he should know the guy. Maybe their paths would cross around town again. That's probably where Dax had seen him.

The town was small enough that he'd notice the newcomer if he saw him again. Then he could introduce himself and invite the kid to stay longer.

OVER THE NEXT WEEK, Sarah seemed to be avoiding him. Besides their working hours, Dax didn't see her often. She claimed she wanted to spend more time with Brielle at the country club. She opted to have someone else take her to visit with her uncle for their Friday lunch.

Dax couldn't help but get the feeling that Sarah wasn't excited about his proclamation of love. At the time, he hadn't seen any apprehension from her. She'd been her usual stubborn self. Now that he thought about it, refusing to say she loved him back was probably a good indication of her feelings toward him.

She'd been at Slate Rock Ranch for about two months now. Had he moved too fast? He didn't think so. The end of summer was coming faster and faster. Sarah could leave and never look back.

The thought of not seeing her again caused his stomach to churn with an unsettling feeling. Perhaps he'd been in denial all this time. Sarah could be spending time with him to humor him.

Tonight, Sarah and Brielle had opted for a girls' night at the country club. Okay, so Sarah hadn't looked like she wanted to go when Brielle brought it up, but she had agreed. When Dax had offered to go to keep her company, she declined.

It was like they'd taken one step forward and two steps back in their relationship. Dax sat on the edge of the porch steps, staring out at the darkness, lost in his thoughts. An unseasonably cool breeze ruffled his hair. He could go on a horse ride, or for a walk. But what he really wanted to do was surprise Sarah at the club. He could hold her in his arms and try to get that connection back that they'd managed to lose.

Dax rose to his feet and strode toward his truck just as the sheriff's car pulled onto the property. He slowed his steps, waiting for the patrol car to come to a stop. The sheriff climbed out and shut the door, his gaze landing on Dax.

For a moment Dax thought the sheriff would head for the house, but instead the man waved him over. "Dax. Just the guy I want to see."

Dax stiffened. "Is everything okay?" The sheriff didn't usually visit the ranch unless he needed to speak to Zeke or Sarah. She'd met with him for lunch earlier that day. Had she said something about him?

This could very well be that meeting a guy had with the girl's father. Except the sheriff wasn't Sarah's father. Dax swallowed hard and shoved his hands into his pockets as he headed toward the sheriff.

"There *is* something we need to discuss."

That sick feeling in Dax's stomach worsened. "Is this about Sarah?"

Sheriff Donahue glanced at the house, then back to him. "Is she here?"

Dax shook his head. "She went to the country club with Brielle."

If Dax hadn't been focused on the sheriff, he wouldn't have noticed the slight way the sheriff stiffened. "She came by for lunch today." He dragged a hand down his face. "And she mentioned seeing someone last week that had caused her some concern."

His brows pulled together. She hadn't mentioned any concern to him.

"She mentioned someone had been watching you two."

"Yeah, someone was watching us when we went outside for some air at the club." His heart beat a little faster. "Did she know who it was?"

The sheriff ticked his jaw back and forth. His reaction was enough to confirm Dax's question.

"Who is it, sheriff?" His hands clenched in his pockets. If this person was enough of a concern for Sarah to mention them to her uncle, then Dax wanted to know what was going on. He wasn't going to let anything hurt Sarah. Least of all some twerp who wasn't willing to show his face.

"That doesn't matter. What matters is that you need to keep an eye out for him. I think he might be hanging around. You should probably go to the country club and help keep them safe." He nodded to the house. "Is Zeke home? I'd like to speak to him as well."

"Wait! Keep them safe? What's going on? I can't go into this blind."

The sheriff gave him a pointed look. "You aren't going into anything. I just want you to keep an eye out. If you see him, call me right away." He moved past Dax and headed for the house.

Dax chased after him. "Who is this guy? Will he hurt her? What's going on?"

The sheriff only glanced at him. "It doesn't concern you. Your job is just to be there. Can you handle that?"

"Sure, but—" Dax hurried around and faced the sheriff. "I'm dating your niece."

He didn't look surprised at all.

Dax let out a sigh. "I'm in love with her, sir. I'm not going to let anything or anyone hurt her. I think I deserve to know what's going on. Does this have something to do with why she's here? She mentioned that she's got a colored past..."

Sheriff Donahue considered him, and Dax almost thought the guy would finally tell him what was going on, but instead he shook his head. "I appreciate your candor, son. But I'm not going to share anything that Sarah hasn't already shared. If she doesn't want to give you any details, then that's up to her." He placed a heavy hand on Dax's shoulder. "You get out to the country club and stay alert. Anything that seems out of the ordinary, call me."

Dax nodded, his shoulders slumping. He hadn't felt this at a loss in a long time. The sheriff headed up the porch stairs and Dax spun around. "You didn't give me a description."

The sheriff paused at the top of the steps and turned around. "Young man. Brown hair. Brown eyes."

That didn't do any good. Half of the people who came through town could be described that way. Dax would have to base his judgment on the way that Sarah reacted if she saw whoever he was supposed to protect her from.

The whole drive to the country club, he tried to remember the shadow person from that night. There were no discernable features. He hadn't been able to tell for certain if the person was male or female. At least now he had something more to go off of.

Dax pulled into the full parking lot and groaned. Tonight was busier than it had been when they'd last come. Great. That meant he'd have to be more vigilant, and that was if he could locate Sarah and Brielle to begin with.

He climbed out of his truck and slammed the door shut. Shoving his keys into his pockets, he headed for the entrance. Right as he climbed the first step, a young man came out and headed down the steps. He made eye contact with Dax for just a moment before brushing past him.

Dax turned and watched the kid go. The stranger from the AA meeting. He nearly called out to the kid, but he had more important places to be. He had to find the girls and let them know what was going on.

He hurried inside, hit by muggy warm air from too many bodies. A country song played over the speakers and throngs of people danced, filling up the entire area. Usually, he could manage to get to the other side of the dance floor without being bumped into, but not tonight.

The nice thing about Shane Owen's country club was that the lighting allowed the visitors to see one another better. Dax scanned the crowd, his gaze landing on several men who could easily fit the bill. But no Sarah or Brielle.

He darted through the crowd, squeezing between large groups who were chatting and laughing. Someone laughed obnoxiously loud and backed into him. She spun around and her margarita splashed all over his sleeve.

Dax stared down at the mess with disdain.

"Oh, my gosh! I'm so sorry." The young woman brushed at his shirt with the small square napkin that she'd gotten from the bar.

He took a step back, muttering, "It's fine." He could smell the alcohol on her breath and had to shut his eyes briefly to focus before memories from his more regrettable stage of life assaulted him.

Some people shouldn't be allowed to drink. Drinking, in general, wasn't a necessity. In his experience, those who partook in the vice had a tendency to share the uglier parts of their personalities.

The girl continued to attempt to dab at his shirt, but he turned and headed toward the other side of the room. While the room was overly crowded, he still couldn't find Sarah. He dodged more people, and his eye finally caught Brielle as she danced with a cowboy who was definitely too old for her.

Her gaze met his and she smiled brightly. "Dax! What are you doing here?"

"Where is Sarah?" he called over the music.

She pulled away from the cowboy, her brows creasing. "She was just here a moment ago. Maybe she went outside with that guy."

His blood ran cold. "What guy?"

She nudged him with her elbow. "You're not jealous, are you?"

He hated admitting to such a thing, but yes. Everything in his body wanted to scream that she belonged to him. But that was bordering on obsessive. Dax swallowed hard. "No. I'm here because her uncle wanted me to keep an eye on you guys."

Again, Brielle looked confused. "Uncle?" Her eyes widened. "Oh, the sheriff."

Her reaction was strange enough as it was. But there was a more pressing matter—whoever she'd gone outside with could be the guy the sheriff was worried about. He spun on his heel, ignoring Brielle's calls for him to slow down.

25

———————

Sarah

Sarah smiled at the cowboy who stood beside her. They leaned against the railing, looking out at the pastures. "It's pretty amazing, don't you think? I didn't even know that horses could be used for therapeutic services."

James nodded, flashing her a wide grin. "When I decided to become a vet, I nearly changed my degree to equine therapy. It's fascinating how animals can even change the chemical makeup of humans just by spending time with them."

"Why didn't you change your major?"

James shrugged. Turning, he rested his elbows on the rail. "I wanted to stay local, and there weren't any businesses that offered that sort of thing here. This place was still barely a pinprick on the map."

She let her gaze travel over the property. "When did Shane open this up?"

"About a year or two ago, I think. But we all thought he was going to build a golf course—it's what all the rich people want, right?" He chuckled, but his words had a different effect on her. She frowned, not meeting his gaze.

"Just because someone is wealthy doesn't mean they're going to do something selfish with their money. I know a lot of selfish people who don't have a lot of money and some wealthy people who would give away every single penny if it meant helping their loved ones."

Out of the corner of her eye, she could see him shifting. Her face flushed. If she had the choice of what to do with her money, she probably would help Dax start up a ranch. He would be so good at training horses for the area.

But that wasn't going to happen. She had to head home, take her job with a smile, and give a large chunk of her money to Kenneth so she could contribute to one more selfish human being in the world. Sarah let out a sigh and finally snuck a glance at James. "So, is anyone else in your family a vet?"

He shook his head. "My dad has a small farm. He grows food, mostly. I took over the veterinary clinic from the guy who used to run it for as long as I could remember. What about you?"

She fidgeted, picking at her cuticles. "Right now, I'm helping out at Slate Rock Ranch for the summer. Then I'm heading back home to work for my parents. They run a financial firm."

His brows lifted. "Wow. That's pretty fancy."

Sarah shrugged. "I guess."

James moved closer, his head ducking as if he would get a better view of her face, but it didn't work. Instead, he hooked his finger under her chin and lifted it. "Seems to me that you don't want to do that."

She huffed. "No, I don't suppose I do."

"Then don't."

"It's not that easy. It's what my parents expect of me." Not to mention she wouldn't get any of the money she needed to keep Kenneth off her back.

"My parents wanted me to take over the ranch. But look at where I am now. They're actually very proud of me after they figured out that I had to do what made me happy."

Sarah sighed. "Somehow, I think our parents don't view the world the same way."

"Get your hands off her."

She jumped, and James dropped his hand to spin toward their interruption. Her eyes widened, finding Dax and Brielle standing only a few feet away. Brielle looked shocked, and Dax looked like he could erupt into flames at any moment.

"Dax? What are you doing here?"

Dax's gaze shifted from her to James and back. His cheek twitched and his hands tightened at his sides. He strode toward her—no, toward James, and his chest heaved with angry breaths. "What do you think you're doing, Pratt?"

James lifted a brow. "You okay, Dax?"

"No. I'm not okay. You're hitting on my girlfriend."

"Dax!" Sarah reached for his arm, but he shrugged her off.

He glowered at James. "You should go back inside. There are plenty of other girls you can hit on."

James chuckled, lifting his hands. "Nothing was going on. We were just talking." His gaze cut to Sarah. "You going to be okay?"

Heat filled her face and she swallowed. "Yeah. I'll be fine," she muttered. But Dax wasn't going to be. She gave James a short nod before watching him head back inside. Then she whirled on Dax. "What are you doing here?" she demanded again. "We told you that we were going out just the two of us."

"Sure didn't look like it was just the two of you," he bit out.

Fury built within her. "Are you seriously admitting that you came here to check on me? We're *not* that serious."

The shock on his face was similar to what she thought it

might look like if she were to slap him. His face drained of color and his eyes widened.

"He said that the sheriff sent him," Brielle murmured beside Dax, causing Sarah to break the stare she shared with Dax. "I guess he's worried about something?"

"Brielle, you should probably go back inside, too," Dax muttered.

Sarah stiffened. Right now she most definitely didn't want to spend any alone time with Dax. He was upset and reasonably so. She wasn't thrilled, and now she had a feeling he was going to make her talk about what she'd just said. She cleared her throat. "No, you can stay."

Brielle hesitated. She glanced from Dax to Sarah.

"*Go.*"

She shot Sarah an apologetic smile. "I'll be inside if you want to come find me."

The second she was gone, Sarah set her dark eyes on Dax. "Was any of that necessary?"

Dax moved closer to her, pinning her against the rail with his gaze. "We need to talk."

"Yeah, we do. You need to tone this relationship thing down."

He shook his head. "What has gotten into you?"

"Me? What about you? I've made it perfectly clear where I stand in this relationship. I'm not ready for something super serious."

Dax let out a harsh breath and ran a hand through his mussed hair. His features contorted into something filled with pain. "The last time we talked..." He shook his head. "I guess I assumed you were more on board than you are."

She hugged herself, her chest aching from the breath she couldn't take. She looked away, refusing to meet his gaze because she knew one look and he'd be able to tell she was lying. "Yeah, maybe you did." She sucked in a sharp, shuddering breath. "I'm not going to be around much longer, Dax. I don't want you to get hurt."

"Well, it's too late for that," he snapped.

She flinched. "It's for the best."

"How can you say that?" he whispered. "I know that I want to be with you. I've told you that I'm in love with you. Isn't that enough?"

Sarah lifted a shoulder. Deep down she knew it would be better to cut him off now before they got closer. But she couldn't bring herself to do it. She lifted her gaze to meet his. "Nothing was going on between me and James. We were just talking."

"I figured." His voice was cold and numb.

"I wouldn't blame you if you don't want to spend any more time with me."

Dax peeked at her. "You have to know I can't stay away from you. If you're set on going home at the end of the summer, fine. But I still want to spend as much time as I can with you."

Chills crawled down her spine and up again. Goosebumps lifted on her arms, an indication that his words had shot like a dart right into her heart. He was too good for her. She didn't deserve him. Even if there was enough time to get him to love her so completely that he would be okay with her secrets, it wouldn't solve the problem she had with her family.

Dax grasped her upper arms, and she looked into his eyes. "Just let me in. That's all I ask."

He wasn't going to drop it. If Dax was one thing, it was persistent. And she was terrible at telling him no. It was best to play along and make him think that everything was going to be okay.

She nodded, but her voice was caught in her throat. She couldn't speak, for fear that the emotion in her tone would betray her.

Dax pulled her close against his chest and rested his chin on her head. She wrapped her arms around his strong body, reveling in the safety he offered her. In a perfect world she could tell him everything, and there would be no issues. He'd come to her rescue and sweep her off her feet.

But this wasn't a fairy tale. She'd managed to get herself into this mess, and she would be the only one to get herself out.

"Why didn't you tell me about the guy who's watching you?"

Sarah froze.

He rubbed her back as if to soothe away the tension, and she was grateful that he couldn't see her face. "The sheriff came by the ranch. He said you were worried about some guy who's been stalking you."

So the sheriff didn't tell Dax anything. The relief she felt was short-lived. Now that Dax knew there was something—or someone—bothering her, maybe he'd ease off a bit and give her some space. Then again, this could be the exact thing that would make him hover.

"How bad is it?" Dax pressed.

She shifted, resting her forehead against his chest. "It's not. He's just some guy from my past."

This time Dax did pull back. She shut her eyes tight. "Sarah," he urged, "what's going on?"

Finally, she opened her eyes. "He's just an ex, okay? He's messing with me."

Dax glowered and his voice tightened as he spoke through gritted teeth. "What?"

"Really. He's harmless," she murmured. Kenneth wasn't going to do anything to jeopardize what he wanted. If he was going to hurt her, he would have done so. He was annoying, and he was committing a crime, but he had all the cards in his hands. She hadn't even been able to tell the sheriff about Kenneth bribing her because there was nothing he could do. She was stuck.

THE MORE TIME THAT PASSED, the worse she felt. The sun continued to rise and set each day, and every so often she'd see Kenneth lurking in the shadows of a shop in town or at the country club. It was getting to the point where she was seeing things. At one point she could have sworn she saw Kenneth hiding in one of the stalls.

Her nerves were frayed and no amount of spending time with Dax could ease the stress she currently experienced. Just like she'd predicted, Dax refused to leave her side. They worked together, they spent their free time together, and they ran errands together. The only thing she did on her own was sleep—but Brielle was there. She hadn't had a single opportunity for alone time.

Sarah stood in the corral with her yearling. The animal was nearly ready to be transferred over to Shane. And while she'd never admit it to anyone, she'd secretly named the spunky horse.

She rubbed Cricket's nose, then leaned into the animal. The only sanctuary Sarah had found was with the animal. She could feel the love the horse had for her simply in the way the horse immediately perked up when Sarah arrived. The yearling had matured from a scrawny baby into a strong, majestic white beast with a beautiful spotted coat.

Sarah ran her hand along Cricket's back, murmuring, "I'm going to leave soon."

Cricket tossed her head and pawed at the ground.

"I know. I'm going to miss you too." She never thought she'd miss an animal so much. It was funny how things had changed since her arrival. She used to shy away from the animals, and all she could think about was going home. But now that couldn't be further from the truth.

Sarah wanted to stay more than she could ever admit to anyone.

The only chore she wouldn't miss was collecting the eggs from the chickens.

"Are you ready to ride her?" Dax's voice drifted toward her, and Sarah turned. He stood at the edge of the corral, his eyes shaded by his cowboy hat and a toothpick between his lips.

Her pulse accelerated as it usually did when he was around. Sarah coiled the lead rope around her hand and moved toward him. "I didn't think we'd be doing that. Isn't that going to be Sean's job?"

Dax's lips quirked into an easy smile. "It's the next step. She's gotten used to the saddle. Now we can put someone in it."

Sarah's eyes widened. "What if she—you know— throws me off?"

"This one knows you. She trusts you more than anyone else. Take it slow, show her she can trust you, and you do the same." He nodded toward the barn where one of the ranch hands hefted a saddle in his arms and was headed toward them. "What do you say?"

The ranch hand slung the saddle onto the rail and Dax retrieved it. Sarah's focus followed him as he secured it on Cricket's back. The horse shifted but didn't dart away like she had the first time. Sarah smiled, pride mingling with the butterflies she still felt with Dax being so close.

He straightened after securing the strap, then held out his hand. "Ready?"

26

———————

Dax

The pressure of Sarah's hand always seemed to ground Dax. Their relationship wasn't fixed by any means, but he no longer felt like he was hanging off the edge of a cliff whenever she was around.

Sarah rode the horse around the corral, a calm smile on her face. That was one thing he had noticed lately. She seemed more in her element when she was around that horse. It wasn't all horses, just this particular yearling. It was as if together they had grown and matured, finding themselves with one another's help.

"Push her into a canter," he called toward her.

She bounced in the saddle as the horse trotted and found a more even gait. She beamed at him; excitement radiated all around her. Sarah was a natural. She belonged in the saddle. She belonged with him.

Except there was one glaring issue.

He still hadn't told her about his secret. Yes, she had some things of her own she hadn't told him, but deep down, he knew his were worse. He was no better than the guy who'd killed her older brother. There was little chance she'd be able to look past it.

All these heart-wrenching thoughts had been the only thing holding him back from revisiting their conversation about her leaving. There had to be a way to get her to stay.

And if there wasn't?

Would it be worth following her? Could he pick up his life to be with her? At this point he couldn't say. She still hadn't told him if she had developed those kinds of feelings for him.

One thing was clear. As he watched her continue exercising the horse, he knew he needed to have another talk with her. Time was quickly running out. He couldn't avoid the conversation much longer.

Sarah slowed the horse to a walk and stopped beside him. She practically glowed. "Did you see that? She's doing so well!"

He cocked his head, holding his hand out to her, and she took it without question. "She's got a good trainer."

She hopped down, still shining with the kind of joy that could only come with the accomplishment that she'd made all on her own. "She's incredible. I only wish..." Her smile faltered as she stood before him. It was short, but he saw it.

Dax brushed her cheek with his thumb, drinking in everything about her that he could. Nothing was ever guaranteed, and after she leaves, he might not still get to have her in his life.

Sarah's lashes fluttered and she let out a sigh. "How do you do it?"

"How do I do what?"

"How can you train these animals and then let them go? How can you not fall in love with each and every one of them and want to keep them for yourself?"

He gave her a crooked smile. "While I like animals, I don't

think I'd want to take care of all of them. That being said, your first is usually pretty special." Dax tucked a strand of hair behind her ear. "You know, if you decided to stay—"

"Dax..." Her voice held a note of warning.

"*What*?" He tried to sound lighthearted with his question, but he couldn't deny the level of gravity that had settled in his chest, making it hard to speak with her.

"You know *what*." She sighed, pulling away. "We've been over this. I can't stay. Once I'm done here—"

He reached for her, capturing her into his arms. "What exactly is it you're doing again?"

She avoided his gaze. "You said I didn't have to tell you if it made me uncomfortable." Her words were barely a whisper, and it set alarms ringing in his head.

"You're right. But sometimes things change."

"Dax," her voice was strained, "I know you care about me, but—"

"*Care* about you? *Sweetheart*, I love you more than I've loved anyone." The realization hit him square in the chest the moment the words left his lips. He traced the edge of her face with the back of his fingers. "From the moment I saw you, I've seen you overcome adversity. Your determination with that horse was admirable. Everything I've ever wanted in a woman—it's you."

She shook her head, a sad smile on her face. "You don't know anything about me. And I don't know you."

Her words shot him so hard in the chest that he nearly stumbled backward. She couldn't possibly know about his past. "Why are you shutting me out?" It was the only question he could ask that he thought she might answer. "And don't tell me it's because I confessed my feelings for you. You've been content to be part of this relationship as long as I didn't push you to stay."

Sarah's face flushed. "I'm not shutting you out." Her response was weak, and she pulled away from his grasp, but he wouldn't let her.

"Come on. Whatever it is, you can tell me."

"It's nothing. I've just never—" She shook her head. "I'm sorry. I have obligations. My parents—"

"The parents who you hate?"

"That's not fair," her voice rose slightly. "My parents want what's best for me."

"If they wanted what's best for you, they would want you to be happy. Would you be happy there? Or would you be happier if you stayed here? With me."

Sarah finally pulled away, forcing him to release her. "Why are you bringing this up now? I thought we were doing okay." She pressed her fingers to her temples. "I only have two weeks left. I don't want to spend them fighting with you over why I can't stay."

Dax let out a groan. "Then just talk to me."

She paced in front of him, her breaths came out in short spurts and she shook out her hands. "The problem is that if you knew everything, I don't even think you would *want* me to stay here with you."

He let out a bark of laughter, startling her. Hadn't he thought the exact same thing? Were they both holding back out of fear? If he'd known that this whole situation could have been avoided with a simple conversation, he would have pulled her aside sooner.

Dax threw up his hands. "You want to know what? You're right. We both have things we would rather keep to ourselves."

She froze, turning to gaze at him, stunned. The thoughts that must be racing through her head at the moment, he could only guess. At this point she could be thinking the worst of him. He needed to clarify what he meant before she jumped to conclusions.

He let out a sigh. "What do you say we go for a walk?" He glanced around the property. They didn't exactly have privacy, and he'd rather not share some of the more intimate details of his life where someone might overhear. As much as the Callahans cared for him and he for them, Dax would still prefer to keep those parts of his life private.

Sarah's large, innocent eyes delved into his as if she could read everything he was ready to confess to her. This conversation would go one of two ways. She would forgive him because that was who she was.

Or she'd be triggered because of her brother.

Then maybe she would be brave enough to share the few missing pieces he didn't have.

Sarah's gaze cut to the horse. "What about Cricket?"

He stilled, his eyes shifting to the horse that wandered nearby. One side of his mouth quirked up. Of course she would name the dang thing. She had grown far too close to the horse. If only she felt the same thing for him.

Dax moved past her, not liking the way she jumped away from him. Her defenses were up. Everything about her had closed down so he couldn't penetrate the walls she'd erected. He uncinched the saddle and slung it over his shoulder. "I'll be right back. We can let her stay out here for a few hours before we take her back to her stall.

Each step he took toward the barn, he went over what he'd say. This didn't have to be hard. He just had to suck it up and tell her exactly what happened and how he'd grown from it. So why was coming up with the words so difficult?

His boots rested heavily against the packed earth. First tell her he was in AA. That would hopefully help ease the ache that would come from hearing how close he'd come to killing someone with his own reckless habits. He was healing and improving.

And if she didn't want to share her story with him? What then? Could he be content with that? He'd once thought that he couldn't allow secrets to be between himself and the woman he loved. But if it came to losing Sarah, he might have to put those desires aside.

Dax placed the saddle on a bar, then rested his palm against a post nearby, feeling the rough texture of the wood grain. There was a part of him that could feel the shift in the air. Hairs on the back of his neck stood on end as if telling him he should think this over.

It was too late. He was going to tell her because that's what needed to happen.

When he returned to the corral, Sarah was tracing her fingers through Cricket's mane. The smile on her face warmed him, easing his anxiousness. She looked up at him, her smile more strained but still present.

He jerked his head toward the trails. Sarah hugged Cricket once more and then headed toward him. They walked for several minutes without speaking and the silence dragged on. Dax grasped her hand, lacing his fingers within hers.

"I can't help but feel that if we were more open about certain things, we might be able to make this relationship work."

Sarah pressed her lips tightly in a thin line. She didn't look up at him but remained focused on the path.

"I've made it clear how I feel about you. I want you to stay in my life."

She sighed. "And I've been upfront about my plans. You're putting me in a position I don't like. Can we just be happy with the time we've spent together?"

As much as he tried to brush off that last statement, he couldn't. Dax turned to face her. "I'm in AA."

Her lashes fluttered and she blinked. "What?" Confusion filled her features. "What does that have anything to do with—"

"About six years ago, I went out with some friends and we drank—a lot. I thought I was okay to drive…"

Sarah's eyes widened, and she grimaced.

"I got in an accident."

She shook her head and stepped away from him, holding up both hands. "Wait, so you're telling me you drove while incapacitated. Did you *kill* someone?"

He closed the distance between them, shaking his head vehemently. "*No*. The guy in the other car was hurt pretty bad, but he recovered." He grimaced. "That experience and Eve passing away was why I had to get sober. I didn't want to tell you because of what happened to your brother." His voice cracked and his stomach lurched, as if he were falling from an immeasurable height.

Sarah pinched the bridge of her nose and let out a shaky breath. "You probably shouldn't have told me," she murmured before lifting her gaze to his.

Here it was. This was the moment he'd been dreading. It didn't change the fact that telling her had been the right thing to do, but almost immediately after he'd said it, he'd regretted every word.

"I think it's great that you were able to make a change." Her features faltered and she tore her gaze away from his, refusing to meet his eyes. "If we don't learn from our mistakes, we can't become better people."

"But?"

She let out a shaky breath. "But something like that is hard for me to get over."

Her flat voice drifted toward him as if they were both in a tunnel. He couldn't trust his ears to translate what she was saying with accuracy. This couldn't be happening. Sarah wasn't like that. She didn't judge people like that.

Sarah gnawed on her lower lip. "I'm sorry, Dax. If there was

even a slim chance that I could stay or come back, I think that...
disappeared."

Dazed. His ears rang and his heart throbbed. Not right. This
couldn't be right. He refused to accept it. Sarah took a step back,
shaking him from his stunned state. His hands shot out and
grasped her upper arms, gentle but firm.

"This isn't about me, is it?"

She refused to meet his gaze.

"*Sarah*. Why won't you look me in the eye? Is it that guy? The
one you said was hanging around?"

Her eyes squeezed shut and a tear escaped. That was enough
proof for him.

"It is, isn't it? He broke your heart and now you're shutting
me out. Well, I'm not him. And this? This right here isn't us. Talk
to me."

Dark brown eyes shot to his, her brows lowered. "Isn't it? I
keep secrets from you. You keep secrets from me. You knew
about how my brother died and you didn't say a single thing.
Strong relationships can't start on lies."

"It wasn't a *lie*." He was quickly losing his footing.

"Yeah? Well, what would you call it?" She threw her hands
up and spun around to head back toward the house. "I don't
know what to tell you, Dax," she called over her shoulder
before she turned to face him again. "Even if I didn't have to go
home in two weeks, do you honestly think that it would be easy
for me to look at you and not see what happened to my
brother?"

Her statement was like a punch to his gut. He'd worked so
hard to get through the darker parts of his past. Sarah's words
cut deeper than he had thought possible. His heart stuttered and
he couldn't come up with anything to say to her that wouldn't
sound like an excuse. There were no excuses. He'd knowingly
got in that car that night. He'd known better.

Sarah stared at him helplessly. She almost looked as sad as he felt, which triggered even more guilt.

Dax shut his eyes, focused on his breathing and told himself he didn't need a drink. He didn't need to block out everything with a bottle. When he opened his eyes, Sarah was gone. He slumped down on a nearby rock, numb and angry. He'd opened up, and this was what happened.

Karma. That's what this was. His past had a nasty habit of coming back to bite him.

27

Sarah

"I can't believe I *said* that," Sarah puffed as she scrambled up the stairs toward her room. Her ragged breaths burned her lungs and hot tears stained her cheeks. Dax hated her now. She could see it the second she'd told him she wouldn't be able to forgive him.

It had hurt more than she thought possible to tell him that. Obviously, Dax wasn't the same guy he was five years ago. He was a good man, and he had done so much to change. But she had become desperate. She needed something—anything—to help him realize that they weren't going to work.

She should just call up the sheriff and see if she could leave early. She'd put in enough hours as far as she could tell. Then she could get out of here and not have to see Dax again. The pain in her chest could be due to how fast she took off, but more likely was a reaction to the conversation they'd just had.

Sarah burst into her bedroom and slammed the door behind her. She flinched, not expecting it to make such a loud noise. That surely would draw attention from whoever might be in the house. She leaned against the door and slid to the ground.

Every nerve in her body was on fire. There had been a point when she'd believed that they might be able to make it work. But that dream had completely disappeared the second that Kenneth had shown up. She wrapped her arms around her legs.

If Dax had thought that there was anything special about her, he didn't anymore. She needed to cut her losses and head home at this point.

While Dax's confession hadn't exactly been positive, she would have been able to look past it. Sarah let out a huff, rubbing her face against her knees. It was ironic that if she had been willing to tell Dax about her family and about her participation in the string of crimes that had occurred, he might have been willing to look past it, too.

She'd almost considered telling him. But then she reminded herself that Kenneth held two issues over her head. Her family's reputation and the relationship she had with Dax. There was one thing she knew without a doubt. Dax wouldn't approve of her giving in to Kenneth. He'd try to find another way to get Kenneth off her back, and then she'd be right back where she started in trying to keep all of this from her parents and out of the news.

Dang it. This was why she had chosen to break up with him. She'd been backed into a corner, and Kenneth had known it from the start.

Sarah let the tears continue to fall until they saturated her pants. By the time she didn't have any more tears to shed, her head ached and her face was tight. The light in the room had dimmed as the sun shifted toward the horizon. Luckily no one had come to check on her. Otherwise, they would have gotten a show.

She pulled herself to stand and wandered on shaky legs toward her bed to lie down. Sarah curled up on her side and stared numbly at the closed door, her thoughts tumbling. She wasn't supposed to meet with the sheriff for a few more days, but maybe she'd ask Brielle to take her to town and discuss her options.

Time was lost as she laid there, not moving. The hole she now had in her heart wouldn't heal anytime soon, but she had no one to blame but herself.

The door opened and shut. The light flicked on. Sarah winced and Brielle gasped, her hand flying to her mouth. She peered at Sarah. "What are you doing in the dark?" She moved across the room, her eyes narrowing. "Have you been *crying*?"

Sarah let out a hiccup and covered her face. "I'm fine. Don't worry about it."

Brielle snorted. "No, you're not. Something's up. Dax—"

Sarah's eyes widened and she sat up, wincing as a sharp pain exploded behind her eyes. "Did you talk to him? It's not what you think."

Brielle's shrewd eyes locked onto Sarah, and she frowned. "No..." She settled on the bed across from Sarah. "But he did mention that you've been distant ever since that night we went to the country club. What happened with Dax today? Did he break up with you?" There was an edge in her voice as if she were ready to storm over to Dax's cabin and have a word with him.

Shaking her head, Sarah reached forward and placed a hand on Brielle's forearm. "He didn't do anything. It was me." She let out a quiet sob, and the tears began once again. "It was all me."

Brielle remained frozen, her face unreadable.

Sucking in a sharp breath, Sarah wiped at her tears. "I never thought I would feel this way about someone—" Another hiccup escaped her lips. "But I can't be with him."

"Why not?" her friend blurted. "He's crazy about you. I can see it. I think everyone does."

Sarah shook her head. "There's more to this than you realize." How much could she tell Brielle? How much did her friend know about Dax's history? It wasn't her place to tell his secrets. She clamped her mouth shut. Telling Brielle about the drinking or the accident was off the table. She couldn't do that to Dax.

That meant one thing.

She'd have to tell Brielle about Kenneth and make her promise not to say anything. Sarah swallowed hard and pressed her lips into a tight line. "This all started a few months ago."

Brielle's features pinched. "Are you talking about the community service thing?"

Sarah nodded. "The guy who shot the sheriff. I knew him."

Shock. That's all she could read in Brielle's face. She scooted closer to the edge of the bed. "Did you tell Michael?"

Another nod, but this time Sarah looked away. "I got my deal by turning him in. I used to date him." Admitting to that fact made the blood drain from her face. She shook her head as she recalled the differences between Dax and Kenneth. She'd been so blind to Kenneth's terrible habits.

She stared at her hands, clenching them and opening them again and again. "He ended up getting a sentence similar to mine."

"But he practically shot Michael!" Brielle blurted.

"I know, I don't know how he got out so soon," Sarah muttered. "But it turns out he doesn't forgive easily."

The air in the room chilled and Sarah shivered. She hadn't even told the sheriff the whole truth. Saying everything out loud right now was even harder than she'd expected it to be.

"Kenneth found me, Bri. He came here, and he watched me."

"*That's* why the sheriff asked Dax to keep an eye on you." Brielle's hushed voice was full of understanding. "Has he threatened you? Because if you tell Dax, I'm sure—"

"I'm *not* involving Dax in this."

"Why? He loves you."

"Yeah? Well, that might have changed after what I said to him tonight." Sarah let out a frustrated sigh. "Besides, he didn't threaten me, not in the way you might think. He's blackmailing me." Sarah finally glanced up to meet Brielle's confused expression. "There's a lot about me that you don't know."

"Apparently."

Sarah flinched, even though there was no malice in Brielle's tone. "My family has a lot of money, and Kenneth wants me to pay for what I did. He's threatening to tell Dax about what I did—"

"You know Dax wouldn't care, right? Dax isn't like that."

Sarah shut her eyes, a flush filling her face. That may be true, but there was no way he'd support her decision. "He also threatened to tell my parents about what happened."

"Wait, they don't *know*? What have you been telling them?" She shook her head. "Never mind. That doesn't really matter. What are you going to do? Did you tell Michael? I'm sure he could help—"

"That's just it. Even *if* the sheriff could help with this, Kenneth would just tell everyone to spite me. He's angry. I get it. I ruined his life. Think of it this way. Since his life was destroyed, mine will be too. Unless I pay him."

"He's a criminal, Sarah. You can't just give him money. He'll keep coming back for more and more until you have nothing left. You have to tell someone. Report him."

"I *can't*! Why don't you understand that? Kenneth has a rope around my neck, and I'm no better than an animal he can lead around. If he tells my parents or goes to the press, my whole family's reputation is at stake because I'm the one who takes over the family business. Sure, maybe Dax would understand and look past the mistakes I made, but there's no way he'd stand by me while I hand over money to someone else. He'd probably put himself in jail by trying to fix this himself."

The look on Brielle's face confirmed everything Sarah had just said. She had to break up with Dax not only to keep him safe from himself and from Kenneth, but to help her family. And now Brielle understood.

Together, they sat in silence, the weight of the quiet pressing down on them. Not even Brielle could come up with a solution to this predicament.

"How did you—what did Dax say—"

Sarah cringed. She knew what Brielle was trying to ask. What had happened between herself and Dax today? Were they broken up? And how did it happen?

There was no way for Sarah to tell Brielle any of it. Not AA, not the accident. She settled back onto her bed and stared at the ceiling. "I told him I'm going home and I don't love him." Her voice was flat, void of emotion. For the most part, her statement was true. Dax wouldn't dispute it. And by the time he vented to Brielle, Sarah would be long gone.

She turned her head and stared at Brielle for a long moment. "You have to promise me you won't say anything to anyone. Don't tell anyone about my family, and definitely don't talk about Kenneth. Not to Dax, not to the sheriff—no one."

Brielle frowned. "You can't be serious. You're part of the family, Sarah. We are supposed to lift up and help our family."

Sarah's heart twinged, tearing at the seams. The people here on this ranch were far more like family than the people who had raised her. She offered Brielle a weak smile. "I appreciate everything you have done for me while I've been here. But it's time for me to leave all of this behind and move on. I wasn't meant to stay longer than a few months anyway."

Her friend moved closer to her and patted her forearm. "I'm going to miss you."

"I'm going to miss you too."

"Will you come back and visit? There's no way I'm going to find a guy to marry without someone who can tell me when I'm being too picky."

Sarah snickered. "The entire time I've been here, you haven't needed my help at all."

"Exactly. I'm not any closer to finding a beau."

Sarah rolled her eyes. "You don't want one."

"So?" Brielle laughed. "You know my dad. He's not going to let Constance date until I find someone. I can't make her wait forever, can I?"

"Since when have you cared about your dad's rules? You're just trying to get me to stay."

Brielle sighed, crawling onto the bed beside Sarah and scooting close so she could share the pillow. They remained side by side, both gazing at the ceiling overhead. "Maybe I am. I've grown accustomed to having you here. You're like a sister to me." She twisted her head and offered Sarah a smile. "I think it would be fun if you were to stay."

"I'm sure it would," Sarah mumbled absently. "Do you think you could take me to town tomorrow? I need to meet with the sheriff."

"What about?"

"I'm going to see if he can get approval for me to end my community service early."

Brielle went so still that Sarah wasn't sure if she would agree. It probably didn't matter. Sarah could catch a ride with someone else if it came to it. Brielle was just her first choice.

"We could get a coffee or go to lunch."

Brielle nodded, still not saying anything.

That was all the answer Sarah needed. If everything went smoothly, she'd be on her way back to the city. She'd call her parents tomorrow as well, asking about the job they'd been holding for her when she was ready. Everything was aligning.

Just not in the way she'd wanted it to. This could very well be one of the last nights she spent at Slate Rock Ranch.

28

———

Dax

Dax stabbed the hay bale with his pitchfork and tossed the contents with a vengeance. His tongue and throat were dry and begging for just one drop of the elixir that would satiate his craving. But he refused. He wouldn't walk down that path again, not even if it meant he'd get some reprieve from his heartbreak.

His muscles pulled beneath his shirt as he tossed more hay into a stall. Sarah had been gone for almost a month. One *long* month and the pain he felt was still fresh. The path to healing would be long and arduous, but he'd done it before, and he would do it again. Sarah was just a girl.

Except she wasn't. She was the girl that he'd fallen so far in love with that there was no going back. No one would come close to making him feel the way he did when he was with Sarah. No one could have hurt him this bad.

He still couldn't believe the last thing she said to him. There was a small part of him that hoped her words had been merely a tool to push him away. But the pain was still there. *Do you honestly think that it would be easy for me to look at you and not see what happened to my brother?*

Her words still haunted him.

The rest of the day followed with more of the same. Dax kept to himself and did every chore that was required of him. He fully planned on skipping dinner, but someone mentioned Sarah and he slowed his steps as he passed the kitchen.

"I can't believe it. Do you think Dax knew?"

"I doubt it. I think we would have all heard about it if even one person knew. I just can't figure out why she was here. Do you think it was some undercover thing?"

"No way. A girl like Sarah Newton lowering herself to our lev—" The young man speaking met Dax's gaze, then dropped his focus to his plate and took a large bite of his food. The others glanced in his direction and did the same.

Dax entered the doorway and leaned against the doorjamb, his arms folded. "What about Sarah?"

They all shifted uncomfortably.

"Come on, guys. She's been gone a month. Do you really think I care if you're talking about her?"

The three young men exchanged glances with one another. The first one who'd spoken swallowed hard and pushed a newspaper toward the edge of the table. Dax pulled away from the doorway and picked up the paper. On the front page was a picture of a small family. A mother, father, and adult daughter. All were smiling, but not in a genuine way. It definitely looked like the kind of relationship she had with her family.

The title of the article read, "Billionaire Business Owners Welcome Daughter."

Billionaire.

He scanned the article, picking out bits and pieces that lined up with the things Sarah had told him. She'd finished her schooling, and she'd gotten hired by her family to run the financial firm. Part of the arrangement was a large sum of money.

His stomach roiled, churning with disgust.

Money. That's all people cared about these days. No one placed value on the hard-working man who broke his back to make ends meet. Was that why she broke it off with him? Her family wouldn't approve of their relationship?

Dax glowered, throwing the newspaper down on the table. She was just like the rich people he'd encountered before. She didn't care about people or feelings. She'd had a plan, and she'd stuck to it. He was probably just one of her playthings—a passing fancy.

Dax spun on his heel and charged out of the kitchen toward the bedroom of the one guy he knew would have some liquor. Blindly, he dug through the mess in the man's drawers until he found the small glass bottle. His fingers wrapped around the familiar shape and feel of the cool glass, and he stormed from the room.

He could already taste the hot burning sensation, his memories filling the void that had been left in his heart. The whiskey would slide down his throat and leave a trail of fire in its wake. There was only one thing he knew for certain.

He'd been more in love with Sarah than he'd realized. And she'd turned out to be just as bad as he had. She was probably with her ex-boyfriend right now, laughing at all the poor people she'd met while she was at Slate Rock Ranch. She'd managed to hide everything from him, and he'd eaten up her lies as she'd served them up to him on a silver platter.

Dax burst through the door and headed blindly as far from the house as he could get. He didn't need the others to witness his destruction. That much was clear. All he wanted was to feel numb again. He didn't want to experience the pain brewing in his heart. Maybe he could have handled a breakup on its own. But to know that she'd broken up with him not only because she thought less of him but also because of his own stupid mistakes, that was the final straw.

He pulled himself up short as he arrived at a large oak tree. His eyes dipped to the bottle in his hand, the weight of it almost grounding him. The amber liquid sloshed around in the small square casing, calling to him, begging him to return to a time when he was happy.

No, it wasn't happiness.

It was oblivion. And that was exactly where he needed to be.

With his left hand, he spun the lid from the bottle and lifted it, stopping when the glass rim was only a few inches from his lips. The familiar smell of the whisky burned his nostrils. It would be so easy to take a sip. To forget for just a few hours about the pain and the betrayal. He could do it without anyone knowing.

His hand lowered and his eyes glazed over as he continued staring at the whiskey.

He'd know. And a small part of him knew that Eve would too.

His face crumpled into an expression of pure agony, and he launched the bottle at a tree. The glass shattered, spraying the immediate surroundings with small, sharp particles and drops of alcohol.

Dax dug both hands into his hair. He'd come so close to losing everything—all the progress he'd worked so hard for— and for what? A woman? If it was any other woman, he'd have brushed it off already. Why couldn't he shake her?

He headed for the barn, whether out of habit or for the sanctuary it offered and settled down on a straw bale. A few minutes later, a shadow crossed the doorway and he glanced up to find Brielle headed toward her horse's stall. She didn't seem to notice him. Good. He wasn't really in the mood to talk to anyone.

She would inevitably bring up Sarah and that was the last thing he wanted to discuss. He remained hunched over, staring at the straw beneath his boots.

It was funny the way he couldn't get past this dismal feeling. When he and Brielle had called it quits, it had been easy to shake off. That was who Brielle was. She never dated anyone for long. That probably had more to do with her father and the rules of their household than anything else.

Although she did get the freedom to date after Adeline got married, it didn't do anything to change her outlook. She still seemed content to live her life the same way.

Dax glanced up again, expecting to find her pulling her horse out of its stall. A yelp escaped his throat and he fell backward into the stack of straw bales behind him. He glowered up at Brielle, who stood over him with her hands on her hips and a smirk on her lips.

"What are you doing? Aren't you supposed to be working or something?"

Stuck in his position, Dax continued staring at her. "Aren't you supposed to be contributing to your family's ranch?"

Her smug smile fell from her face. "I do plenty, and you know it."

He grunted, turning over on his side and scrambling to his feet. Focusing on the straw that clung to his pants, he shook his head. "I'm not really in the mood to fight today, Brielle."

"You started it. What's your problem anyway?"

Dax shot her a sharp look. "You know well enough what my problem is."

She let out a sigh. "It's been almost a month. You can't mope around forever."

He pushed past her. "I said I'm not going to talk about this." He'd nearly drank. He needed to ground himself.

"No. You said you weren't going to fight with me. So don't

fight." Brielle hurried after him, tugging at his arm when he refused to slow down. "Come on, Dax. You can talk to me."

He jerked his arm out of her grasp and shook his head. No, he needed to talk to people who understood him.

She continued pursuing him as he strode toward his truck. There was one thing she was right about. He couldn't keep moping around here. If he did, he'd end up digging out some of the whiskey he knew one of the ranch hands had hidden under the sink in their shared cabin. The temptation had continued to grow stronger, reminding him that he hadn't been to an AA meeting since Sarah had left.

It wasn't wise. He knew it. But he also knew he wouldn't be able to stand in front of the group of his friends and express the heartache he currently felt. He'd been so full of hope the last time he'd attended a meeting.

Dax yanked out his keys, and Brielle jumped in front of him. "Where are you going?"

"It doesn't matter."

"Yes, it does." She peered at him, her eyes shining with concern. "I'm worried about you."

He let out a heavy sigh and his hand dropped to his side. "I'm going to be fine." That wasn't true. Each day that passed, he continued to break apart piece by piece. It wasn't normal. The feelings he was experiencing right now didn't make sense when he'd only known Sarah for a few months.

But they were there, nevertheless.

Brielle refused to move out of his way. She folded her arms and her jaw set tightly. "I'm not letting you go alone. You're not in the right headspace."

She was right again. Dang it.

He frowned. If he let her come with him, he'd have to tell her something he'd managed to avoid all these years. Telling Sarah had turned out disastrous. He couldn't be sure how Brielle would react. He'd like to think their relationship was strong enough that they would survive his confession.

The only way he'd figure it out was if he just told her. Dax expelled another frustrated sigh and raked his hand through his hair. "Fine. Get in."

Her brows shot up and she scurried around the front of the truck to get into the passenger's side.

Dax was either going to regret this or it might just be the thing to help him get out of his funk. Once upon a time, he and Brielle had been close—well, close enough to share some more intimate moments.

He pulled open the door and sat behind the wheel for a few minutes before he finally started the truck and pulled out onto the road. Every explanation he could come up with didn't sound quite right. There was no excuse for the choices he'd made before.

Sarah had done a real number on him. He didn't trust himself anymore. All the work he'd done on himself suddenly didn't feel like it was enough. He wasn't enough for her.

His heart twinged, a sharp pain slicing through his whole soul. It was almost like he couldn't breathe without great effort. Dax glanced at her out of the corner of his eye. "I'm going to a meeting."

She shifted in her seat, her hands clasped tightly in her lap. There was no reaction. Where was her blatant judgment? Maybe she didn't realize what he meant by *meeting*.

He swallowed hard and tried again. "I'm in AA. That's where I'm going."

Still nothing.

He let out a groan. "What?"

"I didn't say anything. I'm glad you're going."

Dax's hands tightened on the steering wheel and he tore off

of the road and onto the shoulder. Shoving the truck into park, he turned on her. "You *knew*?"

"*No*. I mean, I guess I had my suspicions. You were always a wild one when we were teenagers. And you cleaned yourself up a few years back. I guess now that you said it out loud, it makes a lot of sense." She said it with such a matter-of-fact tone that he didn't know how to respond.

All this time he thought he'd been keeping a secret from her that wasn't really a secret. And there was zero judgment on her face—nothing in her tone of voice that suggested she was unhappy with his confession.

Dax blinked back the emotion that he'd been holding back. A weight of sorts had been lifted from his shoulders. There was someone who he cared about who was willing to accept him as he was, and the concept was freeing.

Brielle gestured toward the road. "Well, are you going to get going? I'm assuming these meetings happen at regularly sched-uled intervals. You probably shouldn't be late."

MOONLIGHT SHONE through the front window of his truck as he sat beside Brielle in the dark. He felt naked and alone in front of her. While it had been nice knowing that she wouldn't judge him, there wasn't much left for him to hide.

He glanced at her, then dragged his attention to his hands. "Thank you for coming with me."

"Of course."

"I've not been very stable lately."

She snorted but didn't say anything.

Dax continued. "I found out something about Sarah today that I was pretty upset about."

Brielle's eyes narrowed. "You did?"

He nodded, rubbing the back of his neck. "You're never going to believe this, but she's rich." Dax had expected her to show at least some kind of surprise. But she didn't. He scowled. "Did you know *that* too?"

She lifted a shoulder. "Sarah said a few things to me before she left, and I promised not to say anything. But it's bound to get out. People around here recognized her in that article."

Just her mentioning the article made his stomach swirl unpleasantly. "I can't believe that she tricked me."

"What are you talking about? Sarah didn't trick anyone."

He glowered and faced forward once more. "She moved home for the money, Bri. If you read that article, you would see as clear as day the reason she left. If she didn't pity us, she was definitely embarrassed by us. How much do you want to bet that she would pretend not to know us if we were to ever cross paths again?"

"Take that back. If you really think that's how Sarah is, then you didn't know her nearly as well as you thought you did."

Brielle's words were a slap in his face. He gaped at her, unsure of where to go next with this conversation.

She pulled one leg up onto the truck seat and turned to face him fully. "Sarah was a sweetheart who made a few bad decisions and fell for the wrong guy."

His mouth dropped open. "I didn't think I was *that* bad."

"Not you, dummy. Kenneth."

"Kenneth? Who in heaven's name is Kenneth?"

"The jerk who's blackmailing her." Brielle slapped her hand over her mouth and shook her head.

"Blackmail?" He peered at Brielle and leaned toward her. "What are you talking about?"

Brielle shook her head again. "I wasn't supposed to say anything. She made me promise."

He scowled at her and his voice lowered to a more sinister

tone. "You're going to tell me everything you know." Dax had zero leverage. That was the worst of it. Brielle could tell him where to shove it and he'd have to accept it.

Only, he was counting on their past relationship to help him get through this moment. "I need to know, Bri. It's important."

She gnawed on her lower lip, her gaze darting around the truck before finally landing on his face again. "Fine. But you have to promise me this stays between us."

"I can't do that."

"Dax!"

He held up his hands. "If she's being blackmailed, I need to help her." It didn't matter that she'd broken his heart. In all likelihood, she had meant every word she'd said to him the last time they were together. But that didn't change the way his heart went out to her. No matter what she did, Dax was still in love with her.

Their conversation lasted for about an hour as Brielle went over every detail, lie, and truth that Sarah had told him while she'd been visiting—at least everything that Sarah had confessed to Brielle.

Sarah wasn't related to the sheriff. She'd been involved in something criminal with Kenneth and had gotten caught. Her community service included every little chore she did for the Callahans.

Kenneth wanted money, and Sarah believed Kenneth would walk away once he got it.

Fat chance. Guys like that were never happy with the first payment. Dax could almost guarantee that Kenneth would be around again, holding out his filthy paws for more. And if Sarah had told him, he would have reminded her as such. But it was too late now.

Or was it?

29

Sarah

Sarah hated her desk. She hated her job. And she hated the palpable smog that hung in the air. Okay, so that was an exaggeration. But after spending a little over three months in the country, she could taste a difference in the air. And it wasn't pleasant.

She stared out the window of her corner office down at the people in the courtyard. She used to think that being so high up in a building was the most magical place a person could be. But she'd been wrong.

The exhilaration of riding a horse, the sense of kinship as she shared the property with the Callahans, and even her relationship with Dax had been the best part of her entire life.

Too bad things like that were only rooted in fairy tales.

It hadn't taken long for the bitterness and hopelessness to creep in once returning home. Being stuck in her office and seeing her parents every single day tended to do that. She'd enjoyed her freedom at college—perhaps too much. She'd enjoyed her time at Slate Rock Ranch more, which was ironic seeing as it was a sentence.

Sarah let out a sigh and took a seat at her desk. Her lawyer would arrive soon with the NDA for Kenneth. She didn't care that doing so was just as ridiculous as expecting him to be happy with the money she was about to transfer into an account for him. If it meant preventing Kenneth from hurting her family's reputation, then she'd do just about anything.

Besides, her time at the firm wasn't going to be forever. Even if she couldn't be with Dax, she fully intended on walking away from this place and the misery it gave her. She'd take her money and get a small property outside of the city limits. Maybe get a horse or two.

A smile touched her lips at the thought of being closer in proximity to Dax, then immediately it fell from her face. He wouldn't forgive her. Not after the way she left things. He already had a hard time with trust, and she'd hurt him deeply.

It had taken all of her mental strength not to find him the day she left and tell him she was sorry. There had been truth in her words—a sense of unease surrounding his past alcoholism. But it hadn't been enough to break up over.

That was all Kenneth.

She let out a frustrated sigh. Maybe this was karma. She was being punished for everything she'd done since starting college. She might as well get used to this lonely feeling because there was no one she'd rather be with than Dax.

A light knock sounded at the door and she lifted her head to find her secretary peering into her office. "Your lawyer is here."

Sarah nodded and rose from her desk. "Send him in."

Her secretary held open the door and stepped aside, allowing Mr. Goldblum into the room. The man looked more tired and harried than he'd been when this whole fiasco started.

He'd been the only one out of her family's herd of lawyers that she knew she could trust to keep her affairs private. And he'd followed her requests perfectly.

His grim expression only hinted at the irritation she knew both of them felt regarding this topic. Mr. Goldblum held out a file he had in his hands. "I don't understand why you're even bothering with this. That boy will keep the secret only if it's in his best interest. What are you going to do if he demands more money?"

"I won't give it to him." She accepted the folder and flipped it open.

"If his purpose is to hurt you and he doesn't care about the money, then none of this does you any good."

Her gaze cut to his. "I don't expect you to understand why it is I'm doing what I'm doing."

His weathered hand rested gently on the folder, blocking her from reading it. "Are you sure about this? You don't have to give him a dime. I've got a gal who is amazing at PR. She'd be able to keep most of this out of the limelight. It would just take one call."

The offer he made was more tantalizing than she cared to admit. Maybe she'd made her decision too quickly. There might be other ways to solve this. She hesitated, closing the file and moving back to her seat at the desk. There was one thing Mr. Goldblum didn't seem to consider, however. Her parents could disown her over something like this. She'd seen them do far worse for far less.

She tapped her finger against her lips. If she told her parents before Kenneth could, that wouldn't take away all of his power. The media would have a heyday if they found out what Sarah had been up to over the summer. Heaven forbid her parents' sterling reputation get tarnished.

No. Her decision was made, and she had some plans up her

sleeve that might make all of this more bearable. The offshore accounts had stipulations. Kenneth wasn't getting everything he wanted exactly the way he'd requested, and he'd risk a whole lot of money if he didn't agree to certain terms.

It was risky, weighing his greed over his ego. If Kenneth's thirst for revenge was greater, then none of this mattered anyway and her secret would be out.

Sarah shook her head. "I think this is the best way."

He crossed the room, an urgency in his voice she hadn't ever heard before. "Kenneth is a criminal, Sarah."

"Technically, I am too."

Mr. Goldblum shook his head. "No, you were in the wrong place at the wrong time. You were influenced—"

"May I remind you that some of what happened was my fault? I chose to start this whole mess."

"True, but you had a change of heart. You grew. If you were to go back, you would have done things differently. I'm not so sure about Kenneth."

But if she had the chance to change her past, she wouldn't have met Dax, nor found out just how much she loved being on a ranch. In a way, she had Kenneth to thank for her current outlook.

"Don't let that boy take anything else from you." He offered her a strained smile. "If you were my daughter, I'd want you to stand up for yourself, no matter the consequences. I think your parents would agree." He straightened and strode across the room to take a seat on a couch. "I've got some paperwork to finish while we wait for him to show up. I suggest you think about what you really want."

What she really wanted.

That was easy. Now, getting it was the hard part.

He pulled out a few more files from a briefcase he'd brought with him and got to work. He'd made several good points. As much as she assumed what her parents would do in this situation, she couldn't be one hundred percent sure. For all she knew, they'd be angrier with Kenneth and do whatever it took to completely destroy him.

Once again, doubts over whether or not she'd jumped the gun on this one accosted her. She glanced at her lawyer and frowned. "You know my parents. What do you think they would do if they found out what happened over the summer?"

He lifted his gaze and met her eyes. "I think you underestimate your folks. They want the best for you. And sometimes that comes across differently to you."

She tightened her jaw. There were very few memories where she recalled feeling loved and appreciated by her parents. But if Mr. Goldblum was right, then they wouldn't do much besides scold her for a mistake made and help with damage control.

Sarah had already lost Dax. If they kicked her out, it wasn't like she'd be able to go crawling back to him. Though she might be able to convince Brielle's father to hire her until she could get on her feet.

The possibilities were starting to sound even better with each passing moment. Sarah lifted the document once more, then turned and pushed it through the shredder.

She wasn't sure, but she thought she caught a hint of a smile on Mr. Goldblum's face. "Do you think you could call that PR lady for me? Make an appointment as soon as we're done with Kenneth?"

He already had his phone in his hand and was set to dial. "Of course, ma'am."

She grimaced. "How many times have I asked you not to call me that. It's Sarah."

This time he did smile, and she met his with one of her own. Even if it was for a few minutes, the relief was refreshing and allowed her to clear her head.

Sarah needed to speak to her parents first. Then she'd give Brielle a call. Repairing things with Dax would come later.

"What do you mean you're not giving me the money?" Kenneth's words came out in sharp puffs and his chest lifted and fell with each angry breath. His hands were clenched, and if she hadn't planned on this meeting in a public place, she might have been scared he would hurt her.

The park wasn't full by any means, but at least every few minutes a jogger or a businessman would pass by.

Every ounce of her focus was needed to remain calm. "I don't care if you slander me. As you know, my parents can handle any ding to their reputation. I was the one who made the mistake, and it wasn't me who pulled the trigger. I served my time." It was harder than she thought to speak the words out loud, but at the same time they seemed to free her.

"So it's gonna be like that then. What about your cowboy?" he sneered. "I can go tell him how you're nothing like the perfect princess you made him believe."

Her heart tore a little more. "While he doesn't know the whole truth, that relationship was destroyed the second you pushed my back against the wall. I had to break up with him, and there's no way he's going to want me back. You burned your own bridge with that one." She was bluffing. Kenneth could very well track Dax down and tell him all the sordid details. What was the worst that would happen? Dax would just know the full truth and still not want her. It hurt, but she needed to stop caring so much about what other people thought of her. People who loved her wouldn't care about that sort of stuff.

Brielle didn't care. And soon she'd find out if her parents would do exactly what she thought they would.

Kenneth's face turned beet-red. "I'm going to drag your name so far through the mud that you're going to wish you reconsidered. I know people too. People who wouldn't mind fudging the truth. Everyone is going to think you're the one who brought the gun. I might even see if I can make them believe you shot the cop."

She clutched her hands tightly in her lap and stared up at him. Her calm exterior was nothing like the inner turmoil she felt. "I'm not going to let you control me, Kenneth."

He let out a derisive laugh. "Where did this side of you come from? I'm not trying to control you. I'm getting what I deserve when you stole part of my life from me."

Sarah shot out of her seat and glowered at him, her voice tight as she hissed, "You made your own choices. When you make mistakes, you own up to them and grow from the experience." Just like Dax had.

He didn't blame anyone for the choices he'd made. Dax moved forward and bettered himself. He was the kind of guy she wanted to be with. And she'd ruined it.

Sarah leaned closer to him and whispered, "Do what you want, but you won't get very far. I'm on my way to have dinner with my parents and tell them everything. I'd like to see you get any kind of satisfaction out of messing with me when you don't have any leverage."

When she pulled back, she wasn't surprised to find a deep scowl on his face. If only she'd come to this conclusion sooner—back when he was toying with her in Copper Creek. If only she'd seen the value in being upfront about this with her parents in the first place.

It was just going to be one more mistake that she'd have to learn from.

Sarah fidgeted with her napkin as she sat across the table from her parents. They were still dressed in their work clothes, but then she hadn't expected anything less. They'd always been workaholics. And they'd expected the same from her. That wasn't something she ever wanted, even less now.

They put down their menus, and her mother gave her a strange look. "Why do you look so upset? Is it the article? I told you I didn't have any say in that getting printed."

That was a lie. Her mother had the newspaper editor in her back pocket. One word from her and the article wouldn't have been printed. This was one of the many things her mother did. Little lies. At least Sarah could brush it off as some sort of motherly pride. Her mother had been thrilled when she'd called her after leaving Copper Creek.

Sarah reached for a glass of ice water and took a small sip. "It's not the article. Though you might want to contact the newspapers and get ahead of something."

Her mother's shrewd eyes narrowed, and she pushed the menu aside. Her father's glance bounced between them, but he didn't say anything. "What happened?" As if by the touch of a button, her mother's voice dropped to a flat, emotionless tone.

"It's all been handled. I took care of it. But there's someone who doesn't like me very much—someone from college—he wants to hurt my reputation."

Sarah's parents exchanged glances. "Someone from college? Does this have anything to do with Kenneth?"

She stiffened in her seat and her eyes widened. Kenneth had introduced himself to her parents. She'd completely forgotten. They hadn't mentioned him, so she had no idea what their impression of him was. She nodded. "Kenneth is someone I went on a few dates with, and something happened."

Sarah watched as her parents' eyes met once more. Her

mother nodded and adjusted in her seat. Then her father spoke. "We had a background check run on that young man."

Sarah sucked in a breath. There was no way they didn't know about him and everything he'd been charged with. So why wouldn't they bring it up? Why not tell her that she needed to have better taste in men? Or tell her they never wanted to see him again. She waited on the edge of her seat for them to tell her exactly what they thought of the guy who, not even two hours ago, had attempted to collect on the blackmail he'd demanded over the course of the summer.

Her father continued. "That young man is not to step foot in our home. He's bad news, Sarah."

So they knew. But they didn't know about her own indiscretions. Rats. That meant this wasn't going to be as easy as she'd hoped.

"I'm not dating him. I don't even like him," she muttered. "He was a fling. That was all."

Her parents smiled, though per usual, their grins didn't reach their eyes. The masks they wore were the ones they shared with the public.

"There's more," Sarah added. "Kenneth—we—we were both involved in some stuff several months ago when spring semester ended."

And just like that the air around the table grew colder. Sarah avoided looking directly at her parents. "I didn't actually do anything that caused damages, but I drove the car."

She'd expected her mother to gasp and say her name in that disappointed voice, but there was an eerie silence all around their table.

Sarah glanced up, finding disappointment on their faces. She took a deep breath and let it out through pursed lips. "I made a plea bargain with the arresting officers. I turned Kenneth in, and they offered community service in lieu of something more—serious."

"I don't understand. Why weren't we informed? You're our daughter—" her mother's strangled voice burst through the cold like the sun through stormy clouds.

"I'm an adult. I handled it. I didn't want you involved so I called Mr. Goldblum—"

"Mr. Goldblum knew?" Her mother whirled to face her father, who had remained oddly quiet. "Did you know about this?"

Sarah gaped when her father gave a small nod. He'd known, and he hadn't said anything.

"What?" her mother let out a whispered shriek. "We could have helped her. I'm sure we could have gotten less than community service in some rancher town. You just stood by and—"

"She didn't want our help, Loraine. Goldblum was very clear when he called me that Sarah wanted to handle this all on her own." He turned a small smile that almost hinted at an underlying sense of pride toward Sarah. "And she did. She served her time. She probably picked up some decent skills. And in the end, she told us. I'd say she matured a great deal."

"Howard! You can't be serious."

He reached for her hand and held it firmly. "She's a grown woman. She's bound to make mistakes, and she's going to have to learn from them. It's time we step back and let that happen."

Her mother's face almost matched the red shade of her lipstick. "*Well*," she snapped, "I think we need to revisit the trust we gave her access to. If she's willing to lie and hide everything—"

"*Loraine*." His voice was firm and gentle at the same time. "Sarah has earned every penny of her trust."

Sarah watched the argument unfold, her focus bouncing

from one parent to the next. This was completely unexpected. Her father had always been the quieter one, always agreeing with her mother. But she had no idea he was the more logical one.

Her mother continued blustering, "That money was meant to be—"

"Given to her when she matured and showed she could handle the responsibility. And I think we both know that has happened." He glanced at Sarah once more, then turned to his wife. "There are going to be times we don't agree with what she wants to do with that money, but it's hers now. She has to learn how to be responsible with it, just like she was responsible with the mistakes she made in college."

Sarah's mouth fell open. This couldn't be happening. Her mother was actually calming down as if the fire that consumed her was being doused by her father's words. Loraine glanced at Sarah and then her husband. Finally, she settled back in her seat and let out a sigh.

"It appears I have been outvoted." But instead of the sad disappointment Sarah expected to find etched on her mother's face, all she saw was wry acceptance.

Their eyes met and Loraine tipped her head slightly. "I assume with this freedom you'll want to run away somewhere and do something else."

Sarah froze. "What?"

"Oh, honey. We all know you've never been interested in following in our footsteps. I had always hoped that you'd take the classes and eventually find a joy in it like your father and I have. But it's clear that you're miserable. Your heart isn't in it."

Sarah's eyes cut to her father. He shrugged and pretended to examine the drink menu.

"So what is it then? Are you going to travel the world? Paris? Maybe backpack through Europe? While I don't approve of something like that, I hope you will be smart with your money and not waste it like some kids do these days."

Her eyes rounded and she seemed to lose the ability to speak. Was this actually happening? Was her mother actually letting her make her own decisions when it came to the money they'd given her? This wasn't real. It couldn't be.

Loraine reached across the table and grasped Sarah's hand. "Of course, you will always have a place at the firm. Even though you don't love it, you have a knack for it, and I'd hate to see that talent wasted."

Sarah blinked. "A ranch," she blurted.

Her parents set wide eyes on her.

She swallowed hard and nodded. "I want to buy a ranch. I want to train horses."

Her mother glanced at her father before setting a look that could only be described as condescension. "Dear, do you even know—"

"I worked on a ranch all summer. I'm sure I could get some help from the people I worked with. I just need some land and a barn and—"

"I think it's a wonderful idea," her father murmured.

"*Howard.*"

"What? Did you *see* the way her face lit up just now? It's what she wants. Let her do it." Her father winked at her, and chills washed over her. This was really happening. And she had her parents' blessing.

There was only one thing that could make this better, and seeing as she was more likely to see a pig fly than that, she'd have to settle with this.

30

———————

Dax

*D*ax lifted his phone to his ear as he stared at what could only be described as a mansion. The house could probably fit two or three of the Callahan's house inside it, and that was saying something considering Zeke raised seven girls.

"Are you sure you gave me the right address?"

"I'm positive." Brielle sighed. "That's the address she gave me when I told her I wanted to come visit. Why? Is something wrong?"

"It's just—huge."

"What don't you get about the fact that her parents are billionaires? Come on, Dax. It isn't brain surgery."

He peered through the gate of the house, suddenly very intimidated. This was the kind of home he had stood outside of as a teen and wished he could be part of. On several occasions, he'd been tempted to egg houses like these or break in and steal whatever he could get his hands on.

He'd come a long way since then.

His chest tightened. Neither he nor Brielle had told Sarah that he was coming to visit her. Brielle said Sarah sounded sad the last time they spoke. If she wasn't in a good headspace, then maybe she wouldn't even want to see him.

"Hello? Are you still there? Look, I'm busy tonight, so I'm going to have to hang up. If you run into any problems—"

"Call anyone but you, I know."

"Bingo." Brielle hung up the phone without so much as a goodbye, leaving Dax in the quiet of his truck at the front gate of the property.

He leaned out his window and pressed the button on the intercom. A sharp buzzing sound filled the air and then the intercom crackled.

"Name."

"Um. You want my name?"

"Name," the faceless voice repeated.

"Dax. Dax Heaton."

"Is someone at this residence expecting you?"

He scratched his chin and stared at the house again. "Not exactly, no."

"I'm sorry. I can't let you in."

Dax spun in his seat and placed his hand on the open window of his truck. "You have to let me in. I have to speak with Sarah. She's—we're—please. I just have to see her."

"Miss Newton is unavailable."

"That's a lie, and you know it." His voice seethed with desperate frustration. "She'll want to see me. Just tell her that Dax is here. You'll see."

"I'm sorry, sir. Call and make an appointment." The disembodied voice crackled and disappeared.

Dax pressed the button again and again, but they didn't respond. He let out a groan and stared at the house. He didn't drive several days to turn around and go back home. He wasn't going to leave until he could speak to her and find out exactly what happened.

He pulled out of their driveway and down the street a little way until his focus landed on a tree that grew just outside the property fence. He might be able to climb it and land on the other side. Then she'd have to speak to him.

Dax found a place to park and did just that. His fingers were bruised and his knee banged up against the trunk a little too hard, but he finally managed to get over the fence and make it into the property.

He ran toward the front of the house and hurried up the steps. If he'd known what room was hers, he probably would have just tried getting her attention there, but there were far too many windows and there was no telling if she was even in her room.

Dax pounded his fist on the door and stepped back, waiting for it to open. When no one came right away, he lifted his hand again only to have the door swing inward, revealing a tall, slender man in a suit.

The man's eyes narrowed. "Mr. Heaton, I presume."

"Darn straight. I'm here to see Sarah." He stood on his toes to peer around who he could only assume was her father. "She will want to see me." That was a bold-faced lie, but he wasn't going anywhere until he had a word with the woman he loved.

"Miss Newton is unavailable. I'm going to have to ask you to leave the premises."

"Sarah!" he called. "I'm not leaving until I speak to her."

"Like I said, she is unavailable."

"I don't believe you. You know? I heard about you. She said her parents were controlling, but I never thought they'd prevent her from seeing a visitor. Why not? Is it this?" He grabbed his cowboy hat from his head and threw it on the ground. "Or these?" He lifted his boots. "Am I too dirty or do I work too hard?"

The man's features remained smooth as Dax made a fool of himself. "Sir, you have me mistaken for someone else. Miss Newton is out to dinner with her parents."

His fury evaporated faster than spit on a hot summer sidewalk. Heat crawled up the back of his neck. "Oh."

The man's gaze shifted to a spot behind Dax. "Again. I'm going to have to ask you to—"

"Dax?"

He whirled around to find Sarah standing with two people who were definitely her parents. Behind them was a limousine. How on earth had they managed to arrive without him noticing?

Shoot. Had they seen his little tantrum?

Sarah moved forward a few steps. "Dax, what are you doing here?"

Just seeing her, the way her brown wavy hair framed her face, the way her makeup was done just right, made his heart soar. She almost didn't look like the Sarah he knew. There wasn't a smudge of dirt across her cheek. Gone were the cowboy hat, jeans, and boots. In their place was a blouse and black pencil skirt that came to her knees. She wore a pair of black stiletto heels which made her almost as tall as he was.

She was beautiful.

"Dax?" she repeated as she shot a quick look at her parents.

He scooped up his hat and held it with both of his hands. "I —um—came to see you."

Sarah closed the distance between them. "You should have called."

"I couldn't risk it."

She hugged herself, standing awkwardly in front of him. "Maybe we should take a walk."

He glanced from the man at the door to her parents and nodded. "My apologies." The guy he assumed was her father bit back a smile, but her mother's dark gaze was enough to make his insides go cold.

They walked side by side as they headed around the house along a sidewalk that led through an ornate garden. Flowers, trees, and shrubs grew in perfect harmony, filling the air with a variety of scents.

The yard was large enough it could have been a public park. Lights set the garden aglow, showcasing the property in a way that would have landed this whole scene in a painting. "I can't believe you grew up here," he murmured.

She didn't meet his gaze. "It's not as great as you might think."

"Right."

She'd mentioned as much when they'd shared about their childhoods.

"I guess it's true what they say. The grass is always greener on the other side."

Sarah peeked at him. "I guess so."

They wandered for a few minutes, and all he could think about was how much he wanted to tell her he wanted her back. None of what happened mattered, not if they could overcome it together.

There was just the issue of whether she had spoken the truth about how she felt regarding his alcoholism. Dax stretched out his hand and tightened it into a fist a few times, itching to take hers and lace his fingers with it.

One month apart and now he didn't know how to act around her. He just needed to say something, *anything*. That's why he'd come all this way.

Dax stopped and turned to face her. "I think it's clear why I'm here, but I'm going to say it anyway."

"Dax—"

"I want you to know that it doesn't matter. None of it. None of this. We could have communicated with each other better—right before you left. We could have showed more love for each other. And I want to promise you right now that I intend on doing just that."

She stared at him, unreadable. Dang it, how he wished he could read her mind right now.

The silence was unbearable and he continued to ramble. "I want you, no matter what happened, no matter what your background is. I still think you're the most amazing woman I have ever met. You make me want to be a better man. I never thought I'd be able to find this kind of love, Sarah." His voice grew hoarse. "I can't fall in love without you." He searched her gaze. "Please just say something."

Sarah closed the distance between them and threw her arms around him, burying her face in his neck. Her body shook, and he slowly brought his arms around her to hold her tight. Dax held her like that, letting her use him for whatever comfort she'd been denied for so long.

When her tears stopped and she pulled back, he framed her face with his large hands and brushed at her tears with his thumbs. "What's the matter?"

She let out a watery laugh. "Nothing."

"Then why are you crying?"

Sarah pressed her lips together, turning her face so she could kiss his palm. Chills swept through his body as he waited for her to answer. "No one has ever accepted me for who I am without some kind of demand or pointing out my flaws. No one but you." She closed her eyes briefly. "I'm so sorry for what I said—how I acted when I left. I want you to know that I didn't mean any of it.

You are more of a man than anyone I know. I love you, Dax." She gave him a soft smile. "I didn't think it was possible to find someone who could love me so unconditionally, but I guess I did."

"Oh," he whispered, "there's nothing that could stop me from loving you."

He pressed a soft, firm kiss to her lips and the familiar fire that had been missing since she left returned with a vengeance. It started in his stomach and grew into his chest, warming his whole body.

Being in Sarah's arms was heaven. She was his other half, from their estranged upbringings to the mistakes they shared. If there was such a thing as a soul mate, she would be it. He slipped his free arm around her waist and pulled her closer. Her hands slipped into his hair, knocking his hat to the ground.

A sense of peace filtered through the heat raging within the two of them. A sense of rightness that couldn't be shaken. She was his light, and if they were able to overcome this, then nothing would be able to stand in their way.

He pulled back and tucked a strand of hair behind her ear. "So what do we do now? I mean, I guess I could get used to seeing you dressed like this." Dax lifted his brows suggestively.

She laughed and shoved his shoulder with her fingertips. "I have a better idea."

31

———————

Sarah

Sarah squealed as Dax led Cricket from the back of a trailer and hurried toward them. "I can't believe you were able to get her back! How much did they want for her?"

Dax grinned at her. "I called in a favor. Shane is willing to let you keep training her and keep her, but he wants to be able to use her in sessions if he needs an extra horse."

Her eyes widened. "Really?"

"Really. She's all yours. You've earned her."

Sarah leaned against Cricket, rubbing her up and down her neck and back. The horse was the most beautiful thing she owned—and she'd have the perfect place for her to live. Later today she would close on the property for the small ranch she had purchased. It would be a few months before they could break ground for the house and the barn, but it was all planned out. Everything was finally coming together.

She was happy. And rightfully so.

Her eyes met Dax's, and they shared a quiet moment as if he knew exactly what she was thinking. This was how it had been for the last couple of weeks. They continued to grow closer and share more about themselves. Falling in love with him was easy.

"Oh. You got your horse back."

Sarah turned to find Brielle and her younger sister Constance heading their way. "Yep. Dax pulled some strings."

Brielle glanced at Dax with a smile. "He has a tendency to do that."

"What are you guys up to?"

"Connie's horse is pregnant and the vet is stopping by. The stubborn girl hates being moved, but she's probably close to giving birth and we need her in an open space."

Sarah turned to Constance. "That's exciting. I've never seen a birth before."

Constance grimaced. "It's not as great as you think it is." She got elbowed by Brielle.

"You only say that because the last one you saw went badly."

Constance's features darkened. "If your first birth ended in the baby dying, you wouldn't be so excited either."

Sarah's eyes widened. "It died?"

Constance nodded, pushing her hands into her pockets. "I think it wasn't very healthy to begin with. That coupled with a rough birth and the poor thing just wasn't strong enough to survive."

"That's terrible!" Sarah's eyes darted from each person in their group. "Does it happen often?"

"Not since Dr. Pratt came back from college. He's got to be one of the top veterinarians in the country." Constance smiled. "He's cute, too."

Brielle rolled her eyes. "He's a little stuck up. And he's got a bit of a God complex if you ask me."

Constance sighed. "You don't even know him."

"I know that we're probably just as good at birthing horses as he is. Just because he went to school doesn't mean he knows more than us."

Constance snickered. "I don't think you quite understand how going to school works."

Brielle huffed but didn't offer a retort.

A white truck pulled up onto the property and they all turned toward it. A young man emerged from the Ford and waved to them. His dark hair and bronze skin were the only distinguishing features Sarah could see from this distance. Constance shifted, her voice lowering. "I told you he was cute."

She hurried toward the truck, leaving Brielle with Sarah and Dax.

"I'm with Bri. I don't see anything special about him." Dax's contribution to the conversation caused the girls to laugh.

"See? Dax gets it." Brielle folded her arms, watching as the vet and Constance headed for the barn. "Anyone who thinks they're better than someone else just because they can put the word doctor in front of their name needs to be put in their place."

"What happened, Bri? Did you and the doctor date or something?" Sarah asked.

Dax laughed. "You have no idea—" He grunted when Brielle's elbow lodged into his stomach. His coughs almost covered up Sarah's next question.

"You dated him?"

"I may have gone on a few dates with the guy."

"Try dated him for a couple weeks."

Sarah turned wide eyes to where Constance and Dr. Pratt disappeared in the shadow of the barn. "Does Connie know?"

Brielle snorted. "Why would that matter?"

"She obviously has a huge crush on him."

Brielle stiffened. "What? No, she doesn't. She would have said something."

"She did just say he was cute," Dax offered, garnering a dark look from Brielle. He flinched, holding up his hands.

"Aren't you supposed to be the next one to get married?" Sarah lowered her voice so no one would overhear. "What are you going to do?"

A snort escaped Brielle again. "Me? Nothing. I don't have to do a dang thing. If Constance wants to fall in love, that's on her."

"But your dad—" Sarah started.

"My dad is stuck in the stone age. He's going to have to admit that his daughters are all growing up and we are allowed to fall in love." Brielle threw her hands down at her sides and stormed off without another word.

Sarah turned a concerned gaze on Dax. "What do you think that is about?"

He put his arm around her and pulled her close, pressing a kiss to her temple as they watched Brielle storm off. "I think it might have something to do with the fact that she doesn't want anything to do with getting married, but she knows she's going to have to do something or her sisters are going to struggle."

"She's right, you know." Sarah leaned against him. "Zeke is going to have to come to terms with his daughters growing up. My mom had to. If Constance wants to date the doctor, then no one can stop her. I don't see Zeke being the kind of father to kick her to the curb."

"No, I don't suppose he would. But I'd bet that Brielle is going to need our support. If Constance and Dr. Pratt start seeing each other, she's going to feel a lot more pressure."

"Brielle isn't going to settle for someone she's not head-over-heels in love with. And she's not the type to be bullied into anything."

He chuckled. "You're right about that." He turned to face her. "Now, what do you say we take Cricket for a ride? I think the two of you need to get reacquainted, especially if you're going to get good enough to open your own horse training program."

Warmth spread all throughout her whole body and she beamed at him. "You mean if *we* are going to open up *our* own horse training program."

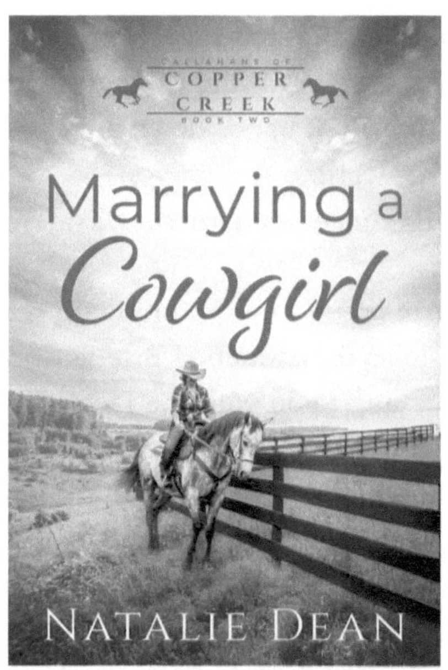

HELLO READER,

If you loved spending time with the Sarah and Dax, you won't want to miss what's next with the Callahans...

Constance has been hopelessly in love with one man for as long as she can remember—Copper Creek's charming veterinarian, James Pratt. Now that he's finally back in town, she's ready to take her shot.

But her old-fashioned father has other plans... and James knows better than to cross him.

When secrets and family rules stand in the way of her happiness, will Constance find the courage to follow her heart?

Look for *Marrying a Cowboy, Callahans of Copper Creek Book 2* —available at nataliedeanbooks.com and other retailers.

ABOUT THE AUTHOR

Born and raised in a small coastal town in the south, I was raised to treasure family and love the Lord. I'm a dedicated home-schooling mom who loves to travel and spend time with my growing-up-too-fast son.

When I'm not busy writing or running my business, you can find me cleaning house, cooking dinner, feeding our three rescue cats, trying to make learning fun and coaxing my son to pick up his toys. On less busy days, you may also find me paddling down a spring run in Florida, hiking a mountain trail in Georgia (on the rare vacation to the mountains), or enjoying a book.

If you love Natalie Dean books, you can be notified of new releases by signing up to my newsletter at nataliedeanau thor.com, where you will also receive two free short stories for signing up. Just click on the "Free Books" tab at the top and you'll be on your way!

Also, as previously mentioned, I've opened my own online bookstore and I'd love your support! As of June 2024, I'm selling my ebooks at Natalie Dean Books. By late summer or fall 2024, I should have audiobooks, regular paperbacks, large print paperbacks, dyslexic print paperbacks and signed paperbacks all available. At the request of my loyal readers, I'll also be adding merchandise, such as glasses, cups, magnets and more. So come check out my small mom-owned author business at nataliedean books.com.

You can also scan the QR code below to be taken to the home page of Natalie Dean Books.

facebook.com/nataliedeanromance